THE FUEHRERMASTER

Also by Daniel Wyatt

Two Wings and a Prayer
Maximum Effort
The Last Flight of the Arrow
The Mary Jane Mission
The Cotton Run
Pennant Man
Route 66

"The Falcon File" series:
The Fuehrermaster
The Filberg Consortium
Foo Fighters

THE FUEHRERMASTER

The Falcon File 1

Daniel Wyatt

Published by
Bladud Books

Copyright © 2003, Daniel Wyatt

Daniel Wyatt has asserted his right under the Copyright, Designs and Patents Act, 1988, to be identified as the Author of this work.

First published in Great Britain in 2003 by Mushroom eBooks

This Hardback edition published in 2018 by
Bladud Books, an imprint of Mushroom Publishing,
Bath, BA1 4EB, United Kingdom

www.bladudbooks.com

All rights reserved. No part of this publication may be reproduced in any form or by any means without the prior written permission of the publisher.

ISBN 978-1-84319-494-1

Foreword

The spring of 1941 was a desperate time for England. In the midst of the Second World War her people were feeling the effects of a winter in which many of their major cities had been bombed night after night. They were on their last legs, standing alone, threatened by Nazism on the continent of Europe. Prime Minister Winston Churchill faced fierce criticism from parliament, his own coalition cabinet, and the English people. His opponents begged him to give in to Adolf Hitler, let the dictator take the continent, and subsequently sign a negotiated peace to end the fighting. Across the English Channel, Hitler felt that the British were ready to cut a deal: a deal for peace, but only on his terms.

In his mind only one man—Rudolf Hess—could pull off such a risky venture.

One

Augsburg, Germany—March 27, 1941
There was little activity this early afternoon at the usually busy airfield opposite the Messerschmitt factory. Most of the aircraft were confined to the ground. Only one, a single-engine fighter, remained in the air. It was circling on final approach by the time Rudolf Hess climbed aboard his powerful twin-engine Messerschmitt BF-110.

The Deputy Fuehrer of Nazi Germany placed his briefcase on the deck inside the tight-fitting cockpit and slid into the seat, waving the mechanics below to the side. Hess quickly started the engines one at a time and brought them to full operating temperature. He cracked the throttles twice.

Then, in his cumbersome and confining flying gear, he emerged from the vibrating cockpit. Stepping onto the wing, he energetically leapt to the ground. One last word to his young adjutant and Hess would be off.

He walked across to his adjutant, who was standing next to a staff car, its engine idling. Captain Karlheinz Pintsch caught a new determination about his superior as Hess handed him a sealed white envelope. Hess leaned into Pintsch's face, trying to keep his voice low yet speak above the clamour of the idling engines. The ground shuddered beneath them. There was a look of suppressed excitement and mystery in Hess's face that Pintsch couldn't help noticing.

"If I do not return within four hours, Pintsch," Hess said to his adjutant, his breath steaming in the cool air, "take for granted that I am on my way and open the envelope."

"On your way, Herr Reichsfuehrer? Where?"

"When you open the envelope, you will understand."

Hess indicated to Pintsch that they synchronize watches. Pintsch fumbled with his watch and the envelope. "Yes, Herr Reichsfuehrer, of course. I will do as you say."

They saluted each other perfunctorily. Hess was obviously eager to begin the flight. Pintsch watched as Hess proudly strode across the tarmac and returned to the cockpit, where he reached up to shut the canopy. The ground crew pulled the chocks away and jogged to the grass clearing. Hess revved the fighter, then swung its ten thousand pound bulk ninety degrees to face the dispersal track. Expertly steering the aircraft to the edge of the far runway, he waited anxiously for tower clearance.

With the airplane in view across the weeded field, Pintsch heard the smooth roar. Suddenly, the camouflaged Messerschmitt was off, speeding down the runway. In a few seconds the aircraft lifted and climbed into the pale-blue sky like a gigantic metal bird.

Pintsch slowly approached the door of the staff car. He glanced at Hess's chauffeur, who looked at him inquiringly. Pintsch motioned that he didn't need him, and he drove away. Pintsch stood there in the open field, wondering where Hess was going. Another mysterious trip, accompanied by secret coded messages to Stockholm. And the letter? There wasn't a letter before. Was it another test of his loyalty to the Deputy Fuehrer? Why not just open it? But Pintsch knew he couldn't do that because what if Hess returned before the four hours was up? The consequences were much too great. He had been Hess's adjutant for only a year, before that on active service in France with the Army. To cross Hitler's right-hand man on such a sensitive matter could spell death for Pintsch at worse, another battlefront as punishment at best. Opening the letter early was out of the question.

The Messerschmitt fighter disappeared over the horizon. Pintsch turned to the operations building several hundred feet across the airfield. Hess, the man he so admired and so envied, again dominated his thoughts. Hess was loved by the people of the Fatherland and respected by most of his peers. What was Pintsch? Just an underling, someone to perform a duty for which Hess would gain the glory. Pintsch wanted to be someone special too, not the ordinary person he felt he was. He was not necessarily good looking at his age of twenty-nine, but he wasn't exactly ugly either. He was of average looks, medium height, and he did ordinary work for Hess that some over-zealous underling could easily do. He did the little things, although sometimes of great secrecy. He appreciated Hess's trust in him. But he was bored. He wanted to be a flier, and wear the dashing leather garb depicting that esteemed vocation. He had expressed such desires to fly on occasion, but hesitantly, only to be immediately quashed with a definite "No!" Pintsch couldn't budge Hess from his decision. It seemed that one star in the show was enough. Perhaps Pintsch was meant always to be an understudy.

Even if his wish had been granted, Pintsch knew he would have to go a long way to match Hess's flying skill. The Reichsfuehrer excelled in flying by instruments and in the skill of following radio directional beams. He had been a test pilot for Willy Messerschmitt. In 1934 he won the Zugspitze, the annual race around Germany's highest mountain, as well as a round-the-houses race in Italy. Hess had even taken lessons from Hans Bauer, Hitler's personal pilot, in the art of dead reckoning, an aspect of navigation which for some strange reason was significantly important to Hess.

Pintsch returned to the tarmac at six o'clock. By then a bitter cold wind was sweeping across the airfield. The dampness sliced through his greatcoat. Pintsch shivered. The sun would set soon and he hadn't left the compound the entire time. He had wolfed down something to eat at the mess, but spent most of the time walking and observing life on the base, studying the solid lines of aircraft, longing to fly. There was no sign of the Reichsfuehrer. No sign of his ground staff either. Did they not expect him to return here? Another airfield, perhaps. Pintsch felt the envelope, secure in his coat pocket. Half an hour more. Thirty minutes until the satisfaction of his nagging curiosity.

Then a familiar sound broke through his thoughts. At first it was far off, so distant that he held his breath to hear more clearly. Yes, unmistakable. The drone of an engine. No, engines. Two. Aircraft engines. Was it the Messerschmitt? The drone grew louder. Yes, a Messerschmitt. He recognized, without a doubt, the familiar hum of an ME-110 in flight. Now the airfield suddenly exploded into action. A truck squealed to a stop near Pintsch and Hess's ground crew scrambled out. The chauffeur pulled up. Then the distinct shape of the ME-110 appeared over the trees, a dark outline silhouetted against the fading light. It grew closer in sight and sound until the roar of the engines filled the air, reverberating loudly off the hangars. The airplane made a low pass over the base, then banked, and lined up on final approach. Pintsch confirmed the fuselage markings of NJ-C11 as the fighter landed and thundered its way to the ground crew. The habitual wave of the hand from the cockpit told Pintsch that the Reichsfuehrer had returned.

Hess shut the engines down and conversed with one of the men who jumped on the wing. Hess eased himself from the snug cockpit, and clambered to the ground. Together they took to the port side of the fighter. The chauffeur opened the front passenger door of the staff car and waited as Hess finished his lengthy instructions to the crew. As Hess drew near, Pintsch walked towards the fighter, his hand on the letter inside his coat, stopping so that he was between the staff car and the aircraft.

Hess met him and took the letter from Pintsch's outstretched hand. "Thank you. Send the message to *Lion*. Mission aborted. Don't give any reason."

"Yes, Herr Reichsfuehrer. As soon as I reach the administration compound."

Hess stuck the envelope inside his briefcase. He took one glance at the fighter, then he whipped off his helmet and rubbed his hand through his matted hair. With a sense of defeat, he strode towards the staff car and ordered his chauffeur to drive him home.

In a thicket of trees running parallel to the airfield, Wolfgang Geis held his binoculars to his eyes until Hess drove off. Geis didn't hesitate. He fought the branches, clearing a path to his automobile a short distance away. He was certain no one had seen him. Ten minutes later he braked in front of the local Gestapo office at Augsburg. He entered the building and flashed his identification at the first uniformed officer he saw.

The officer looked at the card, and cleared his throat. "Gestapo Headquarters!"

"That is correct. I need to use a phone. In private."

"Certainly, Herr Captain. First room on your right."

"Thank you."

Geis closed the door to the empty room and lifted the telephone receiver. "Get me Gestapo Headquarters in Berlin. Hurry!"

He waited until the connection was made. Then he asked for Heinrich Himmler's office.

"Herr Reichsfuehrer?"

"Yes."

"This is Captain Geis."

"Yes, Geis. What do you have?"

"It's Hess, Herr Reichsfuehrer. He flew away again. His own airplane. This time three hours, thirty minutes. Pintsch stayed on the base the whole time, most of it spent outside. Hess handed him something that looked like an envelope before he left and took it back when he returned."

"Where's Hess now?"

"He left the base, heading to Munich. Herr Reichsfuehrer, what do you want me to do?"

"Stay there and keep me informed. Report to me in three days with the details."

"Yes, Herr Reichsfuehrer. Heil Hitler!"

Munich, Germany

Hess greeted his security guards at the gate and entered his large, elaborate country residence outside Munich, along a cobbled stone road called Harthauser Strasse. He then climbed the narrow, ladder-like stairs to the office of his secretary, who had left for the day. He flicked the light on and locked the door behind him. From a window inside the office, Hess looked upon the neat and spacious grounds covered by grass and birch trees. He enjoyed his domain.

Hess turned away. He grabbed a folder containing a thick wad of printed paper and a dozen photographs from inside his uniform, and shoved it into a wide leather briefcase that only he knew the combination to. He snapped the lock shut, and then hid the briefcase in the space carved out behind the bookshelf. This, of course, would only be a temporary hiding spot. The best place was on the aircraft itself. No one would think of looking for the papers there.

Hess sat for a few minutes at his desk, contemplating the change of plans precipitated by yet another abort. This time his fighter had encountered radio problems. Perhaps it was better that he didn't complete the flight on his own, anyway. He was being too impulsive. But no one would know that except him. Now he had to go the official route. All he needed was permission from the Fuehrer for the next stage.

Hess tried to imagine how the mission, if successful, would change the future of the world. His vision spread out before him in a panoramic view. Old ways would give way to the new, a much-needed New World Order. He would be hailed a mighty and powerful conquering hero by many people. He would finally be victorious over his jealous opponents, like his backstabbing Chief of Staff Martin Bormann, Hitler's new apprentice. And what about the Commander-in-Chief of the Luftwaffe, Hermann Goering, and Hess's main rival, Gestapo leader Heinrich Himmler? They were the same foes that were spied on from time to time by Hess's own private Secret Service, comprised of men who were devoted, faithful, and well paid; men who reported directly to him. They would be rewarded somehow for their efforts. Even Hess's wife, Ilse, might display a new respect for him. Hess would make so many proud. Never mind his opponents. They would be taken care of. Quickly.

Hess left his secretary's office and entered the upstairs shower. Stepping from the hot water minutes later, he leisurely combed his wet, greying hair, glancing at himself in the wide mirror. Towel around his waist, hands on his hips, he suddenly stopped and shot his head back in a defiant pose, as if ready to present a speech at a podium before 50,000 fervent Nazis. Hess's image before the Fatherland was always important to him, and the mirror was a good place to practice. He stared into his square face. It was a mask of strong German stock intoxicated with pride and ambition. His eyes were sunken beneath bushy brows that connected above a fleshy nose. He had a determined jaw line, and sharp cheekbones. His mouth was firm, with thin lips. He rarely smiled because he was too self-conscious about his buckteeth. He felt they undermined his generally authoritative appearance. He forbade the German photographers to catch him even so much as grinning. He did not want to appear less than what the Deputy Fuehrer of Germany's Third Reich should be. The German people could only be allowed to see the best side of their Deputy Fuehrer.

Only the best.

Two

London, England—March 30

Eleven minutes after nine in the morning, Colonel Raymond Lampert already had Wesley Hollinger's file on his desk at MI-6 Headquarters. In all his years in public service, he had never seen such a thing. He eased forward and folded his arms. Oh, how times had changed.

The phone rang.

Lampert lifted the receiver abruptly. "Lampert here."

"Colonel! Do you have the file?"

Lampert sat up and straightened his shoulders. Prime Minister Churchill was on the line. "Yes, sir, I do. On my desk."

"Well?"

"I've read it over. Are you sure about him, sir? Personally, I have my doubts. I realize I've never met the young analyst, but I'm just not comfortable with him."

"Too bad. He comes highly recommended by the Office of Navy Intelligence in Washington. He has the kind of experience and potential that our Secret Service could take advantage of. Besides, it's only a temporary assignment."

Lampert drew a breath. "But, sir, we have our own people in Britain. Why do we need an American?"

"Because cooperation with American intelligence services is vital."

Lampert was unconvinced. He flipped through the pages of the open file. "Born and raised in Rochester, New York. It says here he has had his share of carousing, mischief-making and good times, the sum total of which got him expelled from the halls of Cornell University.

Sir, this kind of experience can't be what we're looking for, can it? I wouldn't exactly consider him a pillar of integrity. And to top it all, he's just twenty-three. I fail to see how a young foreigner can be better than one of our own."

"According to Donovan, Hollinger is lucky."

"Lucky? How do you mean, sir?"

"Nothing was going right for the Americans until he arrived at Navy Intelligence. Good fortune seems to follow him. A lucky charm, he is. But he is a little peculiar."

"In what way?"

"Donovan didn't elaborate. He did add that Hollinger was clever, as well as shrewd. Just see this thing through, colonel. The decision has already been made."

The line went dead.

Gloom marked Lampert's face as he returned the receiver to its cradle. So, it seemed to him that he'd have to keep this pretty boy out of trouble. The Secret Service was fast becoming a glorified reform school. Lampert lit his pipe and lifted his heavy six-foot frame from the chair. "Where the blazes is he?" he said to himself, glancing at the clock on the wall. "Fifteen minutes late. Good Lord!" Then he heard the roar of an auto engine. Lampert went to the window and saw a car pull up. A young man stepped out of it.

A minute later, the intercom on the Lampert's desk buzzed. "Yes."

"Mr. Wesley Hollinger is here to see you, sir," a woman's voice explained, politely.

"Send him in."

"Yes, sir."

Lampert's eyes fell on the fashionably dressed American as he entered the smoky office. There was definitely something carefree about him when he shuffled in, twirling his wide-brimmed fedora hat in his hand, unconcerned that he was almost twenty minutes late. His medium-green suit was not off the rack. That kind of fit was only obtained by the best tailors. Up close, he was ruggedly handsome with a slender nose and blue eyes—not a pretty boy after all. Average height, he possessed an athletic build with wide shoulders. Interesting though, Lampert thought, that his hands were those of an artist, long and slender. A large diamond ring bulged on a finger. His dark-brown hair was wavy, a neatly defined parting to the left side. Lampert sniffed. Plenty of pomade and brilliantine, too.

"So, you're Wesley Hollinger," Lampert said, standing.

"So, you're Colonel Lampert," the American replied.

Hollinger flashed a disarming grin and stuck out his manicured hand. Lampert shook his hand and indicated for him to sit down. Hollinger turned and pitched his hat at the coat rack. His aim was perfect. The hat caught the top rung. Then he flopped himself into the leather armchair directly in front of Lampert's desk.

Gnawing on his pipe, the colonel cocked an eye at his visitor, his smile a tolerant one. If this was a job interview and first impressions were lasting impressions, then Hollinger would have been out on the street in a minute.

"Mr. Hollinger, let's get down to business."

"You bet. Sir."

Berlin, Germany

Heinrich Himmler scrutinized the drawings, the numbers, and the detailed items of his latest pet project. It was beginning to take shape. He and the Fuehrer called it the Jewish problem: what to do with all the Jewish dissidents in camps across Germany and Poland.

Himmler was the most feared man in Nazi Germany. He knew it and he relished it. One stroke of his gold pen at his Prinze Albrechtstrasse address, and heads would roll. As leader of the Gestapo and the equally dreaded SS, he kept files on his fellow Germans, including his own agents and the other high-ranking leaders. He knew that Adolf Hitler had once been treated for syphilis, and that Hermann Goering and Josef Goebbels were still running around on their wives. He knew that Hess had homosexual tendencies and that his best friend's wife was a half-Jew. He knew that Martin Bormann had a criminal background. Information as delicate as all this and more was safely tucked away in a large vault to the right of his desk. It was information that he could use someday, sometime, when he needed it most.

A master filer, Himmler was a stickler for details. He never failed to keep track of his own day in a notebook. What time he woke up, what time he bathed, when he left his house and when he entered his office. Everything was down to the last minute. Himmler also made everything in Germany his business. For weeks he had been hearing rumours of German peace negotiations with the British to end the war, and the names of Hess and the Haushofer family as the mediators kept coming up. He wondered what was in the wind, and why the Fuehrer hadn't informed him outright of any peace feelers.

Himmler bent over his desk intercom and pressed a button.

"Yes, Herr Reichsfuehrer," a man said.

"As soon as Captain Geis arrives, send him in to me," Himmler said, closing the Jewish file.

"Of course, Herr Reichsfuehrer."

To Captain Geis, Himmler looked like Satan himself in his black Gestapo uniform at the far end of the eerie office. The spacious room was in darkness except for a bright desk lamp to one side of the SS-Gestapo leader and a fire blazing in the corner.

"Ah, Captain Geis."

It was Himmler's smile that bothered Geis the most. A smile of amusing deceit, as if Himmler knew what you were going to say before you could say it. "Good afternoon, Herr Reichsfuehrer. Heil Hitler!"

"Heil Hitler," Himmler replied, writing down with his gold pen the hour and minute Geis had ventured into the office. The leader looked up through the small lenses of his silver-framed pince-nez. "Anything new since our last conversation?"

"No, Herr Reichsfuehrer."

Himmler's eyes turned cold and his face muscles grew rigid. He glared at his civilian-dressed Gestapo agent, an expert in communications and explosives. Geis was in his mid-thirties, tall, blonde, blue-eyed; what Himmler would call a perfect specimen of the superior Aryan race. "Well, I have something for you. I want the homes and offices of Hess and Goering wiretapped, immediately. I want to know every word they say of importance within minutes. Do you understand?"

Geis swallowed. "Yes, Herr Reichsfuehrer. I'll get my people on it right away."

Three

BLETCHLEY PARK, ENGLAND—MARCH 31

Wesley Hollinger glanced across at his new boss in the passenger seat. Hollinger wasted no time in getting the two of them to their destination northeast of London. He drove his MG convertible sports car as if it was to be his last time behind the wheel and he wanted to make the most of it. Hollinger chose to disregard the rain, the speed limit signs, and the rough-running engine, which seemed to act up in damp weather. He skidded around turns, ignoring all road signs to slow down through villages. Every roadside object, tree, and bush was a blur. Lampert hung on to the window handle with one hand and on his pipe, which had long ago gone out, with the other.

Hollinger didn't know what to expect this cloudy afternoon patched with mist, as he flew past the sooty brick kilns and antiquated, dirty railway yards of Bletchley in Buckinghamshire. He looked forward to the challenge of the unknown, and the air of secrecy surrounding his new post whetted his appetite. Just how good was it going to get? He hoped he would find out soon, as Lampert had been particularly silent on what lay ahead at Bletchley.

Suddenly the country road came to a T, and Lampert motioned for Hollinger to turn left. They soon arrived at the checkpoint gate of the sprawling estate of Bletchley Park. The eighteenth-century two-story mansion, Hollinger noticed after clearing security, was made of red brick, with ornate Victorian gables and a grand porch area. The acres of park had cultivated lawns surrounding the house. Mushrooming throughout the property were hastily-erected out-buildings made of corrugated steel. The Secret Service had an ideal location, whatever they were doing here. It was all very private, very secure. Hollinger braked the MG to a halt at Lampert's direction in a driveway behind one of the large out-buildings.

"Here we are," the colonel said. "Hut Nine." He turned to Hollinger after tapping the contents of his pipe against the MG's side mirror. "With driving like that, you should have been a fighter pilot."

"I had thought about that very thing, sir. Back in the States, that is. But I didn't get very far. I'm what you call a service reject."

"Hopefully, your mind can match the speed of that little machine of yours. By the way, I'd check that motor out if I were you. Sounds like the beginning of a bad wire. Now, grab your suitcase and follow me."

Once past the door, they waited inside a plasterboard porch that led to a hall and several rooms.

"As of now, Mr. Hollinger, you are the senior officer of Committee B, by special appointment of Prime Minister Winston Churchill. Even though you were personally selected by Winnie, bear in mind you still answer to me. This is an important assignment and I trust you can conduct yourself accordingly."

"I understand, sir," the American responded with as much seriousness as he could muster.

Hollinger felt the colonel's coolness towards him for this assignment. In Hollinger's opinion, the stuffy Lampert obviously needed some convincing. The American would just have to prove himself with Committee B; prove himself all over again, as he had done in the States. He smiled, thinking that if any man could be classified as a soldier's soldier, it was the grey-haired Lampert. He was a retired British Army colonel who had fought in the First World War—the only war, so Lampert had often reminded those around him, including Hollinger on the trip to Bletchley. Lampert was proud of his trench-fighting experience, for which he had been decorated. Even though the First World War was to his mind the best one to date, Lampert had admitted to Hollinger that this one twenty years later was certainly shaping up to be quite a challenge.

Hollinger heard quick footsteps coming down the hall. A tall young man, with a freckled face and thick round glasses that distorted his eyes, appeared and greeted the two visitors. "Good afternoon, colonel," he said, cheerily. "Oh, hello there. You must be Wesley Hollinger."

"Hello yourself," Hollinger replied.

"I've heard a bit about you, already. Glad to have you aboard." The man shook hands vigorously.

Lampert turned to the door. "Be a good fellow and brief him, won't you, Winslow? I'm due back in London shortly. Would you be so kind as to arrange to have someone drive me to the train station in an hour or so?"

"Certainly, sir."

Glaring pointedly at Hollinger, Lampert went on. "Someone slow and methodical, perhaps one of the older fellows. In the meantime, is there somewhere I can sample a brandy and have a smoke?"

"In the lounge, sir. Third door on the left," Winslow said.

"You are on your own now, Mr. Hollinger," Lampert said mechanically, disappearing down the hall.

The man with the thick glasses turned his attention to Hollinger. His eyes were friendly. "Glad you're going to be a part of the team. I'm Spencer Winslow, the Hut Nine Chief Duty Officer of Committee B. I must say, it's quite nice to see another young face. For a while I thought it was like a war veterans club here. You might spice up the place a little. However, it's work, work, work, twenty-four hours a day here."

Hollinger liked Winslow's honesty. He was sure they would get along. He dropped his suitcase on the floor, clumsily catching the toe of his right shoe.

"Did the colonel fill you in on what we're up to here?"

"Nope."

"I'll get into it straightaway. You must be aware of *Enigma*?"

"Sure, at least the Japanese version of it. Only the back-room stuff."

"For us, it happened this way. In late 1939 we acquired a copy of the German *Enigma* cipher machine. After much painful toil we cracked their system, thanks to Robbie Langford, our number one cipher expert. Remember the receiving station you were sent to when you arrived in Britain, Mr. Hollinger?"

"Maggie. Blonde dame, about five-four." Smiling recklessly, Hollinger indicated with his hands a robust figure. "Yes, I definitely remember that station, Spence."

"Can't say I've met her, Mr. Hollinger."

"Too bad, Spence. She's a knockout. Maybe I can fix you up with her one day."

"Maybe. Bring your suitcase down the hall and I'll take you to your office. Anyway," Winslow continued as they walked, "the Morse Code your people copied down was sent here by courier and deciphered, then sent out to the appropriate intelligence services of the military branches. You were working with our *Enigma* intercepts, as you well know from your background in America. Our handling of the deciphered traffic is what we call *Ultra*. If the Japanese ever declare war on America, then your secret services would operate in like manner. Without our own code breaking, we might have lost the war by now. In the near future we hope to make a significant contribution by providing our military commanders with advanced insight into enemy movements and strongholds. Ah, here we are."

They stopped at an open door. Hollinger looked in and saw what he had expected—bare walls, ordinary furniture, well used. The word "chintzy" came to mind. "Spare no expense," he mumbled.

"Pardon me?"

"Nothing. Just thinking out loud."

"Would you like a brief tour of the place before dinner?"

"Sure. Let's go."

They stood outside on a stone roadway before Winslow spoke again. He looked around at the peaceful surroundings. The bushes and trees broke up the expanse of lawn, all a subdued green. He pulled a cigarette from a pack in his breast pocket and fired it with a butane lighter.

"Let me try to give you a good example of what I was trying to say before. The German *Blitzkrieg* through Europe required perfect timing to deploy. Radio signals from unit to unit were absolutely vital. Dive bombers and tanks, followed by troops, were all controlled by what they believe to be unbreakable radio signals. The secret was speed. Britain, France, and the Low Countries could not decipher the enemy's radio traffic at that time. I hope that for the rest of the war we will anticipate Germany's every move, perhaps before their own generals will. The *Enigma* people are in that hut over there," Winslow said, pointing over a slight rise. "As you know we have housed some Americans here, and will continue to do so, I understand."

"So, our East Anglia Morse Code was put to good use."

"Very good use, indeed. Bletchley is deciphering secret German wireless traffic every day."

"So, why am I here and what is this Committee B?"

"We are a special as well as the newest section of Bletchley. The Germans are using another machine, a more complex one called *Enigma II* that we have not been able to decipher. Yet. Lucky for us they are in short supply and are quite possibly used only for diplomatic purposes for the time being, not in the battlefield. However, that scenario could change quickly. We have one here in Hut Nine, stolen from the German forces in Norway. This took some doing."

"I bet."

"As was the case with the first *Enigma*, our foreign agent had to make the Germans think that their cipher machine was destroyed, or else they would have gotten rid of all their machines and switched to another system. We had to blow up a Gestapo office building in Oslo where this particular *Enigma II* was stored. We left behind parts of another cipher machine in its stead to make the Germans think the machine blew up with it."

"Clever. I'd like to see this *Enigma II* right now, if I may?"

"Don't you want that tour first?"

"Nah, there's plenty of time for that."

"Right you are. I'll see to it."

Minutes later, they found themselves in Hollinger's office. A new piece of furniture was added, a metal stand in the middle of the room. On it was what appeared to be a large, clumsy typewriter, much larger than a regular Underwood. Hollinger threw his hat on top of the filing cabinet, his eyes never leaving the machine. Although he had helped in breaking the Japanese version of *Enigma*, he had not actually seen one of the objects up close. He had only done the back-room cryptography. The keyboard, he realized, resembled a universal typewriter, but the numbers, punctuation marks, and other extras were missing. Behind the keyboard was a plate with another alphabet repeated in the same order, and above that a set of six wheels attached to what seemed a long roller.

"I'll go get Langford."

"Do that, Spence. I'd like to meet him."

Winslow opened his mouth to say something, but changed his mind and left instead, returning in a few seconds. Hollinger, his back to the door, continued to study the machine, oblivious to a striking redhead in a dark-blue skirt and white blouse entering the office with Winslow.

"Wesley Hollinger," Winslow declared after a few moments. "I would like you to meet Langford, our head cryptographer."

Hollinger spun around.

"Roberta Langford," Winslow said distinctly.

"How do you do, Mr. Hollinger? Welcome to Bletchley," she said confidently, extending her hand. She blinked, opening deep-brown eyes, smiling at the same time.

Wesley extended his hand slowly, as if partially paralyzed above the waist. The last thing he expected was a woman. So young and so pretty. The two exchanged glances, and he examined her with a touch of curiosity. Her clothes and hair set her off from most of the badly dressed English women he had encountered in their mousy business attire. She was in her mid-twenties with a slender face and long legs. Her brilliant long red hair, tied in the back, had sausage curls on the sides, which waved and bobbed, creating an aura-like frame about her pretty face. Except for her speech, she could have been easily mistaken for a high-class New Yorker.

"Wesley Hollinger is our new senior officer sent by the London Secret Service," Winslow informed the cheery woman. "He's a cipher analyst coming to us from the Office of Naval Intelligence in America. And this is *Enigma II*, Mr. Hollinger. By the way Robbie, keep in mind that Mr. Hollinger has some prior knowledge of cryptography."

Winslow offered Langford a cigarette, which she accepted with a nod. He lit hers, then his own.

"Thanks, Spencer." Langford cleared her throat. Blowing out a thick cloud of smoke after a deep, breathy puff, she folded her arms and began. "The original version of the *Enigma* machine was invented and patented by the Dutch in 1919," she said in a Yorkshire accent. "*Enigma* is—"

"Just a minute, here," Hollinger interrupted. Winslow and Langford shot a glance at each other. "There is a new rule I'd like to establish right off the top. There will be no smoking in my office." He approached the two smokers with the desk ashtray. Winslow butted his smoke out, but Langford wavered. It was the ammunition Hollinger needed. He snatched the cigarette from her mouth and butted it out himself.

Langford pressed her lips tightly together, her cheerful disposition gone. Her eyes flickered to Winslow then back to the American. "I could have done that myself, thank you."

"Now, let's hear what you have to say," Hollinger said, sitting on the edge of the desk nearest her, looking down at the machine.

Langford glanced over at Spencer, who shrugged and moved closer. Her cheeks were an intense red. She slowly removed her glasses. "*Enigma* is the Greek word for puzzle. And it has been that, a puzzle. This machine was a Polish invention, later developed to a higher degree by the Germans. They further altered it to a point where it became more complicated than the original. Basically, *Enigma* is a transposition machine, which means that every letter typed is turned into another letter on paper." She stopped to see that Hollinger was nodding, as if he understood. "It has a regular keyboard, backed up by another set of letters in the same order, just as you see before you."

"And the second set starts the transposing?"

"Exactly, Mr. Hollinger. To start with, the operator hits the letters of his message on the keyboard. Each time he presses a key, a letter lights up on the second alphabet. An assistant makes a note of the lit letters, then sends those letters by Morse Code on the wireless."

"And we here at Bletchley receive these messages from the receiving stations."

"Right again, Mr. Hollinger. The party receiving the message takes the collection of letters and taps it out on his own machine in order to get the appropriate message. But the secret is in the plugs and wheels inside and how they are arranged. They are the actual mechanisms that, for example, make the letter N come out as a C one time, a K the next, and so on. The transposition is supposed to be done in such a tricky manner that it is nearly impossible for any eavesdropper to know what goes on inside the machine, especially since the sender and the receiver have their machines set exactly the same, simply by turning each of their wheels to the same starting point letter. There are so many letter permutations to consider that it is overwhelming. We have a computer housed in another hut to organize the variations in the deciphering, although a lot of our work is still done manually."

"Very good."

"After thousands of hours," Langford went on, "we cracked the original *Enigma* cipher with its five wheels and three slots. Not all the wheels are used at one time. But *Enigma II* has eight wheels and six slots, with more variations to consider."

"I think I get the drift of it, Langford. In your estimation, how close are you to cracking this *Enigma II*?"

Langford shrugged, glancing at Winslow. "Months, at least," she answered slowly. "Unless we get awfully lucky."

"That about covers it," Winslow said during a long pause in which Langford and Hollinger tried to stare each other down.

"Now, if you'll excuse me," Langford said, breaking off first, "I have a cigarette to finish. I won't trouble you any longer. Cheerio." She disappeared without speaking another word in a streak of legs, skirt, and red hair, taking the ashtray with her.

Half an hour later, Winslow showed Hollinger to his living quarters. They were located inside a large garage that had been converted into several rooms for the senior officers at Bletchley.

"Not bad," Hollinger commented, throwing his suitcase on the bed.

"You weren't too impressed by Langford, were you?" asked Winslow.

"What would make you say that?"

Winslow chuckled. "Well . . ."

"All right. Yeah, she seems to know her stuff, I'll grant her that. She's a looker all right, and lots of spunk. It's just that I have an aversion to redheads."

"That's probably best, anyway."

"Why?"

"Because if you're thinking of moving in, I'd advise you against it. She's already taken. She's pretty serious about a navy officer up in Scapa Flow. I'm sorry we couldn't accommodate you with a brunette or a blonde."

Hollinger caught the humour, and laughed. He glanced at his watch to see it was nearly four in the afternoon. "When do you have tea around here? I'm starved."

"It's coming on the hour."

Hollinger sat on the edge of the bed, testing the springs. "Good."

"All the comforts of home, Mr. Hollinger. We want to make things the best we can under the circumstances. Solving *Enigma II* is top of the list of priorities at Bletchley."

Hollinger stood. "This *Enigma II* thing has got me interested. If the Germans weren't such a maniacal lot, I'd admit to their brilliance. My first impression is that they are more methodical than the Japanese. They are quite clever."

"I agree. They're giving us a good run."

Hollinger looked through the window at the grey sky. "Will it really be months before we break this thing?"

"It appears that way, yes."

"Great," Hollinger said with no enthusiasm. "So I might be hanging around here for a while."

"You're stuck here."

"What are you talking about? You make it sound so final."

"We are the crème de la crème of the Secret Service, with the best mathematical and scientific minds in the British Isles, Canada, and America. We know too much. Once in this line of business, never out. Maybe when the war is over . . . Some of us have tried for postings elsewhere, but we've all been turned down."

"Really?"

"You seem surprised. Didn't you know that? Although, if you have an in with Winnie . . ."

"I don't think my in is that good. I've only met Churchill once. Besides, why would anyone want to leave that badly?" Hollinger bent over his suitcase and unsnapped it. On top were his monogrammed shirts. He wondered if he had packed enough clothes for a prolonged stay. Maybe he could send for more. From underneath his clothes he pulled out a dartboard and a brown paper bag full of multi-coloured darts.

"Chess is my game," Winslow said, glancing at the dartboard. He opened the door to the room. "Getting back to the question of why anyone would want to leave that badly you'll find out soon enough. We are granted a day off once a week, except for emergencies, for some outside activities. It's best to get away and clear your mind."

"No doubt," Hollinger replied. *Emergencies, eh?*

"Four or five trains come and go into Bletchley on weekdays and two on Sunday. Traveling through the countryside makes you forget there's a war on, at least for a day."

"It feels as if I've been committed to a prison or an asylum."

Winslow laughed. "Very accurate deduction."

"What's so funny?"

"A Royal Air Force regiment guards the grounds. They warn their

NCOs to look lively or they'll be thrown inside the compound." He lowered his voice. "I'll have someone bring your tea and biscuits over," Winslow said, closing the door. "Toodle-oo."

Hollinger stood at the window and watched Winslow take the stone path that returned him to Hut Nine. Toodle-oo. Cheerio. These English were a strange bunch. What was wrong with a goodbye or a see you later?

Apparently, it was going to be a longer siege than Hollinger had first imagined. Three years in the business and this was where he ended up. He smirked, bringing back the summer of 1938 and the football accident he had suffered at Cornell that left him with a bum knee, thus ruining his dreams of an air force career. That autumn, one of Hollinger's professors saw a certain ability in the young man, and recommended him to an important person within a highly secretive organization; Colonel William Donovan, an intelligence adviser to President Franklin Roosevelt. At just twenty years of age, Hollinger showed amazing aptitude at breaking simple ciphers and codes in his early training with the agency. Then he was sent on loan to the US Navy Intelligence Service. There he laboured with a team of engineers instrumental in cracking the Japanese codes and ciphers that were being transmitted between Tokyo and the Japanese Embassy in Washington. After reporting back to Donovan, Hollinger was transferred to a receiving station off the coast of East Anglia, England, to learn the British decoding system as part of another team that received coded wireless messages from the European continent. Quickly promoted because of his brilliant mind and keen intuition in translating coded signals, he did not go unnoticed by MI-6 and the British Prime Minister in London.

Hollinger looked up to the sky again. Rain had been forecast. So, what else was new in Britain? Now, if only the sun would show itself and brighten not only the day but his spirits as well. With a sigh, he turned to his suitcase and continued to unpack. What had he gotten himself into?

Four

Berchtesgaden, Germany

High in the Bavarian Alps, one hundred miles southeast of Munich, Rudolf Hess and Adolf Hitler walked onto the balcony off the main sitting room at Hitler's mountain residence. They looked over the glittering expanse of the snow-covered valley below, dotted with cedar and pine trees.

This was the Fuehrer's remote hideaway called Berghof, purchased with the royalties of his book, *Mein Kampf*. What once was unspoiled Bavarian landscape was now crowded with guest houses, garages, and air-raid shelters, and crisscrossed by numerous roads. Surrounding the property was a secured park of barbed wire, complete with alarms and armed SS guards around the clock.

Bundled in a thick knee-length coat, Hitler, just out of bed, leaned over the balcony ledge with his hands on the wood rail, and inhaled deeply. He looked right and left. The cold mountain air filled his lungs. Adolf Hitler was an ordinary-looking man, outside of his square moustache and common-soldier haircut, which he considered was indicative of his identification with the German working class. It was early afternoon, shortly after one-thirty; another late night for the leader who usually hit his stride after midnight. His red puffy eyes caught a flock of swift-moving nightingales far below in the valley. Always fascinated by birds, he followed their flight until they disappeared into some trees. By then the fresh air was beginning to revive him.

"More problems, Hess?"

"Yes, mein Fuehrer. Radio malfunction."

"Three times, three aborts. I have no tolerance for failure," Hitler said in his rural Austrian accent, the direct opposite of Hess's articulate and educated upper class Bavarian tone.

"I have a solution, mein Fuehrer. May we go inside to discuss it?"

Hitler smiled sadly, conscious of Hess's First World War lung injury. For over twenty years since, Hess had trouble breathing in such high altitudes. Hitler decided not to give Hess the upper hand and motioned him to a set of steel patio chairs beside a wide, white table.

Hess took a deep breath of the cool air, and waited for Hitler to seat himself first.

"What is that in your hand?"

"A map, mein Fuehrer," Hess replied between punctuated gasps, desperate to show no physical weakness before his leader. "I have brought it to clarify the entire situation for you." Hess spread out a crisp, creased paper nearly as big as the table, pointing out England, Scotland, and Wales. Hitler took immediate interest, fishing for his reading glasses in his pocket and sliding them on.

"The original plan," Hess began, "was to fly to Aalborg in Denmark and hand your peace proposal package to a specially-trained ME-110 crew which was to fly to a secluded, predetermined point in England." Hess pointed to a large X in the northeast corner of England. "Here, near Ainwick. The crew would drop the package to our contact, *Lion*, on a low-level pass over the beach due east of the town."

Hitler reached into his pocket for his small chocolates. He handled them gently, selected one, unwrapped it, and popped it into his mouth. "I know all that, Hess. So what is your solution?"

"I will fly to Denmark, refuel, and then set out for Great Britain myself."

"And drop the package?"

"Oh, no, mein Fuehrer," Hess uttered slowly. "I will present the peace initiatives to *Lion* personally."

Hitler quickly gulped down the chocolate in his mouth and stared at his deputy. "What! Are you crazy, Hess?"

Hess shook his head. "No, mein Fuehrer. It is the only way to test the appeasers' reaction to your generous proposals. It will not be as dangerous as you may think."

"Not as dangerous? But where would you land?"

"A place known as Dunhampton. An RAF aerodrome in Scotland. Our aerial intelligence has discovered the secret RAF base not far from the Duke of Hamilton's castle, from which the British fly our captured aircraft. My fighter, you see, mein Fuehrer, won't seem out of place."

Hitler nodded, calming down. "Yes, I do see."

"I have not confirmed my plans with *Lion* as yet, but I'm sure that the Duke of Hamilton will assure my safe arrival. If he can provide our Denmark crew an untouched corridor as promised, he should allow me the same privilege."

"Where is this Dunhampton? Show me."

Hess's finger found the general area, south of Glasgow, east of Eaglesham. "Here, in the moors where it's thinly populated."

Between more short gasps, Hess went on to describe what would be the turning points coming off the North Sea. He began with the lighthouse at Holy Island, which stayed lit because of the treacherous local waters despite the blackout. The Farn Islands would lead him to the Cheviot Hills and another lighthouse at Troon. He recited names, distances, and whether he would have to vector left or right at various points. He mentioned the towns of St. Abb's, Coldstream, and Peebles as if he had already been there. And why not? Hess had gone over the maps dozens of times in the last few days, arming himself with names, repeating them again and again.

"This is interesting," Hitler said.

"I will use a radio beam, mein Fuehrer. I should arrive during the remaining hours of daylight, thus enabling me to see my turning points and destinations, giving me the night for an unchallenged return."

Hitler rubbed his chin, his puffy eyes moving from Hess to the map and back to Hess. "And if you are not successful? What if you are captured? What then?"

Hess bolted upright, hands on his hips. "I am prepared for that. Just say that I went crazy. And you can say that neither you nor anyone else in the High Command had any prior knowledge of the flight. I will take full responsibility, for the sake of the Fatherland's future. The risk is mine. Mine alone."

Hitler smiled and reached for a new chocolate. He could see the seriousness in Hess's face, a sense of no turning back.

"Peace with England is essential to our plans. No sacrifice should be too great in winning Britain's friendship. Remember? Your very own words, mein Fuehrer," Hess exclaimed, quoting *Mein Kampf* to its author.

"Don't I know it." Hitler brought to mind their prison days together in 1923, when the two shared their thoughts and minds on paper. Hitler spoke and Hess wrote. The outcome was *Mein Kampf*. "As usual, Hess," Hitler smirked, "your planning is extremely thorough, and it is certainly feasible the way you present it. And you do seem bent on this. You always were stubborn in your ideas."

Hitler fell silent for a long time, eyeing the mountains. He dug for another chocolate. He had to think. His deputy had just offered to lay his life on the line for his country. Goering or anyone else in the High Command hadn't offered to do that. If successful, Hess could move up the chain of command and dislodge Goering, whom Hitler had appointed as Germany's successor only the year before. Wouldn't that be something? Peace with Britain was the key. The flight was a desperate move on Hess's part to gain back the acceptance he once had. If the mission failed, Hess was expendable anyway. Other individuals were in line to take over, men like Martin Bormann. As far as Hitler saw it, he had a lot to gain and very little to lose.

"Make the arrangements, Hess," Hitler said, at last. "You have my permission."

Hess grinned. "Mein Fuehrer, I failed to mention it, but I thought you might appreciate the name I have chosen. In honour of your passion for birds, I am calling the mission *Operation Night Eagle*."

Hitler looked pleased. "Very well. If that is all, you may go. I have work to do. Bormann will see you out."

Hess gave the Nazi salute, his arm outstretched, his heels clicking together.

Smiling, Hitler lifted his arm, his thoughts elsewhere. As Hess walked away, Hitler barked, "Rudolf!"

The Deputy Fuehrer turned around. "Yes, mein Fuehrer?"

Hitler's eyes rested on a distant snow-capped mountain, his back to Hess. "Remember, your mission is for the good of the Fatherland, and not your own."

"Mein Fuehrer," Hess answered, his breathing laboured. "I will never do anything to hurt the Fatherland."

"See that you don't."

BLETCHLEY PARK, ENGLAND—APRIL 2

Wesley Hollinger swaggered down the long hall of Hut Nine, stopping when he saw Langford through her open door. Hollinger snuck in, knocking on the frame at the same time. Her office was a small room, half the size of his own. Her desk was piled with papers. There she sat, massaging her forehead lightly with her hand. She lifted her head up slowly, her face showing obvious pain, her pale, wrinkled forehead the proof.

"Pressures getting to you?"

She attempted a weak smile. "I've had this headache all day. Doesn't seem to want to go away."

Hollinger put his hands in his pockets and rocked on his heels. Langford had some light make-up on and her perfume smelled of lilacs. He hadn't realized until that moment just how pretty she really was. "While I'm here, I want to apologize for my rude behaviour a couple days ago. I shouldn't have snatched the cigarette from your mouth. The trouble is, I detest smoke in any shape or form. So, I'm sorry if I embarrassed you."

She waved her free hand, her head down, giving Hollinger the impression that her headache was her immediate concern. "That's quite all right. You're forgiven."

Hollinger hadn't expected such leniency from her. The other redheads he had known weren't so easy-going. "I don't apologize to many people, you know."

"I'm sure you don't."

"I just don't want to have Bletchley's number one cryptographer mad at me. Spencer said I should be good to you."

"How decent of him. Don't fret. I'm not mad at you. At least not anymore."

"I guess we have something in common. Never hold a grudge, my father used to say. May I sit down?"

"By all means. Go ahead."

"Thank you."

Hollinger looked about. The condition of the furniture in her room wasn't much better than the pieces in his own office. He made a mental note of what he saw, then boldly reached for a framed picture on her desk, a recent shot of Langford in a tennis outfit, complete with sweater and shorts. She was holding a racket and her hair was tied back.

"You like tennis, do you?" he asked her.

"Whenever I get the chance."

"I've played a bit, too, back in the States. Couple times over here."

They glanced at each other uncomfortably. There was a long, uneasy pause as Hollinger returned the picture to its proper place. For a time the only sound was a ticking clock on the wall.

"How did a nice girl like you get mixed up in this nasty business, anyway?"

"I was selected."

"Yeah, really? Me too." He sat up. "What's your related background?"

"Physics and mathematics."

"Teacher?" Hollinger probed.

"Quite right. You?"

"Engineering."

She suddenly lifted herself from her chair, rubbing her forehead harder and harder. "Mr. Hollinger, if you don't mind, I really think I should lie down somewhere. Soon."

"Of course," he said, watching her twist around the side of her desk.

"I'll be back in an hour or so."

"Fine."

She rushed away, leaving Hollinger alone with the aroma of her lilac perfume and a rear-view glimpse of her slim body heading down the hall. Another quick exit, thought Hollinger. Can't she leave normally?

Five

LONDON, ENGLAND—APRIL 9

Simon Brenwood's steel empire and various financial interests spanned the globe: Great Britain, Sweden, Africa, Canada, the United States. At forty-three he was one of the richest men in the British Isles. He was a man of influence. He also had strong political connections.

Brenwood left his office late in the afternoon and told his chauffeur to drive to the General Post Office on the River Thames, a distance of eight miles through bombed-out streets. Once there, Brenwood went about his twice-daily ritual of unlocking his private post box. Today, he fingered through six letters, five posted in Britain, the bottom one from Stockholm. He didn't expect another letter from Stockholm so soon. There had been a lot of activity coming through neutral Sweden over the last few weeks, enough for Brenwood to worry himself sick over. What if one of these letters was ever intercepted by the pesky Secret Service? So far, he had no reason to believe that they were tampered with. He slammed the box closed and was out of the post office in less than two minutes.

Forty minutes later, at his two-story home in the northern suburbs of London, Brenwood removed his coat, handed it to his butler inside the door, and went to the study, asking not be disturbed until he came out. Brenwood locked the door behind him. He took a key from his desk drawer and unlocked the tall, polished mahogany cabinet next to the window to reveal the German *Enigma II* decoding machine. Paper was already in the roller. He flicked on the desk lamp and angled it towards the machine. He dug out the Stockholm letter and fumbled with it. The garbled message was long, the longest he had seen so far. Brenwood sat down in front of the machine, anxious to know the contents. With one finger, he carefully tapped out each letter as it appeared on the paper in his left hand. Like magic, the machine transposed each tap into its proper letter coordinate. Three words came to life . . . five words . . . seven words for a full sentence. One full paragraph later, he had a sinking feeling in the pit of his stomach. Brenwood then completed the second and last paragraph, and sat back in his chair, every nerve in his body tingling.

He couldn't believe it. Good Lord, Hess was coming in person!

At the start of the negotiations, the scheme seemed so simple. When he joined the British chapter of the Anglo-German Fellowship Association in 1936, he thought he was doing the only decent thing he could do. Through the organization he met a member, the Duke of Hamilton, and the duke's best friend, a German named Albrecht Haushofer, who had been personally appointed by Rudolf Hess as the adviser on British Affairs to the German Foreign Office. Together, Brenwood, Haushofer, and Hess decided that Germany and England should stay on the best of terms for the good of Europe and the world. Brenwood remembered dining with Hess during the Berlin Olympics in 1936. The Deputy Fuehrer took him on a tour of Luftwaffe bases, where Brenwood was awed by the German aeronautical advancements. His opinion of an Anglo-German coalition still hadn't changed in five years, despite the war. Now it was more important than ever. The lobby group had to be solidified once and for all. But why this way?

Brenwood's collaboration with other prominent Englishmen who shared his own views of European peace was becoming risky. Prime Minister Churchill had already purged the alliance with some success. He had banished the previous leader to a government position in the United States. But the list still grew. Military officers in the army, navy, and air force, and businessmen like Brenwood, held stubbornly to their political viewpoints of "peace with Hitler at all costs." The only Englishman from the alliance who had met, talked, and dined with Rudolf Hess, Brenwood had been appointed the unofficial leader of the clandestine peace group in 1940. He accepted the post with enthusiasm, at first. A year later he wasn't so sure. It was becoming more difficult as the months passed. Too many problems, too many delays. All he wanted was to see the thing through as quickly as possible before the plan backfired on the lot of them.

Brenwood crumpled the paper in his hand. He knew the next step would not go over too well with the Duke of Hamilton.

Bletchley Park, England

Roberta Langford picked away at her dinner of mutton and Brussels sprouts at a corner table in the cafeteria. She wasn't that hungry. She was lost in thought, reflecting on her last leave with Arthur. *The late meal at the country inn near the North Sea . . . the overnight stay . . . the intimacy . . . the romance . . . and the drive out to the sea in the morning.*

In the midst of her daydreaming, she didn't notice Spencer Winslow seeking her out in the throng of bodies, smoke, and conversation.

"I got your note."

She glanced up. "Oh, yes. Sit down, Spencer."

"Sorry I missed you. I was in a meeting."

She stabbed at another piece of mutton on her plate, although she couldn't bring herself to eat it. "That's quite all right."

"Care for a cigarette?"

"Don't mind if I do. I've been appreciating them a little more of late." She gave out a low, husky laugh.

"Don't we all know it. Allow me." Winslow struck a match and lit her cigarette, then his own.

"Thank you," she said.

"So, what's on your mind?"

"Since you are the acting head of Committee B in Hollinger's temporary absence, I wanted to let you know I've discovered something this morning about the *Enigma II* rollers."

"Hollinger just got back. Some workmen are taking boxes into his office as we speak."

"In that case, I'll save it for him."

Winslow shrugged. "Suit yourself. I hope you don't mind my tagging along, though?"

"Not at all. Tell me, how did he ever get out before the weekend?"

Winslow frowned. "He seems to have the knack of getting his own way. You'll never guess what he was doing when I left him."

"I'm afraid to ask."

"He was putting up NO SMOKING signs in all the hallways of Hut Nine."

Langford laughed. "The crazy bugger."

"Do you find some humour in that? I certainly don't."

"He's in a class by himself."

"I'll second that," Winslow agreed.

"Did you get a gander at that ring of his? How vain."

"If you only knew the whole story about him," Winslow grunted. "You don't seem to mind him, do you?"

Langford thought of Hollinger's apology the day before. "No, I don't, really. Leastwise, he has some good qualities."

"Name one."

"He has blue eyes. Like Arthur."

Winslow shook his head.

"After how he embarrassed you, you compliment him? Well, did you know he doesn't like redheads? He said he has an aversion to them. He told me so."

"Oh, does he?" she pouted.

"It's true. He looks like the type who's shacked up with a few Yankee girls. Dames, as he calls them. He doesn't really strike me as a Cornell man."

"Who can you compare him with? How many other Americans do know who went to Cornell?"

"None," Winslow admitted. "All I know is it's a very prestigious private university in New York State. Nevertheless, he's a bit off and kind of clumsy. And, speaking of Cornell, do you know he was nearly kicked off the campus?"

"No!"

"You want to know why? Get this, he was caught in bed with the dean's wife."

"Good grief! The dean's wife! Who told you?"

"Lampert. It's in Hollinger's file. The whole thing was dropped when the dean discovered his wife had been sleeping around on him for years." Winslow exhaled a cloud of smoke. "To tell you the truth, I don't mind him either. He a likeable enough chap."

For the next few moments neither one spoke, until Winslow said, "Your hands are shaking. Are you not feeling well?"

Langford extended her fingers to study them. "I'm tired. Haven't had much sleep with the *Enigma II* push on. I could use a long rest."

"How's Arthur?"

"Fine. We're planning a weekend in London, the first or second week of May. I got a letter from him today. But he didn't quite sound himself. No energy to it. Not like the others. Something's wrong."

"Must be the war," Winslow said.

"Maybe."

Winslow stood up. "Well, shall we go, my dear? Doesn't look like you're going to eat the rest of that lot. Our American cousin awaits us. I'm anxious to hear what you've uncovered about the rollers."

Langford didn't budge. "So, he hates redheads, does he? He can wait then."

"Change your mind?"

"Yes. Let's have another smoke."

He smiled. "Just in case it might be a long meeting?"

"Right you are, Spencer," she said, flipping a cigarette from her purse. "Sit down."

It took Wesley Hollinger less than a week to realize what Spencer Winslow had referred to when he said, "You'll find out soon enough," on his first day at Bletchley. The major portion of the American's work turned out to be boring, with mounds of *Enigma II* paperwork to plug through and a long list of menial administrative duties to take care of. Piled high in the registration room were neat rows of flimsy paper, the garbled *Enigma II* dispatches distinguished only by the call signs and the medium or high-range frequencies recorded by the English receiving stations. The stacks were gaining height every day, as Hollinger and the Hut Nine workers laboured around the clock in three shifts in an all-out effort to conquer the secrets of *Enigma II.* In preparation of an extended siege, Hollinger decided that his office needed a new desk, some new chairs, and more file cabinets, all charged to one of those mysterious Secret Service accounts that only a few in the organization were supposed to know about, let alone use.

Taking a break, Hollinger slouched in his new office chair, head back, legs spread-eagled on his desk. He faced the dartboard on the far wall, fifteen feet away, with a fist full of darts. He began to throw one at a time. On the sixth try he hit the bull's-eye. Then he heard two sets of footsteps down the hall. He quickly threw the last dart, just as Winslow came through the door.

"Hey, watch it."

Hollinger scrambled to his feet as Winslow and Langford stood there, inside the entrance, blank looks on their faces.

"Sorry," Hollinger said, red-faced.

Winslow grinned. "Nice chairs. Upholstered, too. I do hope we aren't keeping you from something important." When Hollinger didn't reply, Winslow continued. "I was talking with Robbie. She might have something for us."

"Let's hear it." Hollinger adjusted the knot in his tie. "Any news is good news."

"I'm sure it is," Winslow said, glancing at the dartboard and the darts stuck to it and in the wall.

Langford withdrew and returned with the *Enigma II* machine on a waist-high trolley. "Well, Mr. Hollinger," she began, "the Germans were very clever in putting this machine together. But I may have uncovered a flaw. The two wheels at the far right side of the rotating roller do not flip up every letter of the alphabet." She pointed to each roller with a sharp pencil. "Only ten letters each. The same ten letters. The one next to these two displays only half the alphabet. The three other wheels work perfectly."

Hollinger gripped his desk and leaned sideways in his chair. "Why do you think it might be a flaw?"

"Well, we know that sometimes in an airplane factory, at least so I've been told, one mistake can be made that is handed down to the next line and might not be corrected until a few planes are finished and in service. Let's think back to what we know of *Enigma II*. They are in the experimental stage. There are only a few of them out. Less than ten was the last estimate, according to our garbled dispatches."

Hollinger swung the chair a quarter turn to look at the lawn shrouded in a light fog. When Langford paused, he said, "Are you suggesting that it might have been rushed into production?"

"Yes. The Germans probably haven't caught the error yet, at least not with six wheels. There are too many. Or maybe they have, but haven't done anything about it. Why should they? Even with the flaw, it's more complicated than the mother *Enigma* with the standard roller. And as far as they know, we haven't cracked the first *Enigma*. So to them there's probably no urgency."

It was good news to Hollinger, and so soon after his arrival at Bletchley. He stood up. "You know, if your hunch is wrong, and only this machine is flawed and not the others . . . We have got to find ourselves another *Enigma II* machine so that we can be sure."

"Yes, sir."

"Fat chance of that," Hollinger huffed, eyeing Langford. "If we continue to work out the permutations of this one and we are unable to decipher any of those stacks of messages in the registration room, all this has gone for naught."

"That's about it, Mr. Hollinger."

Hollinger glanced away from his visitors. "But what if you're right about the flaw? How long would it take to monitor all the possibilities so you can start deciphering?"

Langford thought about it. "The computer could break them down in a few weeks, at the most."

Hollinger nodded, saying nothing.

"What should we do?" Winslow asked.

Hollinger sauntered over to Langford and with conviction said, "Keep going. Assume it's not just this one they've buggered up. It's all we got. Hell, don't stop now."

"I won't," Langford promised.

"Good. Oh, and Langford . . ."

"Yes."

Over the last few days, Hollinger had realized how important she was to the project. Winslow was right. She was the best, red hair and all. "Nice work."

"Thank you, sir." She smiled, and glanced across the room at Winslow, who glanced back.

"How are those headaches?" Hollinger wanted to know.

"I'm still a little lightheaded today, but I do feel better. Thanks for asking, Mr. Hollinger."

"You're welcome. Keep me posted on your work."

She smirked. "And I'll leave you to your darts game."

Six

MUNICH, GERMANY

The train carrying Nazi Germany's Deputy Fuehrer clanged its way into the station, hissing clouds of steam, before banging to a stiff halt. Night had fallen and there was a chill in the air. Rudolf Hess emerged from his private compartment and scanned the quiet crowd, mostly made up of soldiers, until he spotted his old friend, Professor-General Karl Haushofer, on the far side of the dimly lit platform.

The professor was a tall man with a hook nose, a moustache, and grey hair. Hess guessed that none of the soldiers would know who the elderly man was. Haushofer's background was a worthy one. He fought in World War I, and was a former military attaché to Japan. He later received his Doctor of Philosophy, majoring in geography, geology, and history. As a result of combining these three subjects in his own unique way, he became the Professor of Geopolitics at the University of Munich in 1921. He taught many students who eventually embraced his new beliefs of geographical imperialism, a new and controversial study of political geography as seen from a German point of view. To him and the new recruits, the Germans had been stabbed in the back by their government in the First World War. They all saw a new vision for Germany, one of power and force. Their destiny was to control the continent by divine right.

One of the professor's prized pupils was a fanatical youngster named Rudolf Hess, who had found himself disillusioned following the war. In Haushofer, Hess saw the father figure he had been searching for. They began to socialize. Haushofer loved Hess like a son. The professor provided the educational training that fixed Hess to the vision. Adolf Hitler later provided the political training. During the ill-fated Beerhall Putsch of 1923, in which Hitler and his henchmen attempted to seize power by force and were subsequently left scattered when the police moved in, Haushofer hid Hess in his home for a time during the roundup of the ringleaders. The deputy minister never forgot Haushofer's brave act of mercy. The professor's wife was half-Jewish. Once the anti-Semitic laws were enforced in the 1930s, Hess, who was second in command to Hitler by this time, threw his personal blanket of protection over the Haushofer family. And for that the German High Command never forgave Hess.

The professor looked up as Hess walked towards him across the platform. His former student was clad in a greatcoat, hat pulled down over his forehead. He entered on the passenger side of the professor's vehicle and slammed the door. Haushofer joined him in the front seat.

"Good evening, Professor."

Haushofer smiled and nodded at the man who had risen from a World War I veteran-turned-student to such glorious heights in the last twenty years. "Good evening, Rudolf. Chilly night."

"That it is. Thank you for coming."

"You are very welcome."

Haushofer started the ignition. He waited until he drove onto the road before he asked with a note of anxiety, "Are you still going to attempt your mission?"

"Yes, of course I am. All is ready."

"Must you? The North Sea in spring can be awful. You are heading right into the jaws of the enemy. Let diplomacy decide the fate and process of peace. Albrecht is still making contacts. He thinks it's wrong to fly to Britain, regardless of the English position and their recent military defeats."

"I know. Your son has told me. But Albrecht can't seem to break through."

Hess stared into the darkened night as the professor roared over the open road. Hess had never doubted his mission before and he wouldn't now. Two nights before he had dreamt he entered an old country castle carrying a briefcase, and proceeded down a long, high corridor lined with oil paintings of Scottish and English country settings. It seemed so real at the time, as if he had been there before. The dream meant one thing to him. It confirmed the importance of completing his mission. And the only way to do that was to appear before the British group. In person.

"The Fuehrer is using you. You're his sacrificial lamb." The professor could always talk freely with Hess, without reprisals. "The others," he went on, "Goering, Himmler, Goebbels, do not care at all. Albrecht knows the British. He has been to the Isles. He can vouch for them. Give him a chance."

"I know your son's views, professor," Hess said, cutting his friend short. "He hates any war, this one especially. But what tangible progress has he made with his own peace feelers? Nothing! I have to reach the appeasers myself."

"When?"

"Any day. Two, three weeks at the most."

Haushofer was horrified. "*Mein Gott!*"

"Professor, all I want is your support. It's my decision to fly to Great Britain. My mind is made up. Please, there is nothing else to say on the subject." Hess stared into the night, as the car raced over the road. "How is your dear wife?"

Seven

Near Eaglesham, Scotland—April 4

Wing Commander the Duke of Hamilton strolled the gardens of his Dungavel Castle country estate in the moors, as the sun poked through the surface mist that had rolled off the Firth of Clyde at dawn.

The handsome and wealthy Royal Air Force Commanding Officer in charge of the aerial defence of Scotland and northern England greeted his visitor Simon Brenwood with a firm handshake. A former amateur boxing champion, the duke was now closing in on forty, not a tall man, but wiry. A one-time member of the House of Commons, he was internationally known for being the first pilot to fly over Mount Everest in 1933.

"What brings you here, Simon?"

"See for yourself, Douglo," Brenwood said, using Hamilton's nickname.

Hamilton read through the long, decoded *Enigma II* message handed him. It was from Rudolf Hess to Brenwood, identified not by their surnames but by their appropriate codenames of *Deputy* and *Lion*. Now it seemed that Hess would be using the new codename of *Falcon*. And there was also a new name for the undertaking—*Operation Night Eagle*. Hamilton read on, then stopped.

"I've seen enough. He can't be serious. Can he?"

"I'm afraid he is, Douglo."

"How did he know about Dunhampton in the first place? Who told him? You?"

Brenwood looked insulted. "Of course not. I don't doubt that German intelligence is up on these things."

Hamilton gave the creased sheet back to Brenwood without bothering to read the final part. "I suppose the group expects me to give him free passage all the way in now."

"Yes, we do. You have the means to do it for us."

"I might have the means, but has anyone thought of the risks? We've gone from an unknown Luftwaffe pilot dropping a mere package on a secluded North Sea beach, to the Deputy Fuehrer flying across Scotland and landing with peace proposals from Adolf Hitler. Anything could go wrong. Anything! It was my understanding that I would not appear connected with the group in any way other than allowing the airplane's safety along the length of the beach. Now he wants to land? Germans are a strange lot. He's got to be mad!"

"I don't like this any more than you do," Brenwood conceded. "I want this whole mess to be over with myself. My nerves are on edge." He sighed. "I was thinking on the way here. Hess must feel that his ME-110 landing at Dunhampton would not seem that peculiar, seeing as it is an aerodrome for captured German aircraft. Besides, we're forgetting something."

"We are? What?"

"Hess must be bringing some very important papers with him, papers that he couldn't trust anyone else with."

Hamilton shook his head. His silence spoke volumes to Brenwood. They walked further into the garden, away from the stone house. They came across a brick path and followed it past roses in early bud. Brenwood looked up at the famous officer who was nearly a head taller than he was. He knew Hamilton was a moody individual, a hard person to get to know, almost as if he were two people. Behind his watchful face loomed a complicated man.

"We're in this too far to stop now," Brenwood said. "The good of Britain is the vital thing here. Churchill's policies are ruining us. The bastard wins every debate, while our fighting men lose almost every battle. Rommel is whipping our boys in North Africa and he's threatening the Suez. The German U-boats are sinking more than their share of our supplies coming over from Canada and America. Furthermore, if the bombing in London keeps up, there won't be anything left of it in another year or so. If Hitler is offering us a generous peace, we should take it. Why keep fighting him?"

Hamilton stopped and faced the businessman. "And what about your own interests? Obviously you don't want anything to happen to them if Hitler expands into new territory."

"That's not the only matter on my mind. I am an Englishman first; loyal to my country."

"Oh," Hamilton replied, his eyes telegraphing that he was unconvinced of Brenwood's outward sincerity.

"What else can we do? All the other attempts at peace have failed. We're in too deep. The group and Hess want to know if you can secure a safe flight and landing at Dunhampton."

Hamilton weighed the suggestion. "On one condition."

"And that is?"

"I never meet Hess. I told you before I don't want anything to do with him. Conduct the negotiations without me."

"Yes and no. Dunhampton is twenty-four miles away. You see, for convenience sake, we were thinking of using your castle for the negotiations."

"Oh, no." The colour drained from Hamilton's face. "Certainly not."

Brenwood showed Hamilton the final portion of the message. "It's all here in the last part of the message. I'll look after everything, and I'll pay off your servants for the day so they are not around."

"My word. Bring Hess to my house! You've really done it now."

"If not, we may be forced to call the flight off."

"Then call it off."

"We can't because we need more suitable and less hostile surroundings to confer with Hess. Another thing, I will provide the interpreter. The last time I met Hess he spoke very little English."

"You're going to provide the interpreter. Now there's a load off my mind."

"Please, Douglo. We need your cooperation."

"Oh, do it then," Hamilton finally agreed, after a long interval. "I won't be here. I'll make damn sure I'm on duty."

"That's quite all right with me, my good man. Just let him fly in safely. We'll do the rest."

BLETCHLEY PARK—APRIL 5

Colonel Lampert thought it unusual that a cluster of men and women were under the porch at Hut Nine, smoking and shielding themselves from the light rain, when they should be inside. He steered the car over to the shoulder of the gravel road, got out, and closed in on the crowd.

"Good afternoon, sir," Spencer Winslow greeted the colonel. He puffed on his cigarette, flipping up the collar of his trench coat.

Lampert stared oddly at the group, then at the butts on the gravel. "What the devil is going on? What are you doing out here in the rain?"

"New rules, sir."

"It's more like the beginning of a reign of terror," said an elderly woman in the back, who Lampert knew as Grace Dealey, a secretary transferred from another hut to handle the extra *Enigma II* load. "I've never been so embarrassed."

Lampert's eyes fell on Winslow. "What's the meaning of this? What new rules?"

"Since yesterday there is a total smoking ban inside Hut Nine."

"Who made such an asinine rule like that?"

"Our American cousin, sir," Dealey spoke up.

Lampert carefully pulled out his pipe, pushed some tobacco in the end, lit it, then dropped the match to the gravel. "We'll see about this."

"They're starting to refer to him as the Tyrant of Hut Nine," Winslow said, an amused curl on his upper lip.

"I wonder why?" Lampert said, entering the building and slamming the door behind him.

Dealey tapped Winslow on the shoulder. "That's it for our new boss. Lampert will eat him up and ship him back to Washington."

"I wouldn't take bets on it, Grace."

Lampert removed his coat inside the hut and tucked it under his arm. Right off, he saw two hand-written NO SMOKING signs in extremely large letters pinned to the walls in the bare lobby. Livid, he stomped the length of the hall to Hollinger's office, where he expected to see the standard stark furniture. Instead, to his amazement, the office had been outfitted with a new desk and chairs, and a dartboard, of all things, on one wall. Lampert went over to Hollinger's desk and fingered a pair of steel-rimmed sunglasses, which he took to be an American make, similar to the type worn by the American pilots in the RAF.

"Why, colonel."

Lampert spun around to see Roberta Langford at the door.

"This is a pleasant surprise," she said. "Welcome back."

"Welcome back, *my eye*. Where's Hollinger?"

"I believe he's in the workroom, sir."

"Take me to him this instant."

"Yes, sir. Follow me."

Langford led the colonel to a large room at the extreme rear of Hut Nine. Inside were four or five-inch-high stacks of paper neatly arranged on long benches. Hollinger sat beside one of the benches flipping through one of the stacks, the sleeves of his monogrammed shirt rolled up.

Lampert approached the youngster. "Hollinger, what's the meaning of this ridiculous rule of no smoking in the building?"

Hollinger stood slowly and cautiously, glancing over at Langford. "Why don't we go over to my office, sir, and discuss it?"

"Your office? That's another thing. Good God man, where did you get all that furniture? It must have cost a king's ransom. And a confounded dartboard? Do you have that much time on your hands? We're not running a country club here!"

"The dart board is a pressure release, sir," Hollinger replied.

"I'll vouch for that, colonel," Langford said, keeping a straight face.

"As for the furniture," Hollinger continued. "When I was appointed your understudy at Committee B, I was told that I could make any improvements that I felt were in the best interests of the Secret Service. Therefore, I decided that if I was to spend considerable time with visitors and work associates," he nodded at Langford, "then I should make use of more comfortable furniture. I also outfitted Langford's office. She needed new chairs badly. The old ones were falling apart." Langford smiled at Hollinger, but turned away when Lampert shot a glance at her. "As for the 'no smoking' signs, well, sir, you can't knock my reasons. Two days ago we nearly had a fire in here from a dropped cigar ash. Some people are far too sloppy for their own good when it comes to smoking. There are far too many important papers in this room and the entire hut. We do not want any setbacks due to human carelessness, do we now, colonel? With that in mind, I banned smoking in the whole hut. If anyone has to light up," he went on, staring at Lampert's smouldering pipe, "then he or she will have to do it outside in the cold."

Lampert didn't know what to say as a rebuttal. It was radical, but his reasoning too sound to argue with. Hollinger had him. He took the pipe from his mouth and banged the tobacco into an empty waste-paper bin, watching the ashes until they burned themselves out.

"Thank you, colonel."

"Anything new since the last time we spoke?"

"No, sir," Hollinger answered. "The computer and the mathematicians are still breaking the cipher variables down. If Langford is bang-on with her discovery, we'll know any day."

"We hope," Langford added.

"The minute you get anything, I want to know. And, I want any ciphers with the destination of Stockholm brought to me in person."

"Why Stockholm, sir?"

"Never you mind."

"Yes, sir."

"I want them as fast as you can drive them up to me. But I still want them in one piece. Don't kill yourself racing them to London." Lampert began to suck on his pipe, then looked at it strangely, suddenly realizing it was not lit. He quickly yanked it from his mouth. "And I do not want you to discuss the contents of these Stockholm intercepts with anyone else. Understood?"

"Perfectly, sir," Hollinger replied. "Got that Langford?"

"Yes, sir," she said.

"Carry on."

"Yes, sir."

When Lampert turned for the door, Hollinger gestured a stiff thumbs-up to Langford across the room. All she could do was frown and mouth *you're lucky*.

Eight

Berchtesgaden, Germany—April 8

Martin Bormann, Rudolf Hess's Chief of Staff and Adolf Hitler's constant companion at Berghof, appeared at the door to Hitler's reception room. It was a magnificent room, containing the largest picture window in Germany. Lining one wall was the Fuehrer's collection of rare and tropical birds. Bormann found Hitler feeding a brightly coloured toucan with orange and apple slices.

"That's my boy. You won't die like the others, will you, Frederick," Hitler said softly, dropping the fruit pieces inside and closing the cage. He wore his most common attire today, a wrinkled grey coat and baggy black trousers, his World War I Iron Cross pinned to his breast. Hitler was especially fond of the Central American toucan, enjoying the way it would jab at the fruit with its long beak. Visitors over the years had brought foreign birds to Hitler at Berghof as presents, but many of them had died in the harsh mountain air. Two years before he received his first toucan, which had lived for barely three weeks. So far, Frederick, which Hitler had named after the Prussian leader, Frederick the Great, had made it through two months with no ill effects.

"Excuse me, mein Fuehrer."

Hitler brushed his hand across the bars of the cage to catch the toucan's attention. It jerked its head and looked up. Hitler mimicked the bird by nodding his head at it. "That's my boy. *Yes*, Bormann, what do you want?" Hitler asked sharply, his eyes on the bird.

"I'm sorry to disturb you, mein Fuehrer. But Reichmarshall Goering is on the telephone from Karinhall."

"I'll be back, Frederick." Hitler looked over at his heavy-set, round-faced confidant. "I'll take it on the scrambler."

"Yes, certainly, mein Fuehrer."

Hitler trotted into his study, hands behind his back, and sat down at his desk. A metal box rested beside him. It was about two feet square with a series of wires and contact plugs connected to the desk telephone. Hitler turned to his left and punched a button on the side of the phone, engaging the scrambler.

"Goering?" Hitler's voice was now split into five smaller garbled bands that raced through the telephone lines and reassembled at the receiving telephone.

Hitler listened as the Reichmarshall opened the conversation.

"Yes, Goering. You heard it correctly. It's true," Hitler said, as he reached into his coat pocket for a chocolate. "I want the modifications to Hess's aircraft approved. Yes, whatever he wants. Do it. Never mind about Croneiss," he said, referring to Theo Croneiss, the Messerschmitt technical director at Augsburg. Hitler listened, nodding. "Yes, it was proper for him to follow the chain of command and call you. But I want it done."

Hitler waited to hear Goering's itemized list of changes. "Why all those you ask? Because Hess will fly to Great Britain." There was no reply on the other end. "Goering, are you still there?"

Dolln See, Germany

Hermann Goering dropped the receiver into the cradle and folded his arms over his loud, medal-garnished Luftwaffe uniform. He would soon be off to Berlin, two hours driving time from his lavish Karinhall chalet on the Schorf Heath, a picturesque Prussian terrain of forests and lakes that stretched to the Baltic coast.

The Luftwaffe Commander-in-Chief laughed heartily. Goering hated intellectuals like Hess; an abstainer, a vegetarian, a man who prided himself on such culturally elite subjects as geopolitics. The two had loathed each other for years, and were often separated at party rallies to prevent any confrontation that would embarrass the High Command. Goering recalled Hitler's general order forbidding all Nazi leaders from piloting their own airplanes for obvious reasons of safety. How had Hess been getting away with it? Hess had to be a fool. The whole thing had to be his idea, the buffoon, not the Fuehrer's.

Since the outbreak of the Second World War, Goering had assumed that if any German should meet any British peacemakers that he would be the natural choice. After the attack on Poland, he had informed the Fuehrer that he would fly to Britain to explain the situation. But Goering later reconsidered and thought it much too dangerous. And now Hess was about to try it more than a year into the war. Goering was a pilot, too, although he was now far too fat to squeeze into a fighter cockpit.

Goering seethed with jealousy. Hess was trying to make him look bad.

BERLIN, GERMANY

Wolfgang Geis shut the door to Himmler's office behind him, walked toward his superior's desk, and came to a halt. "Begging your pardon, Herr Reichsfuehrer?"

Himmler stirred behind his desk. "What is it, Geis?"

"Herr Reichsfuehrer, I have something for you so important that I rushed to tell you myself. My men picked up a word-for-word conversation today between the Fuehrer and Goering. Hess is going to fly to Scotland to seek a negotiated peace with the British."

"He's going to what?"

"Here it is, Herr Reichsfuehrer."

Himmler snapped the typed sheet from the Gestapo officer and studied it closely, silently waving Geis to sit. The wire-tap had paid off already. Goering had questioned Hitler on some modifications to Hess's personal aircraft, including a more powerful radio and auxiliary tanks. Hitler told Goering details of Hess's *Operation Night Eagle. Falcon* would be his codename. The Deputy Fuehrer needed daily weather reports and maps of the safe areas to fly. So, Himmler concluded, the rumours of peace negotiations were true. And Hess was in on it.

"Very good, Geis," Himmler smiled. "I am pleased with you. Keep it up and you may make colonel."

"Thank you, Herr Reichsfuehrer."

"Keep me informed. Dismissed."

Geis sprang to his feet. "Heil Hitler!

Nine

Augsburg, Germany—April 15

Rudolf Hess arrived at Augsburg unannounced, threw on his flight gear, and had his chauffeur drive headlong to the aircraft. There, Hess climbed the wing and bent over his cockpit. He glanced around. He took out a screwdriver from inside his flight suit and promptly removed one side of the thin metal plate along the fuselage to the right side of the pilot seat. Then he slipped the leather folder of papers and photos behind the plate, and screwed the side in place. He had to hurry now. His ground crew, as expected, were racing towards him in a truck. He finished with seconds to spare as the two men drove up, skidding to a halt off the fighter's port wing.

"Sorry we are late, Herr Reichsfuehrer," one of them said as he pounded up the wing in heavy boots. "We had no idea you were arriving."

Hess calmly seated himself and looked to the young man in the brown cap. "Don't worry. It wasn't a test of speed on your part. I decided at the last moment to take a morning flight. That's all. I should have notified you first. It will not go on your record."

The man looked relieved. "Thank you, Herr Reichsfuehrer."

"Now, please get me ready, sergeant."

"It will be a pleasure, Herr Reichsfuehrer."

It was raining when Hess returned to base thirty minutes later. He was earlier than expected due to mechanical problems that needed attention. He ordered the crew to fix what he thought was a sticky rudder so that he could fly the aircraft again that evening at 1800 hours. Then he headed for the compound.

As Hess swung open the door to the pilots' room, he saw wet footprints on the concrete leading up to the front of his locker. He stopped and glanced around. No one else was there. It wasn't raining before he left, so they couldn't have been him. Had someone been in his locker? He unlocked it and checked the contents inside. His clothes had been moved, just a little, but enough for him to know that they had been disturbed. It was an amateurish job. Who wanted to search his locker? Did someone doubt his intentions? Himmler? Hitler? Goering? The opportunity to stash the papers on the aircraft could not have come at a better time. But did someone see him do it?

BLETCHLEY PARK, ENGLAND—APRIL 20

Wesley Hollinger had his late evening meal brought to him in his office because he didn't want to leave. Hut Nine was buzzing with excitement after Langford had spread the word that something was coming down within the hour on an *Enigma II* breakthrough. He stole a glance at his watch. Almost eleven. He brought the cup to his lips and swallowed a mouthful of dark tea, the way he liked it. He was getting used to British tea since his arrival on the island, especially when it had a little dab of good American whiskey in it.

A door slammed. The quick footsteps were familiar to him. Langford entered the office, her expression immediately convincing Hollinger that Bletchley's luck had suddenly changed for the better.

"It works, Mr. Hollinger. It works! Feast your eyes on this. We tried some of the older ones first." By the sound of her voice she was tired, but a spark of electricity showed in her eyes.

Hollinger wiped his mouth and read one of her deciphered communiqués sent from Adolf Hitler's Chancellery in Berlin to the Luftwaffe attaché in Moscow, dated March 18. It was trivial, requesting the appearance of the attaché in the German capital as soon as possible. Nothing really, but at least *Enigma II* was being deciphered. A wide, satisfied smile appeared on Hollinger's lips, the kind of smile that Langford and the others had not seen on Hollinger for days. Bletchley had finally broken *Enigma II*, and that was plenty to be happy about.

"I like it. Yes, ma'am. I like it."

"Good news for the colonel."

"Hell, yeah."

"How far back should we go with saving the ciphers?"

Hollinger slid his fingers through his thick mop of hair, and mulled the question over. Would there be anything of worth in the past diplomatic ciphers? "Make it the beginning of the year."

"Right you are."

"What else do you have there?"

"The next few are somewhat unusual. I added a notation in each corner."

Hollinger looked at the top sheet of the set handed him and was taken aback by her hand-written inscription on the left side of the paper. "The original cipher was sent in English, not German?" he asked, puzzled.

"Yes, sir."

"Don't you think that's a little . . . weird?"

"Yes, I do."

"Call sign NPL."

"Not only that, sir, but it's from Stockholm. So are the other ones in the pile."

Hollinger rubbed his chin and went down the sheets. "So they are. What do you know about that. Thanks. I'll get onto it."

"Toodle-oo, then."

"Yeah. So long." Hollinger's eyes dropped to the first sheet.

NPL
URGENT
CODE 33658
TO STOCKHOLM LION KPG/1140
FROM DEPUTY AUGSBURG
3526/52 0800/01/25/41
LEAVING AUGSBURG 1200 01/27/41
WEATHER PERMITTING
DESTINATION AALBORG
ARRIVE AINWICK 1700
END

"Ainwick!" Hollinger whispered aloud.

He knew the place, vaguely; if it was the Ainwick he was thinking of. He had been there once. Nice place too. He jumped from his chair and studied the wall map of the British Isles behind him. Ainwick was on the North Sea shore of England near the Scottish border.

"If that don't beat all," Hollinger said to himself as he searched his desk directory for the RAF intelligence branch involved with *Enigma*. He found the phone number, took the receiver and dialled, hoping the contact he had spoken to earlier that week was still in. "Group Captain Walker, please. Priority Red."

"Yes, sir," the receptionist answered.

Seconds later.

"Hello."

"Group Captain Walker?"

"Yes."

"Wesley Hollinger at Bletchley. I know it's late. But I need your help."

"Let's go on scramble before we say another word." Walker's accent marked him as an upper-class Englishman.

"OK." Hollinger hit his telephone button and waited. "Are you with me?"

"Yes, I can hear you clearly. Password?"

"Hut Nine."

"What's keeping you up so late, Mr. Hollinger?"

"Like you. Burning the midnight oil."

"Priority Red is it? What can I do for you?"

"I need some information. A few things actually. Got a note pad?"

"Righto. Fire away."

"Have you ever heard of a place called Augsburg? In Germany, I believe."

"Indeed, I have, my man. It's outside Munich. A test aerodrome for the Messerschmitt factory."

"Is that right? The next one. Aalborg?"

"Denmark."

"Can you tell me if there is a Luftwaffe station there?"

"As a matter of fact there is. ME-110 night fighters. They do a lot of patrol duty in the area."

Augsburg... Aalborg... Ainwick. Hollinger was beginning to picture a flight plan before him. "Now, I have some numbers for you. They are, let's see, 3-5-2-6-dash-5-2. Can you tell me what they might represent?"

"I'll do what I can. Off the top of my head I'd say they sound like an aircraft serial number. Quite possibly a German series. I can check it out. Is that the lot?"

"Yes, sir. When can you let me know?"

"Stay there. I'll ring you back in a few minutes, but it may require some additional research."

"Thanks. I won't move."

Hollinger hung the receiver in place. Why was the message sent in English? That had to mean something. Was the contact in Stockholm an Englishman? An American? Or maybe a Canadian?

For the next twenty minutes, Hollinger checked the gist of the other intercepts to discover they were unimportant. Then the telephone rang. He grabbed a note pad and put the receiver to his ear. "Hollinger here."

"It's Walker."

Hollinger hit the scramble button. "Yes, sir."

"Where in the King's name did you get that serial number?" Walker's friendly tone had disappeared.

"It's a long story, group captain. Is it a German series?"

"It is."

"Well?" Hollinger clicked his silver, ballpoint pen.

"I do hope there's no security leak here."

"What are you talking about? What security leak?"

"The MI-6 have a spy in the Messerschmitt factory at Augsburg."

"They do? I didn't know that."

"I didn't either. I checked his file. His transmissions have been released to Royal Air Force Intelligence."

"And? I've been cleared, remember?"

"Apparently those numbers belong to Rudolf Hess's personal airplane, a D-version ME-110. We even know his fuselage markings because he uses the airbase at Augsburg for his flying."

"So, what are the markings?"

"N-J-C-1-1."

"Oh, shit! Hess?" Hollinger's eyes shot to the message in his hands. Bingo! Rudolf Hess, the Nazi Deputy Fuehrer. So, that's who "deputy" was in the dispatch.

"Yes, Hess. What's this all about?"

"Thanks, Walker. I'll be in touch. Ah, toodle-oo."

Before Walker could reply, Hollinger hung up and wrote the fuselage markings down. He slumped in his chair, realizing that he was on to something even bigger than the *Enigma II* breakthrough. He shook his head, attempting to pull some sense out of it. Had Rudolf Hess really tried to reach Ainwick on the coast of England on January 27? Who was he to meet? What did Lampert have to do with this, if anything? Why did he want all the Stockholm ciphers brought to him in person? And who the hell was *Stockholm Lion*?

Hollinger drew a breath and buzzed his intercom. "Langford?"

"Yes, Mr. Hollinger?"

"You're still up?"

"Too excited to sleep."

"Thanks again."

"You're more than welcome, sir."

"From here on I want every cipher with the call sign NPL put directly on my desk. Check all the ciphers going back to last year for the same call sign, which means fishing for them in the garbage. Retrieve everything."

"Yes, sir."

"Tell the next shift that too or, better yet, leave a note somewhere, because we're driving to London. Now."

"We? Now?"

"Yes, *we, us, now*! Lampert wanted these Stockholm intercepts delivered in person and that's exactly what we're going to do. I thought I'd bring you along because you could use a break, a couple days off to see your family. So, be ready in fifteen minutes."

"Good grief, fifteen minutes?" she choked. "How can you expect a woman to pack in fifteen minutes?"

Langford dashed to pack and was ready on time. Hollinger checked out at the gate and raced his MG over the country roads through the darkness. Ten miles outside Bletchley, Langford asked Hollinger to stop.

He pulled the car over and said, "What's the matter with you?"

"I'm not feeling very well. I could use some air."

"Now?"

"Yes, now."

She got out, slamming the door behind her, then knelt down beside the ditch and vomited. When she finished, Hollinger helped her up and gave her his handkerchief to wipe her mouth.

"Thank you," she said, her breath steaming in the cool night.

"Keep it."

She walked back to the MG and reached inside her purse for her cigarettes. With trembling hands she opened the pack.

"You're pregnant, aren't you?"

Langford dropped the pack to the ground. Hollinger calmly picked it up and held it out to her. "Well, aren't you?" he repeated louder.

"How dare you ask a woman that?" she replied, her voice rising an octave, as she snatched the pack from him.

"I'm no idiot. I've suspected for some time."

"Oh, have you."

"Yeah. You can hardly eat. You're always tired. Your headaches. Now the vomiting. Well, are you?"

She still didn't answer. Instead, she turned around, bent over, and threw up some more. This time Hollinger went ahead and wiped her mouth for her with the handkerchief.

"Hell's Bells. Don't you think I can do that myself?"

Hollinger stepped back. "OK, OK. Don't bite my head off. You still haven't answered me. I'm waiting."

"All right! Yes, I am what you might call knocked up." Her voice quivered as she held back from crying. She stumbled to the sports car and steadied herself against the fender. "And I don't know what to do."

Hollinger stood beside her. "What about your navy boyfriend? Does he know?"

"No. I want to tell him myself when we get together in two more weeks."

"Do you love him?"

"Yes, I certainly do."

"Well then, if he's any kind of man and has any thread of decency in him, he'll marry you."

She sighed. "I wish it were that easy. My parents are the problem. They'll die. My father's a minister."

"Oh, I see. The embarrassment."

Langford began to sob, softly. It had all come to a head. Her pregnancy. Too many long hours at Hut Nine. Too many sleepless hours worrying about Arthur in Scapa Flow. Too much stress trying to break the *Enigma II* secrets. Too little food. "They won't have anything to do with me," she said, wiping away the tears. She took a deep breath and straightened up.

"Strict and proper Englishman, I take it? You'll have to tell them. Why not on this trip to London?"

"Oh, no." She shook her head. "I couldn't. Not now. Not until I tell Arthur first."

"Being the father, I suppose that's proper."

"Yes, it is."

"Beautiful night, you know," Hollinger said, searching for something to say. Anything. "No wind. The stars are bright. Look at them." She glanced up, unconcerned. "Don't get me wrong, and I don't mean to be disrespectful towards you in your condition, but in the universal realm of things your problem is just a speck, just like those stars out there."

Langford smirked. "As an analyst, is that your final assessment?"

He gently placed his hand on her shoulder. "Hang in there. You'll get through this. You're too damn tough of a woman to give up. A lot of people are counting on you, Roberta, especially that new life you're carrying."

"You called me by my first name."

"Yeah, I guess I did," Hollinger chuckled. "It's a nice name. Maybe it's high time you started calling me Wesley."

Langford could feel herself warming to him. "Maybe I will."

"OK, then."

They stood there staring into the dark night.

"By the way, Wesley, what do you suppose is in those ciphers that has us firing off to London?"

He shrugged. "Nothing much, really. Ever hear of Rudolf Hess?"

"Good grief, who hasn't?"

Hollinger informed her of the conversation with Walker, then said, "Actually, I asked you along because I need your help."

"So, there's a catch?"

He nodded. "I need you and your Secret Service ID to get us into some files that I wouldn't be able to get into on my own. And the middle of the night is probably the best time to pull it off."

"So that's it. You devil."

"Yeah, that's me. You game?"

"Oh, why not. I'm in enough trouble as it is."

Bowing, he said, "After you, my lady," and he opened the passenger door for her.

She turned her nose up and laughed. "Thank you, kind sir."

"There, you see, you're looking better already."

But when they got into the MG and he turned the ignition, the engine wouldn't start. Hollinger pounded his fist on the steering wheel. Reaching for the flashlight in the glove box he got out, opened the hood, and examined the wires. He then went for his toolbox on the floor beneath his seat. Langford got out with him and together they looked the engine over.

"Sounds like a bad distributor to me. No bloody spark," she said.

"How the hell would you know?" Hollinger grunted. He set the tools down and checked the wires for wear, twisting them with his hand.

Langford removed a pair of pliers from the box, popped the distributor cap, and flipped it upside down. "Look," she said, while Hollinger shone the light for her. "It's filthy."

"Yeah sure, make me look like a schmuck, why don't you?"

"Clean the contacts every now and then, dearie." She removed the handkerchief from her coat pocket and wiped the inside of the cap. As she put it back on, she noticed a crack on the outside. "See that?"

He bent over the fender with her. "Yeah?"

"Might be trouble. Better get it replaced in London."

"Thanks for the advice."

"If it can start, it should at least get us to our destination."

"It better or we'll have to thumb it."

"I beg your pardon," she said.

"You know, hitchhike. It probably wouldn't take us too long. I was left stranded once with this gorgeous blonde back in the Adirondack Mountains in New York. My car ran out of gas on a highway. All she did was show a little thigh and the first car stopped. Some old geezer—"

"That's quite enough. I have no intention of displaying my thigh in such a fashion."

"Don't worry about it. Nobody out here, anyway." He shook his head.

"What's the matter with you?"

"You never cease to amaze me. How do you know so much about cars?"

"My father taught me a few things. He used to be a mechanic before he went into the ministry."

"Figures."

Hollinger slipped behind the wheel and turned the ignition. This time the engine cranked and started. He revved it a few times for good measure. It was running rough but it would have to take them to London as it was.

Langford slammed the hood down and got in on her side. "Put 'er to the floorboards, cowboy, and get the hell outta here."

Ten

LONDON, ENGLAND—APRIL 21

Hollinger prepared the reel of film on the projector inside the MI-6 Secret Service Headquarters. He turned out the lights, switched on the machine, and took a seat close enough to rescue the projector if anything should go wrong.

He glanced over at Langford in the seat beside him. Both were tired after the auto trip from Bletchley so late at night. "Let's see what we got here."

The screen began to show some footage taken a few years before the start of the war, one of the annual Nazi Party rallies at the enormous Nuremberg outdoor stadium. At least 100,000 people had to be in attendance, the majority in uniform. The camera slowly panned the faces of German High Command members . . . Hermann Goering . . . Josef Goebbels . . . Heinrich Himmler . . . and finally . . . Rudolf Hess.

"There he is," Langford exclaimed.

"Yeah." Hollinger fixed his eyes to the screen.

The Deputy Fuehrer removed his military cap and took the podium before a half-dozen microphones. Draped behind him was a huge swastika flag. Hess was a tall man with a solid build and broad shoulders. His deep-set eyes, square jaw, and high cheekbones almost gave him an American Indian appearance. Then Hollinger saw something. "How about that?"

"How about what?"

"His mouth. He has buckteeth."

"In the entire realm of things, should that mean anything?"

Hollinger grinned. "Probably not."

Together, they seemed to enjoy the piece of film. Hess's oratory that sunny afternoon bordered on insanity. He hollered almost as much as Hitler was famous for. Obviously Hess, too, could incite a crowd into a frenzy. At the conclusion to his charismatic speech, the crowd broke into a chorus of *Sieg Heil*. Hollinger grimaced. The film reaffirmed what he had concluded since Hitler's rise to power. The Nazis were a bunch of theatrical rabble-rousers.

Hollinger looked over at his companion. A few minutes before, she had lain down onto two chairs and gone to sleep. He shut the projector off and flicked on a small desk lamp to his right. Careful not to disturb her slumber, he grabbed the papers Langford had found in a section of top-secret MI-6 files, the same place they had found the film.

He was amazed to find that the Secret Service had been keeping some unusual files, one on Rudolf Hess. Here, in Hollinger's hands, was Hess's military and political career, and medical records. It stated on the second page that Hess had suffered a near-fatal wound through his left lung in the First World War that had left permanent scars on his chest and back. Interesting. Next, Hollinger scanned a typed list of Nazi decrees enforced from 1934 to 1939, authored by Hess and his Chief of Staff, Martin Bormann, mostly of the anti-Semitic and anti-religion variety. Compulsory military service for all Germans. All persons who criticized party policies were to be reported to the Gestapo. All Jews were denied the right to vote or hold public office. Jewish doctors were forced to treat only Jewish patients. Jewish lawyers denied the right to practice their profession. Jews forced out of the business community. Any party members joining the clergy or caught studying theology were to be refused party status...

The words leaped out at Hollinger. Hess was one powerful man. And a cutthroat too, when called upon. From the information on hand, Hollinger quickly worked out Hess's involvement in the *Night of the Long Knives* in 1934. During Hitler's early years, before he had obtained absolute control of Germany, he had formed a strong-arm group known as the SA—the Sturmabteilung—who were nothing more than a pack of thugs who beat up Hitler's opponents and broke up the public meetings of other democratic parties. The leader of the SA was Ernest Roehm, a drunkard and child molester. By 1934, Roehm had three million in his private army, stronger in numbers than the combined forces of the German army, navy, and air force. He was out of control and secretly planning the takeover of the Nazi Party. Something had to be done. Hitler called a meeting with Goering, Hess, and Himmler. A list was quickly drawn up of those SA leaders "not faithful to the Fuehrer." Roehm's name was at the top. He was arrested, sent to prison, given a loaded gun, and ordered to use it on himself. He refused. Within the hour, a man entered the cell and shot Roehm dead. Unconfirmed reports credited Rudolf Hess with pulling the trigger. Hitler then used the roundups as an opportunity to rid himself of all opponents in a vast witch-hunt across the country. Over the course of a few days hundreds of Germany's unfaithful were liquidated as the world sat and watched in horror. From then on, Adolf Hitler was the dictator of Nazi Germany. And Hess helped to propel him there.

Hollinger closed the folder and placed it beside the other files that he and Langford had found. The contents of the other folders were just as strange. Prominent British politicians were being spied on by the Secret Service. He nudged Langford until she woke.

"Come on, Robbie. It'll be sunup soon. Let's scram, pronto. I'll drive you home."

She sat up, stretched, and yawned. "And where are you going, may I ask?"

"A hotel for a few quick hours of sleep, then I'd better get the MG fixed. After that, I'm going to pay a little visit to someone at 10 Downing Street."

"Churchill?" she asked, startled.

"Yep."

"You're kidding, right?"

"Not me. I never kid."

Berchtesgaden, Germany

Adolf Hitler entered the room that was one of the most important to him on the Berghof estate. Large maps lined every wall. Europe, Asia, North Africa, and major cities on these continents, came to life before his eyes. A map of London was his favourite. It was the biggest and most detailed, and was in three sections, showing the neighbourhoods and individual main buildings. He could actually see the exact location of the House of Commons and 10 Downing Street, the home of his enemy, Winston Churchill. Today, the Fuehrer shuffled over to the newest addition to his room: a long, colourful map of Scotland. Glasses to his eyes, he stood, alone, studying the route Hess had given for his flight to Dunhampton. He saw Holy Island, the Farn Islands, Cheviot Hills, Troon, St. Abb's, Coldstream, and Peebles; all the landmarks mentioned by Hess.

Twenty minutes later, Hitler met Karlheinz Pintsch and Martin Bormann at the entrance to the reception room.

Pintsch extended the Nazi salute. "Heil Hitler."

Hitler turned to Bormann. "I do not want to be disturbed for anything."

"Yes, mein Fuehrer." Bormann clicked his heels, spun around, and withdrew, closing the door behind him.

Hitler shoved a chocolate in his mouth. "Come with me, Pintsch."

"Yes, mein Fuehrer."

They walked over to the cages, Hitler with his hands behind his back. Although Pintsch had been to Berghof twice before, he had yet to see the reception room with its huge window that framed the Bavarian Mountains. It was quite a view. The cages and the birds to one side reminded him of a zoo. It seemed that Hitler's fascination with birds was not just a rumour.

"Do you like birds?" Hitler asked, over the chirping.

"Yes, I do, mein Fuehrer. But I'm afraid I do not know that much about them. Some of these look tropical."

"Over here are the birds native to Europe. The skylark, the bee-eater, the thrush. Farther down are my parakeets, my cockatoo, and my prized toucan, Frederick the Great. But Frederick hasn't been eating lately. I hope he doesn't die too, like the last toucan. He's my most loyal bird of all. He eats right out of my hand. Loyalty is very important to me, Pintsch."

Pintsch's nerves tightened as Hitler stared at him. Hitler suddenly stood at attention and shot out a Nazi salute with his arm. "Do you know that I can stand before my soldiers—my loyal soldiers—as they parade past me, and I can keep my hand raised for two hours. Did you know that, Pintsch?"

"No, I didn't, mein Fuehrer."

"Of course you didn't. But I can." Hitler dropped his arm down. "Goering can only hold his hand up for thirty minutes. No longer. Why? Because he's made of flab. I am built of muscle. Your superior, Hess, can hold his hand up for an hour. That is it." He paused for a moment to catch his breath. "Do you think Hess is loyal to me, Pintsch? What did you find?"

"Nothing at all, mein Fuehrer."

"No papers hidden anywhere?"

"Nothing."

Hitler drew closer. "Nothing at Augsburg when you searched his locker?"

Pintsch cleared his throat, stepping back. He remembered how he had to scramble when Hess came back early. "I couldn't find a thing."

"Has he been acting out of the ordinary?"

"Not that I can see, mein Fuehrer."

"Has anyone been to his house?"

"I've kept a close watch. Only those on official business." Pintsch licked his lips. "Mein Fuehrer, may I ask what I'm looking for? Perhaps then I could be of more help to you."

"Very well! Stay here." Hitler left and returned with three typed sheets in his hands. "I can't tell you everything, Pintsch. However, I will say this. For weeks Hess has been attempting a flight to Scotland to conduct peace negotiations in my name with the British."

Pintsch prayed his knees wouldn't buckle on him. He brought to mind his superior's mysterious flights at strange hours, the coded messages to *Lion* in Stockholm. Mission Abort, three times. Sometimes he would send the *Enigma* messages himself, but most of the time Hess did it. And then there were the modifications to the Messerschmitt. Extra fuel tanks. Stronger radio. "I never suspected," Pintsch exclaimed. "But when I think back, now it makes sense."

"You, Pintsch, must find out if Hess is acting for me or on his own. And there is only one way to do that. Look, look at my proposals. If Hess is in possession of any other proposals, then he is a traitor to the Fatherland, and disloyal to me. Then he will be dealt with. Now read them!"

When he took the papers, Pintsch realized he was entering a new dimension, beyond anything he had experienced in duty to his country before. And it made him feel uneasy because espionage and politics were not his fields. He had no training in either of them, and frankly, he didn't really want anything to do with them. Hitler motioned him to sit. Finding a chair, Pintsch forced himself to read. First, a membership board, a coalition of European countries, including England, would be set up and called the Council of Peace. Hitler would be its chancellor, naturally. A common currency would be established, based in Berlin. The pound sterling and the British parliamentary system would be abolished. All British interests would be either controlled outright or monitored by I.S. Filberg, the German business cartel. Lastly, England had to promise never to go to war with Germany again. Pintsch finished and looked away to the birds. The Fuehrer couldn't be serious. The British on their last dying breath would never agree to such terms. They would rather fight.

"What do you think, Pintsch?"

Pintsch swallowed. He knew he had to be careful with his reply. "I am no politician, mein Fuehrer. But they do seem to be harsh."

"Harsh! You want to see harsh? If the British don't comply with these points, we will bomb their cities day and night and crush them with a channel invasion!"

"Yes, mein Fuehrer."

"One other thing, Pintsch. Be discreet."

"Mein Fuehrer?"

"Hess must not know what you are doing, just in case he is as loyal to me as he claims."

Pintsch suddenly felt as if he was the one Hitler was watching and not Hess.

Eleven

Berlin, Germany

Captain Wolfgang Geis sat at a table at a popular outdoor restaurant in the capital and tilted back his schnapps. He saw the delivery truck turn down the alley behind the restaurant, and caught a pretty fair glimpse of the man behind the wheel. His boys in the Gestapo had found the man and passed on his route; they had done their background work with precision. Himmler would be pleased.

Geis quickly drank up and took to the pavement. The rear of the truck was thirty feet away at the end of the alley. The man stepped out and walked towards the kitchen entrance, oblivious to anybody watching him. Geis ran up and got a better look. The man was older, thinner for sure, and a bit taller than his counterpart, but it was the facial resemblance that staggered Geis.

"You there!" Geis said, holding his arm across the door, blocking the driver's way.

The man stopped cold. "What do you want?"

"Gestapo." Geis flashed his identification.

"What do you want with me?" the driver asked with some contempt. "I didn't do anything."

"I didn't say you did. I want to talk with you."

"Can you hurry up? I have a busy schedule."

Geis smiled. Even the eyebrows were nearly identical. "Remove your cap, please."

The driver hesitated as if he knew what the Gestapo agent was going to say next. He frowned and obeyed. "There. Better?"

"Has anyone ever mistaken you for someone else?"

"You mean Rudolf Hess? Yes, all the time."

LONDON, ENGLAND

Requesting and receiving an immediate audience with Winston Churchill at 10 Downing Street, London's most famous row house, on a few hours' notice was a proud accomplishment for Wesley Hollinger. Colonel Lampert would never have tried to reach the Prime Minister's office so early in his career. But Lampert didn't have the vigour and the gall of the wavy-haired, blue-eyed American senior officer of Bletchley's Committee B.

The two undercover civilians, Lampert and Hollinger, so opposite in style, were now standing in Churchill's wide library where the smell of stale cigar smoke lingered in the air.

Lampert nodded at Hollinger and said, "At least the timing was perfect. The Prime Minister finished his afternoon nap and it's tea time. I like his tea blend."

Hollinger was tired, and looked it. "Me, too. Thanks for coming, colonel. I didn't want to go over your head."

"This better be good, Hollinger. I still don't understand why you can't tell me without involving the Prime Minister."

"I want the Prime Minister to hear it from yours truly."

"Hear what, my boy?"

Hollinger whirled on his heels to see a short, very stout man in half-moon reading glasses saunter towards them, steadying himself on a cane. He wore a dark-blue night coat, and brandished a long lit cigar in his mouth. His feet and chubby hands were small, his hair a wispy white. This squatty man could easily have been mistaken for a ditch digger, or a counter clerk in a Brooklyn delicatessen, not the leader of the greatest sea empire in the world. This was the man who seemed moderately popular with the ordinary English people, and who at the same time was known to the outside world as the individual who was not only carrying the bulk of Great Britain on his shoulders but that of the whole Free World as well.

Awed in the presence of greatness, Hollinger had not seen Winston Churchill since the American's second day in Britain. His face and hands were more wrinkled than Hollinger had recalled from that short meeting on January 2. He seemed heavier and more stooped. But what remained obviously unchanged was the inner strength that the 66-year-old leader seemed to draw from, as if it were always on reserve for the taking. Hollinger could see that strength in his eyes, his confidant walk, despite the cane, and his keen expression. He certainly was not the warmongering drunk his opponents thought him to be. He was fighting for his country's survival against overwhelming odds.

Churchill was the son of an American mother and an English father. He was the extreme Man of War, a seasoned politician whose aim on the home front was to solidify the coalition government in Britain. It was proving to be a hard struggle. In the 1930s, while his peers were ignoring the danger signs in Nazi Germany, Churchill was a lone voice against Hitler's expanding war machine. Churchill had campaigned for more defence spending and was tagged an extremist. But he did have support from those who saw the danger. Men such as Colonel Raymond Lampert, others in the Secret Service, as well as a selected group of Americans, starting with Franklin Roosevelt and his intelligence adviser, Bill Donovan. Churchill had allies. The right people positioned in the right places.

"Good to see you again, Wesley," Churchill said in his lisp. His handshake was strong, his voice the same recognizable blare as in his radio broadcasts: hard, gruff, full of fight. "So, how is the Tyrant of Hut Nine?"

Hollinger froze at first. Damn. Churchill didn't miss anything. He'd heard about the "no smoking" signs. "Fine, Mr. Prime Minister. Just fine."

"I hope you don't mind if I smoke?"

"Not at all, sir."

"Have you been in touch with my friend, Mr. Donovan?"

"Yes, sir. He wrote me following my evaluation report of Bletchley. He said to give you his best."

"Good man that Donovan."

"Yes, sir. He is."

"What about those Japanese? Are they going to start anything in the Pacific?"

"If they do, sir, I'm confident our forces will be ready to take them on."

"And you, Colonel Lampert?" Churchill jabbed Lampert in the stomach with his forefinger. "How are you keeping? Have a seat, gentlemen."

"A little tired, sir," Lampert replied, easing into a padded chair.

"Hah," Churchill chuckled from behind his smoky cigar. "Try keeping the hours I do. Look at Wesley, here. He looks like he hasn't slept for twenty-four hours. The colonel working you too hard at Bletchley, boy?"

Hollinger had heard of Churchill's late nights. The Prime Minister very seldom dropped off before two in the morning. "Actually, sir, I did manage to catch an hour or so in a hotel before I came over."

"Care for a drink, anyone? It is tea time, is it not? Wine, whiskey, champagne, brandy."

"I could be persuaded to try a brandy," Lampert said.

"I thought you might. And you, Wesley?"

"The same here, sir."

Churchill snapped his fingers at a butler who withdrew and re-entered the room with three drinks and a container of ice on a tray. He served the drinks and shrank away like a cat, not making a sound, clicking the library doors closed as he retired to the hall.

Churchill settled into his favourite armchair, his cigar in one hand and a glass of iced scotch in the other. "Now, young Wesley, what's so damn important to get you out of Bletchley?"

"Yes, Hollinger," Lampert muttered. "I'm dying to know myself."

Churchill laughed, heartily. "You didn't tell your superior? Wesley, you got the nerve."

Hollinger blushed, and Churchill nodded at him to begin.

Hollinger bent down to his leather briefcase and nervously handled the small stack of papers inside. "Sir, it's *Enigma II*. We've broken it," he started out, his voice cracking.

"You have?" Lampert said. "When?"

"Last night."

"And you kept it from me until this afternoon? Why? I was supposed to be the first one notified."

Hollinger cleared his throat. "I wanted to tell you both in person. Actually, that's only part of it. It's the content of the intercepts themselves that... well... a series of them sent from Augsburg, Germany to a contact in Stockholm by the codename of *Lion*, are extremely unusual. They use a call sign of NPL." He set the papers on his armrest. "These are the same Stockholm intercepts that you asked for, colonel. None of them had to be translated because, strangely enough, they were sent out in English. Of course, I was suspicious right off. The first one was this one, dated January 25, from *Deputy* THREE-FIVE-TWO-SIX-FIVE-TWO." Hollinger handed the sheet to Churchill. "For your benefit, colonel, I had mimeographed an extra copy."

"Thanks for thinking of me."

Hollinger nervously passed the copies to Lampert, but dropped some sheets to the floor. "Sorry, sir. I'll get them."

Churchill looked at his sheet and glanced at Lampert as Hollinger retrieved the dispatches. "Go on, Wesley."

"There are many more from Augsburg to Stockholm where the same codenames of *Lion* and *Deputy* keep cropping up. When I checked with the section of RAF Intelligence attached to *Enigma*, I discovered the RAF have a spy at Augsburg. The Messerschmitt factory is at Augsburg, and it also has an airfield. According to the RAF files the numbers THREE-FIVE-TWO-SIX-FIVE-TWO are the serial numbers of a Messerschmitt-110 belonging to none other than Rudolf Hess, the Deputy Fuehrer of Germany."

"Hess?" Lampert asked, calmly.

"Yes, sir."

"Exactly what are you implying, Wesley?" Lampert demanded, glancing at Churchill.

Hollinger coughed. "This, sir. On the night of January 27, almost three months ago, Rudolf Hess attempted to fly his personal ME-110 from Augsburg to Aalborg, Denmark. But he didn't make it." Hollinger shifted uneasily. He handed out the rest of the deciphered Hess-Stockholm *Enigma II* intercepts. Something wasn't sitting well with him. Churchill and Lampert should have been more surprised. "See for yourselves," Hollinger said. "Later, on the twenty-ninth of January, *Deputy*—that is Hess—sent Stockholm another cipher stating he was forced to return to Augsburg due to a fuel leak. At first I thought Ainwick was his destination. See the bottom of the intercept where it states *arrive Ainwick 1700 hours*. But the last stage of the flight I now know was meant for a rendezvous aircraft, not Hess's plane."

"How did you conclude that?" Churchill asked, peering over the top of his glasses.

"We've deciphered several messages indicating that Hess has new plans to fly to Scotland in person very soon and meet with *Lion* at a base called Dunhampton, not far from Wing Commander Duke of Hamilton's Dungavel Castle. The codename for the flight is *Operation Night Eagle*, and Hess's codename is *Falcon*."

Churchill's eyes were fixed to the appropriate paper. He didn't look up this time until Lampert stared across at him. Then their eyes met.

Hollinger hadn't noticed. He reached for a thick file in his briefcase. "Mr. Prime Minister, how familiar are you with the Duke of Hamilton and his social and political connections?"

"Why would you ask me that?" Churchill answered.

"Because the Secret Service has a file on him, along with Hess. And here it is." Hollinger held it up and wiggled it in his hand. "It's all here. The Duke's pro-German leanings before the war. How he became friendly with several German pilots during a visit to Berlin in 1936 at the time of the Olympic Games. He attended a banquet at the chancellery hosted by Hitler and the Nazi Party. Two of his acquaintances were Professor-General Karl Haushofer and his son. Both just happen to be close friends of Hess. The same Professor Haushofer, by the way, whose Geopolitical views have influenced others so much, including Hess and Hitler, and certain Englishmen. Haushofer believes that Germany should lead a United Europe, side-by-side with her British brothers. One a land empire, the other—"

"You can skip the Geopolitics lesson, Wesley," Churchill interrupted. "The colonel and I are familiar enough with it."

"Yes, sir. Forgive me, sir. The professor's son, Albrecht, is the bizarre one," Hollinger continued. "He's a teacher at Berlin University and the adviser to the German Foreign Office on British Affairs, appointed by Hess. He's presently being investigated by the Gestapo for some alleged homosexual affairs with young boys. Albrecht and the duke had gotten together on a number of occasions before the war, in Britain and Germany. And let's not forget that the duke was a member of the Anglo-American Fellowship Association, and that he had stated, as a conservative in the House of Commons only a month after the war started, that he stood for a just peace. And that's not all. I also have in my briefcase a copy of a letter from Albrecht to the duke, dated September 1940. It was sent via a German spy named Mrs. V Roberts in Lisbon, Portugal—a letter the MI-6 intercepted before the duke saw it. There is also some information on Hess's life. Apparently he was part of a homosexual ring in Munich and Berlin. Even his marriage some twenty years ago didn't stop the rumours. There seems to be evidence of another homosexual ring in these files involving Albrecht Haushofer, maybe even Hess, the duke, and other noted British politicians. It's a potential scandal."

Hollinger dug for another folder in his briefcase. "There's more. The Secret Service has been gathering information on many leading British politicians. Lord Halifax, for one, and his deputy, Mr. Butler. And your own Secretary of War, sir, Oliver Stanley. Then there's the British Minister to Hungary, Owen O'Malley. And there's William Strang."

Churchill sprang from his chair, and with the help of his cane trotted over to Hollinger. "That's quite enough, young man," he said, snatching the folder from Hollinger's grasp. "You are one bright boy. Too bright. You have walked into a hornet's nest, Wesley." He turned to face Lampert. "We'll have to tell him, now, colonel."

Lampert shook his head. "We have no other choice, sir. Damn you, Wesley, you had no business rummaging through our confidential Secret Service files."

Hollinger searched the faces of Churchill and Lampert. They were fuming. "You both know about Hamilton, don't you? And about the letter."

"The letter and a lot you don't know. The aborted flights to Denmark. And we know Hess has communicated with Simon Brenwood using *Enigma II*."

"Brenwood?" Where had Hollinger heard that name before? "You mean the steel industrialist? You don't suppose he's the *Lion* mentioned in the intercepts."

"He is," Churchill replied. "It's handled through one of his Swedish business firms and two-a-day mail deliveries to London. And we know the *Falcon-Lion* meeting is set for Dungavel Castle."

Hollinger was astonished. It took several moments for his brain to catch up with what his ears had just heard. Churchill was right. Hollinger certainly had walked into a hornet's nest. "Why is Hess trying to reach Brenwood in particular?"

"Because Brenwood is the figurehead of a small but powerful lobby group in Great Britain composed of influential business people and politicians—men like Stanley, Butler, O'Malley—who want to sign a peace treaty with the Germans, and the Duke of Hamilton is a key collaborator. It's the duke's air sector that Hess plans to fly through for the meeting. Some people I know would rather make amends with Hitler to save their own cowardly skins! The cards are in place to overthrow me." Churchill sat down, throwing the file on a nearby nightstand.

"I've suspected collusion for some time, going back to Dunkirk," he continued. "Lord Halifax wanted our government to sign a peace pact right after the evacuation, while Hitler was still in the mood, as he put it. The traitor! But I fixed him so he wouldn't bother me. I banished the bugger to Washington. Made him our ambassador." Churchill threw back part of his drink. "His wife came here on her knees begging me not to send them to America. I had no mercy."

"So, that's what happened," Hollinger said, remembering the news of Halifax's appointment to Washington.

"Still, behind my back, members of my own party wanted me to give in to Hitler and let him take the continent. This outstretched hand of peace, as Hitler refers to it in his broadcasts. I thought the signing of the American Lend-Lease this month would change everything. It hasn't. And your President Roosevelt had offered us a blank check. All the supplies and war material we ask for. Getting back to Hess, how does he fit into all of this? He may be the missing part of the puzzle. He is definitely a peace messenger. The go-between. The message for Brenwood and his group of appeasers must be a vital one. Why else would Hess risk his life to fly here?"

"Can't these appeasers be put behind bars?" Hollinger suggested.

Churchill stood up and went over to the drinks tray, puffing on his cigar. He turned to the rugged, young analyst. "You have a lot to learn about diplomacy, lad. There's a broad line between being a traitor and an appeaser. Besides, if all these influential people were arrested for rising up against my leadership, it would ruin public morale in Britain. We can't even arrest Brenwood yet for fear of losing an excellent chance of trapping Hess. We have to make it look as if no one suspects Brenwood. We have to be strong and united in this country, not weak and divided while that Nazi swine with the stupid haircut and his sewer rats are knocking at our door. Anything I have to do must be accomplished behind some backs, the way it's always been done."

Hollinger suddenly wondered if he would ever have been told the

Hess secrets behind *Enigma II* if he and Langford had not been so snoopy. "Now I know why breaking *Enigma II* was such a priority. You wanted the jump on Hess," Hollinger said.

"I like the jump on everybody." Churchill dropped a fresh ice cube in his drink and sat down again. "Wesley, do you know how I was able to keep tabs on the German military machine long before the war began? I needed funds. I went straightaway to the King. He helped me establish my own Secret Service within the MI-6. Public money, lad."

"I never knew that."

"And Prime Minister Chamberlain didn't know a thing. Not a thing! Because the King and I didn't trust him. I'll tell you something else, too. I have a spy in the appeaser group. Even the colonel doesn't know who it is."

"No, I don't," the colonel confirmed.

"So, you're holding the trump card, sir," Hollinger said. "You know when Hess is coming because we can intercept the ciphers at least twelve to twenty-four hours before the plotters see them. Why don't you shoot Hess down while he's over the North Sea?"

"Why do that?" Churchill grunted.

"Why not? Get rid of him. RAF Intelligence could be brought in on it. They have night-fighter crews, experts on airborne radar. They could track him coming out of Denmark."

Churchill looked over at Lampert and grinned, reflecting on Hollinger's idea. "I like your spunk, lad. But why on earth would we want to kill him? Why not see what he's bringing with him?"

"Well, then, if you want him alive, let him be escorted to Scotland. If he's expected at Dunhampton, let's make sure he gets there and doesn't crash-land somewhere else where the information may fall into the wrong hands."

Churchill paused to consider the new suggestion. "You might have something there. I'd get working on it. With the colonel's permission, of course."

Lampert nodded, his face fixed. "With *Enigma II* cracked, we can spare him."

Hollinger exhaled a sigh of relief. For a time there he thought he was going to lose his job altogether. "What do you suppose Hess is bringing, anyway?"

"Wesley," Churchill said. "The Germans are mobilizing several Panzer divisions combined with air and ground units along the Polish-Russian border. It appears, to our sources, that the Germans are planning to attack the Soviet Union."

Hollinger was awestruck. "Would Hitler really do it?"

"I wouldn't put it past him. There's a strong anti-Communist movement in Britain, especially in the appeaser group. Ridding Europe of communism would only make them happier. It's rather simple. The appeasers overthrow me, sign a peace pact, and let the Germans knock off Stalin. The Geopolitical vision becomes reality. If Hess is carrying top secret plans for an attack on Russia, then he must be locked up as soon as he sets foot on our soil."

"You're absolutely right, sir."

"German scientists are also working on splitting the atom. Atom bombs, my friend." Churchill shook his finger at the American. "Destruction like you have never seen in your life. They would be able to control the world. Now, pick these papers up and return them. And don't go poking around," he said firmly. "From now on, if you want to know something, ask. We're on the same side. Keep that in mind."

"Yes, sir."

"As for the escort idea, get on it right away. Call Group Captain Walker at RAF Intelligence today. Keep in touch. And get some sleep. You look bloody awful."

"Yes, sir. I will get some sleep." Hollinger gathered the papers and slipped them into his briefcase. It had been quite the afternoon. "Goodbye, sir." He nodded at Lampert. "Colonel."

"Mr. Hollinger."

After Hollinger left, Lampert rose to his feet and said, "I still don't like the idea of him breaking into the files. He had no business in there. Now, another knows."

"I guess it was bound to happen sooner or later. He was too close to the intercepts not to notice. He's too smart, and like I said before, he's lucky. What arrogance."

"I'll drink to that."

Churchill smiled. "You know, colonel, he reminds me of someone."

"Really? Who?"

"Me."

Twelve

Berlin, Germany—April 22

Himmler looked through the one-way glass at the middle-aged man slouched in a chair next to a table in the interrogation cellar. "So, this is the delivery driver your men discovered for you?" he asked Geis.

"Yes, Herr Reichsfuehrer."

"How did you find him?"

"A friend of a friend. A conversation or two between people and—"

"Did anyone see you bring him in?"

"No, Herr Reichsfuehrer." Geis handed his superior the file; he had the man's information committed to memory.

"Felix Schubert," the Gestapo leader said, springing open the manila folder.

"Yes, Herr Reichsfuehrer. A distant relation of the Austrian composer. A former bank clerk. He had training as a Luftwaffe pilot after World War I, but washed out. Fifty-years-old. Wife and two daughters, both married to officers in the service. He's financially broke. A past criminal record and a heavy drinker. He used to be an informant for the German State Police under Von Hindenburg. Served only nine months in prison of a three-year term for robbing a jewellery store in 1931. Then someone on Hess's staff found him and recruited him."

Himmler closed the folder. "Recruited him for what?"

"Schubert was Hess's double during the 1932 elections."

Himmler's eyes sparkled. "He was?"

"Between the two of them they covered twice as much ground campaigning. In fact, on one occasion they were in two different places many kilometres apart at the same time giving the same speech. When I heard that, I thought that he could be of use to us in some way."

"That is why you brought him here?"

"Yes, Herr Reichsfuehrer."

Himmler didn't know that Hess had a double. It had to be the best-kept secret in the Third Reich. In an instant, a plan developed in Himmler's mind that was so bizarre that he grinned foolishly. But would it work? Why wouldn't it? "Yes, he can be of use to us."

Captain Geis looked pleased. "I hope I can help, Herr Reichsfuehrer."

"Yes, you can. Does he speak English?"

"Enough to get by."

"Same as Hess. What luck. Someone is looking favourably upon us, Captain Geis. He certainly looks like Hess."

"Yes, he does, Herr Reichsfuehrer. He is thinner, older, and taller, but his face is perfect, except for having no buckteeth. And it's unfortunate he's not exactly the smartest person walking the streets."

"He has no money, you say?"

Geis nodded. "He drank a lot of it away. His wife finally had to give him an ultimatum. One more drink and she'd leave him. He told me he hasn't had any alcohol in over a year."

"He's perfect, then. He's needy."

"Are you thinking, Herr Reichsfuehrer, that he can be used to play Hess once more?"

Himmler smiled. "I'm thinking exactly that, Herr Captain. All he has to do is follow orders. Listen, I want you to do two things for me."

"Of course, Herr Reichsfuehrer."

"Number one, see to it that this Schubert creature is drilled on every piece of detail you can find on Hess. Immediately. What I have planned for him will be far beyond playing Hess on the campaign trail. Two, there is a person I want you to see. Professor Karl Haushofer's son, Albrecht. He is Hess's friend and the adviser on British Affairs to our foreign office. He has spent time in England. I want the names and backgrounds of anyone in this British peace group we have heard about who have ever met Hess face to face. Ask the questions in the name of national security. I'll tell you when the time is right to contact Albrecht. Work on our delivery driver first."

"Yes, Herr Reichsfuehrer."

"Now, I wish to speak to Schubert. Alone, Colonel Geis."

"Of course, Herr Reichsfuehrer. Did you say—?"

"Congratulations. A new rank is in order as a reward." Himmler smiled at Geis.

"Thank you, Herr Reichsfuehrer. You are happy with me, I trust?"

"Yes. Very."

"I will always be grateful."

"I'm sure you will be." Himmler then entered the chamber, Geis closing the door for his master. The delivery driver looked up.

"Felix Schubert?" Himmler said, standing before him. "Do you know who I am?"

The man remained slouched in his chair, his hands on the table in front of him. "Yes."

"Good. We know everything about you, Herr Schubert. You cooperate with us, and you will never have to drive another truck for a living again. You played Hess once before. We need you to play him again."

"I have a feeling I don't have a choice."

"Now, now, Herr Schubert, we at the Gestapo reward our workers for services rendered. We can make you a rich man for the first time in your miserable life." Himmler snuck behind Schubert and pulled back on his chair, causing him to fall backwards to the floor. "Now stand up when I'm talking to you, and listen!" Schubert scrambled to his feet. Himmler was waving his finger now. "If you defy me or mess up this mission, you, your wife and your daughters will rot in a Gestapo prison. Do I make myself clear?"

Schubert cleared his throat, terror in his eyes. "Yes, Herr Reichsfuehrer."

Thirteen

Southern Scotland—April 22

Flying officer Jack Croucher heard the noisy batman tramp into the Nissen hut. "Good morning, gentlemen. It's eight o'clock."

Croucher tucked the covers under his chin and grumbled. "So. Get lost. This isn't an ops day. We're supposed to be sleeping in."

"Sorry, sir. Not anymore. I was told to wake you. The CO wants to see you and Pilot Officer Jones in his office at oh-nine-hundred."

"Why us?" Croucher argued. "I thought we were going on leave." He kicked his navigator in the bunk beside him. "Ted. Hey, Ted. Rise and shine."

Jones rolled over. "Huh."

"Get up. Got to see the CO in an hour. Gotta get moving."

Pilot Officer Jones grunted and sat up in his bunk. He looked bleary-eyed at his pilot, then at the sergeant stomping out the door. "I don't get it."

"Me neither," Croucher said.

Both in their early twenties, Jones and Croucher were a polished, experienced two-man crew. Accumulating nearly fifty-five hours of operational time in radar-equipped Bristol Beaufighter night-fighters, they had shot down six German aircraft to date, including one during the night only a few hours before. The crew took turns washing their faces over the basin before they slid into their battle dress. Croucher, the bachelor, was the last to leave the hut, adjusting his officers' cap to sit at just the right angle on his head. Outside, the fog clung to the ground at the RAF aerodrome near the Firth of Clyde, as they hopped on their bicycles for the half-mile ride to the officers' mess. Over powdered eggs and sausages, tea, toast and jam, they complained about their bad luck. They had both been looking forward to the leave they were promised at the beginning of the week. How dare it be cancelled on them?

Croucher was still brooding as they rode through the damp grass to the commanding officer's hut. The sun suddenly appeared as a faint orange glow through the fog. "Damn it all, anyway. Why us?"

"You don't suppose it has anything to do with that brawl at the pub in town, do you, Jack?" Jones asked.

"Couldn't be. We took off before the police came."

"What then?"

"Hell if I know."

The commanding officer of the base, Squadron Leader Bailey, a stout, no-nonsense Welshman, waited for the two to lean their bicycles against the hangar wall, then confronted them outside his office window. There would be no need for the service men to enter, sit, and talk. There was nothing to talk about. It would be short and sweet. "Jones, Croucher," he barked in the damp air. "Your leaves are cancelled. I want you to know this is beyond my control. Just do what you are told." Then he pointed to a car in the parking lot. "There's your man."

Wesley Hollinger had the back passenger door to the Secret Service staff car already open. He caught a glimpse of his unshaven face in the rear-view mirror and he was not a pretty sight. He licked his dry lips to moisten them. He had driven the car most of the night with no sleep at all. His hair was matted and his tie undone. He quickly zipped his tie up to his neck and felt his swollen eyelids. He silently wished for a damn good stiff coffee laced with rum or whiskey to keep him awake. Then he removed his fedora and dragged a comb over his scalp, neatly parting his hair which had not been cut in weeks.

He got out and shook hands with the RAF officers. "Flying Officer Croucher, Pilot Officer Jones. I'm Wesley Hollinger of the United States Naval Intelligence on special assignment to the British Secret Service, otherwise known as MI-6." He handed the airmen a sheet of paper. "It requires your signatures."

"By Jove," Jones said to Croucher. "It's the Official Secrets Act!"

"Yeah, so it is."

*RAF D*unhampton, *S*cotland

Hollinger drove the MI-6 staff car west for about eighty miles over bumpy roads through the Scottish moors to another aerodrome. In the last few months he was growing accustomed to driving on the left side of the road. It wasn't that bad.

The more Hollinger saw of these dull, barren Scottish moors the more he missed the English countryside near Bletchley with its neat hedgerows, rolling grain fields, and attractive thatched-roof houses. Here in the moors the absence of buildings made the views look worse. Apart from the occasional herd of sheep, it looked like a desert. No wonder the RAF picked a secluded spot like this for a test base for German aircraft. It was peaceful at the same time as it was ugly.

The aerodrome came into sight. It was nestled in a ravine and one side was bordered by a thicket of trees. Past the front gate and inside a sectioned area stood one large hangar and three smaller ones, and a mile-long runway. There were also a few small maintenance buildings, a two-story house, and a control tower. Every structure was sandbagged. It was all strangely silent, with no aircraft in sight.

Hollinger yawned and drove through the gate checkpoint, then up to the largest hangar. Turning to the fliers in the back seat he said, "Welcome to Dunhampton. This is an RAF base used for the testing of captured German aircraft. You've noticed that none are about. That's because they're put away when they're not being flown. If you think you'll be flying German aircraft, you are wrong. Your job, gentlemen, is about to be made clear."

A dark-haired man, about thirty-years-old, came out of a service door and proceeded to slide the wide hangar door open. Hollinger drove through. There, in the middle of the concrete was the biggest surprise of all—a twin-engine fighter with Royal Air Force markings and airborne radar aerials protruding from its nose and wings. Two mechanics in coveralls were working on it, but they backed away when Hollinger and the officers stepped from the car and came closer.

"What on earth!" Croucher said, pounding the belly of the aircraft overtop his head. "It's made of *wood*."

"Plywood to be exact, boys," Hollinger corrected the pilot. "Good old Alaskan spruce, birch and fir from Canada, Ecuadorian balsa, and English ash."

"What is it?"

"This, Flying Officer Croucher, is a de Havilland Mosquito. In the next year or so hundreds, if not thousands, will be coming off your production lines. My government back in the States would love to get their hands on this baby. Yes, sir."

"I get it. She's an untested prototype," Croucher said, with a certain amount of apprehension. "Why us?"

"It's more than tested. It works. Why you? Because I heard through the RAF grapevine that you two are one of the best airborne crews in the area. Is that simple enough? Now, if you'll please allow me to feed you the dope on this bird."

"Let's hear it," Croucher said, staring at the aerials.

"This model has twenty-five hours of flying time on her. The airborne radar, an advanced version of the A1-Mark IV, has been tried, tested, and approved for combat. It works better than the Beaufighter, I'm told."

"Let my navigator, here, be the judge of that, Mr. Hollinger."

Hollinger ignored the remark. "I'm sure you will miss your Beaufighter's roomy fuselage and cockpit, and its general sturdiness, but you have to admit, your old Beaufighter was slower than a turtle."

"True," Jones admitted.

"Anyway, the Mosquito, with her light weight and two mighty Merlin engines, has a top speed of four hundred miles per hour in level flight. *Nothing*, I repeat, nothing, in the Luftwaffe will catch you. You can bet on that!" Hollinger then proceeded to pull out a note pad from inside his suit jacket, in which he had two pages of written information. He saw Jones grabbing one of the nose guns. "For armament, four Hispano twenty-millimetre cannons under the floor, three hundred rounds each, four .303 Browning machine guns, two thousand rounds in total, in the nose. No changing ammunition drums in mid-flight here, guys, like in the Beaufighter. The cannons are belt fed. All the engine nacelles are equipped with divided flaps into inner and outer segments. And, bulletproof windscreen. Nice safety factor there. Now," he lifted his head, "take a look inside. Go ahead. Don't be shy."

Croucher climbed the ladder of the opened hatch under the nose and squeezed his body through the hole. "Hey, Ted, we're right beside each other," he yelled down to Jones, who climbed the ladder and poked his head inside.

They both settled into their respective seats.

"A little nip and tuck, there, Jack," Jones said, leaning his face into the radar screen below the feathering buttons.

Hollinger yawned, referring once again to his notes. "For your information Pilot Officer Jones, your radar version operates on VHF, a circular pulse of energy," he called up the ladder to the men. "Maximum range is five miles and minimum range is one thousand feet. Outside of that, you will not receive a pulse echo. If the target is further away from the radar than the ground or water, then the geographical image below will smother your screen. The rest," Hollinger concluded by flipping the note pad closed, "you will find out for yourself as you get used to the aircraft."

Croucher climbed down the ladder and jumped to the concrete from the second-last rung. "When do we take her up?" he asked. Jones followed behind. They both looked impressed with the fighter.

One of the mechanics walked up. "You can give her a go right now."

Jones smiled. "I can't wait; four hundred miles per hour!"

"What I want to know is, what do you have in mind for us?" Croucher asked, his eyes narrowing.

"Excuse me?" Hollinger said.

"What are we going to do with her? I smell some secret operation. Am I right?"

Hollinger rubbed his chin. "We'll let you know when the time comes."

Fourteen

London, England—May 7

"We have a terrible task in front of us," David Lloyd George raged in the House of Commons chamber. "No one man, however able he is, can pull us through. I invite the Prime Minister to see that he has a small war cabinet who will help him—help him in advice and help him in action."

Prime Minister Churchill sighed and glared at David Lloyd George as he sat down. Churchill was in a pinch and he knew it. The battle lines were drawn. Today was the anticipated showdown between his leadership and those who opposed his handling of the war. A crucial vote of no confidence was sure to follow before the day was out. This could be his last day leading the British people at such a perilous time.

Churchill had to admit that the war news was growing worse by the day. His censors were scrambling for any light in the ocean of gloom and darkness. But Rommel, the "Desert Fox," still reigned invincible in North Africa. He was now threatening the Suez and her oil supply. The Germans and the Italians had joined forces to kick the British army off mainland Greece. Malta, the British-held Mediterranean island, was under a terrible German siege. On the Atlantic, the enemy wolf-pack U-boats continued to destroy Allied shipping from Canada and the United States by torpedoing one in ten vessels, on the average, to the bottom of the sea. And at home the relentless bombing of Britain's cities continued. Yes, good news was hard to come by. Many leading figures in the house voiced their opinions that day, but none to the degree that former Liberal Prime Minister David Lloyd George had done when he accused Churchill of trying to run the war all by himself.

As the war of words continued unabated, Churchill sat and trained his mind on other matters such as Adolf Hitler. Recent *Enigma* intercepts revealed that another one of his Panzer divisions had been sent to Poland. There was no doubt now that Hitler was mobilizing his forces for an attack on Russia. That meant that Hess was probably still planning to bring the details of the offensive to scare the British into signing a negotiated peace. Churchill frowned. The proposed attack and flight were far off, secondary now.

When the opportunity came for Churchill to speak, he lifted his squat, overweight body, ready to respond. Standing erect, he had the full attention of the men who a few moments before were cackling like a chicken coop of hens. The House of Commons turned deathly quiet. He smirked, wondering if this was how it was for Julius Caesar at the Ides of March. Were the knives being sharpened, ready to stab him in the back? He looked around at the many faces in the room, some old, some young. How many were on his side? Not too many. He clutched his notes in his hands; the speech he had stayed up for hours practicing in front of a mirror.

He began to speak slowly until he felt more comfortable. Then the words came quicker. He spoke of cooperation and the dangers facing them as a nation. Nothing would come easy. But they couldn't give up. Not now. Not ever. After some minutes, he sensed he was drawing some of the members to his side. But would it be enough to sway the anticipated vote of no confidence? The longer he spoke, the bolder he became. Minutes later, he concluded by exclaiming, "When I look back on the perils which we have been over, upon the great mountain of waves on which the gallant ship has been driven, I feel sure we have no need to fear the tempest. Let it roar and let it rage. We . . . shall . . . come . . . through!"

Then he sat down, his throat dry and sore.

Simon Brenwood sat in the back seat of his 1937 Rolls Royce, his eyes glued to the great stone steps of the House of Commons, expecting the inevitable. Churchill was in a pickle. He didn't stand a snowball's chance in hell in there. Brenwood imagined what England would be like with another leader, a leader more sympathetic to the Nazis and their pseudo-science Geopolitical views. There was no stopping Hitler. Couldn't Churchill see that?

Brenwood turned his attention to the House of Commons doors as a horde of men rushed down the steps. Brenwood got out and advanced on the crowd. He recognized two newspapermen, both probably running off to their offices to write their stories. So this was it. Churchill had had it. His short reign was over, lasting but one year. By later today or early tomorrow every paper in the world would carry the news of Churchill's demise.

He stopped one of the reporters. "Well, Mr. Coan, is Ol' Winnie done for?"

"Done for?" the white-haired man answered with a question. "Are you joking? Churchill stole the floor."

"He did?"

"He sure did, Mr. Brenwood. He was magnificent. Got a standing ovation, he did. He took the vote by 447 to 3." Then the reporter hurried off.

Brenwood stood open-mouthed. How the bloody hell did that bastard do it? Suddenly, in one instant, all the negotiations with the Germans in the last few months were in serious jeopardy. Tortured inside, Brenwood staggered back to his Rolls Royce, bumped twice by the last of the reporters fleeing the building. He glanced at his chauffeur who had the door open for him. "Take me home," he said in a trance.

"Yes, sir."

Munich, Germany

Karl Haushofer arrived at Hess's estate that afternoon.

"A little further, professor," Hess advised. "Let's keep walking. Make everything look normal. Even my own house doesn't feel safe anymore."

Hess didn't feel satisfied until they came to the creek a hundred yards behind the house. "There."

"Churchill won a vote of confidence today."

"Yes," Hess replied. "The Fuehrer notified me."

"Doesn't that change your plans?"

"No. I'm still going."

"You mean the Fuehrer granted you permission in spite of Churchill's victory?"

"No. He ordered me to call it off, but I'm going anyway. We can't afford to wait until Churchill gains a stronger control over his government. You said you had something to tell me about your son?"

"Yes. A Gestapo agent came to Albrecht's house to ask him questions regarding his British friends."

"The Gestapo!"

"Yes, Rudolf."

"When?"

"Yesterday. They wanted to know who in the British group has had any previous contact with you."

"You mean before the war?"

"Yes. I don't like the Gestapo in this. How much do you think Himmler knows?"

Hess thought about it, and turned to his friend. "More than I first suspected. Thank you for coming, professor. I will see you to the front gate."

"Be careful, Rudolf."

"I will."

Augsburg, Germany

Hess reached down and gently moved the stick towards the windscreen. The green fields below rushed up to meet him. Fifty feet off the ground, he eased on the throttles and watched the ME-110 speedometer climb to over three hundred miles per hour. Buildings, roads, and trees flashed past him almost like a solid line of colour and shapes. There was nothing that Hess enjoyed more than racing across the German countryside at low level, the roar of the engines in his ears, the slipstream whistling over the cockpit. Low level was the only way to get the true sense of an aircraft's speed. "Like riding on the wings of an angel," he once told the envious Karlheinz Pintsch.

The twin-engine fighter was running on cue, all the controls responding to his moves. The ME-110 was ready. Hess was ready. The world was ready. Hess saw the base and the sprawling Messerschmitt factory on his port side. He heaved back on the stick. The aircraft climbed sharply, sticking Hess to the back of his seat. Then he let up on the throttles and gave right rudder. In a wide turn, he contacted the tower for landing clearance and dropped the landing gear. On the downwind leg, he turned onto final approach. Careful to keep the speed at the required ninety-five miles per hour, he levelled out by adjusting the rudder pedals. Lower and lower he came towards the ground, until the runway was only inches underneath him. Lower . . . then he chopped the throttles. The wheels banged with a screech. He rolled to the end of the runway and spun the aircraft around with a blast of throttles.

At dispersal, Hess climbed from the cockpit and leaped to the concrete. Pintsch came forward to meet his master.

"Does everything meet with your satisfaction, Herr Reichsfuehrer?"

Hess smiled, delighted with the ME-110's performance and handling. "Yes. Wait for me. I am going to communications." He waved to a man behind the wheel of a refuelling truck.

"Certainly, Herr Reichsfuehrer."

A tall, blonde-haired cipher clerk greeted the deputy minister inside a private cubicle in the communications sector attached to the administration building. "Good afternoon, Herr Reichsfuehrer."

Hess locked the door, unzipped the front of his flying suit and pulled up a chair close to the *Enigma II* machine. "Good afternoon, Forster," he said to the only subordinate he had briefed on his flight to Scotland. Forster was a recently married young man who could keep secrets, one of Hess's inner army. "I have a message for you to send to Stockholm. Are you ready to record?"

"Yes, Herr Reichsfuehrer." The eager clerk quickly grabbed a notebook and sat beside Hess. As the Deputy Fuehrer slowly typed from a sheet in his left hand, the clerk stood back and alertly jotted down each letter dictated to him by Hess as it appeared on the second keyboard above the first. After several minutes, Hess stood to his feet, and waited for the clerk to jot down the last letter of the message.

"Wire it at once," Hess demanded, turning away from the young man and leaving the way he came in.

Outside the building now, Hess stopped cold. He saw Pintsch more than a hundred yards away on the wing of the ME-110, leaning into the cockpit. Hess's first reaction was that his adjutant was deliberately searching for something. Could it have been Pintsch who rummaged in his locker two weeks ago? Hess had suspected his adjutant as a culprit but couldn't break down and accuse him because he didn't want to believe it and he didn't have the proof. Until now, that is. Was Pintsch doing this on his own or was he working for somebody? The Gestapo, perhaps? It had not crossed Hess's mind until now to stick a private spy on his adjutant, the one person—next to Forster—he thought he could trust. Then again, maybe, just maybe, Pintsch wasn't up to no good at all.

Pintsch's heart beat rapidly as he studied the cockpit's interior, intent on finding anything unusual among the dials, the gauges, and the levers. He climbed into the seat and ran his hands behind the rudder pedals. *Nothing.* He looked behind him between the back of the seat and the wall of the navigator's compartment. Nothing there. Then he heard a truck approaching. He got out and stood on the wing just as the truck drew alongside the staff car.

Hess stepped out, still in his flight gear. "Is anything wrong, Pintsch?" Hess asked firmly, looking up at Pintsch on the fighter. "What are you doing?"

"Just wishing, as always, Herr Reichsfuehrer," Pintsch answered. "Just wishing."

"Wishing what, may I ask?"

"That I could fly."

Hess smiled. "Not that again. Come down from there."

Fifteen

Bletchley Park, England

Wesley Hollinger shuffled down the hall of Hut Nine. He was about to open the door and go for a spell of fresh air to clear his mind of the day's work, when he heard Winslow call out to him.

"Wesley, wait," Winslow said, jogging over, handing a sealed envelope to his boss. "This is for you, from Robbie."

"I thought she was on duty."

"Not anymore. She asked me to put in for her."

"Where is she now?"

"Her room."

"OK. Thanks."

"Don't mention it."

Hollinger returned to his office, and slammed the door. He opened the envelope to find a decoded *Enigma II* intercept stating that Hess was going to take another run at a flight on the evening of May 10. Hollinger was flabbergasted. Hess would be risking a lot after Churchill's recent convincing victory.

Hollinger reached for his scrambler and dialled. "Colonel?"

"Yes, Mr. Hollinger."

"It's what we've been waiting for, sir. A Stockholm intercept. Hess will try for Dunhampton, May 10th. Ten o'clock our time."

Hollinger heard an audible sigh on the other end. "We'll be ready for him. See you in London."

"Yes, sir."

Hollinger hung up, and headed out of the door in the middle of a misty rain for a separate out-building at the end of a stone road a short distance from Hut Nine. Emerging inside a plain, multi-roomed white-washed structure, Hollinger brushed the rain off his coat and threw it on a hangar in the foyer. He was met by Langford's young assistant coming out of one of the washrooms to the side. She had just taken a shower. Her hair was wet and she had a towel wrapped around her, exposing her bare arms and legs several inches above her knees.

"Mr. Hollinger," she said, shocked to see a man in the female quarters. "What are you doing here?"

"Where's Robbie?"

The woman pointed with one hand, her other holding on to the top part of her towel. "Second one down. Other side."

"Thank you."

Hollinger walked up and knocked twice on the door. "Robbie. It's Wesley."

"Go away," came Langford's voice from the other side.

"Let me in or I'll break the door down."

"Are you deaf? I said, go away."

"No, I won't."

A small crowd of curious women began to gather in the hall. He glanced at them and said, "Business."

They stared back.

Langford opened the door a little and peered out. Her face was flushed and her make-up was smeared. She had let her hair fall free, and it was quite long, down to her shoulders. Hollinger eased the door open the rest of the way and entered the tidy room lit by a large lamp stand near the bed.

"What's going on? Why aren't you on duty?" he asked, while she pushed the door closed.

She sat on the bed. Then began to cry, head down, hair across her eyes.

"What's the matter?"

She wiped her eyes with a tissue. She got up for a letter on the dresser and gave it to him. "Here."

It was not good news for Langford, Hollinger discovered, as he read the slanting style of a left-hander. The contents were what the Americans would call a Dear John Letter. Her navy boyfriend had found another woman. He threw the letter on the dresser, where his eyes rested on a photo of a navy officer and a faded wedding snapshot taken twenty or so years before, by the look of it. Her boyfriend and her parents, without a doubt, he thought.

"So, he dumped you before you could tell him he's a papa. Seems you're in a bit of a jam." He looked over at the picture of the officer and wondered how much longer it would stay in her room before she threw it in the garbage.

She sniffed. "What am I going to do?"

Hollinger stood beside her and put his arm on her trembling shoulder. "Now, now, it's not so bad. These things happen."

"Not so bad?"

"Hush. Keep your voice down."

"How can you stand there and say it's not so bad? You're not the one in this predicament. And don't tell me that in the world realm of things it doesn't count."

"I wasn't going to. That statement's a little worn out. Have you told your parents?"

"No."

"You can't keep putting it off, Robbie. I'll drive you to London first thing in the morning. I have to see Lampert anyway."

The only sound now was the clatter of rain on the window. He took the opportunity to look closer at the two pictures on the dresser. Langford was a good blend of her parents. She had her mother's eyes and face, her father's chin. "Your parents, I take it?" She nodded. "They look like understanding people. You said your father's in the ministry. Then he should practice what he preaches. You know, forgiveness."

She said nothing.

"Look, why don't you take the rest of the evening off."

"I was going to anyway."

"Oh, were you?" Hollinger grinned. She still had her sense of humour. "Get a good night's sleep. I'll be in the car at seven-thirty." He turned towards the door.

Langford blew her nose in the tissue. "I'll be ready. Wesley?"

"Yeah," he responded, looking back.

"Thanks for caring," she sniffed. "You're the only one who knows, so far."

He smiled at her and said, "Hang in there." Then he left quietly.

BERLIN, GERMANY—MAY 8

"There you are, Herr Schubert," Heinrich Himmler said, standing over several items on the table in the interrogation cellar. The Gestapo leader polished his pince-nez, then jabbed it in place on his nose. "Luger, stiletto, sunglasses, briefcase. Inside the briefcase are the peace terms. Study them when you are alone aboard the submarine. No one, other than the British group, are to see them. Is that clear?"

"Yes, Herr Reichsfuehrer."

Schubert scooped up a bulging manila envelope and glanced across at Colonel Geis, who was standing in the corner. "And these others?" Schubert asked, glancing down at the table.

Himmler nodded at Geis to take over.

"Hess artefacts," Geis said, stepping forward. "They are to prove your identity. Two pictures of Hess and his son, in addition to a picture of Hess at Hitler's mountain retreat in Bavaria; two visiting cards from Karl Haushofer and his son, Albrecht; an assortment of drugs and vitamins Hess has been known to take. If you happen to get lost at any time, we've supplied you with a Scotland road map, some identification, and an envelope marked Captain Alfred Horn, an identity you can assume if someone thinks that they recognize you. Keep these particular artefacts on your person. In your trousers. Your shirt pockets."

"Of course."

"Now, the codes. The name of your mission?"

"*Operation Night Eagle.*"

"Your codename?"

"*Falcon.*"

"Your British contact?"

"*Lion*, the only British appeaser who has met Hess in person."

"Very good. Be careful with him. Don't say too much. Don't say too much to anybody. Let the peace terms do the talking. Use only English. Understand?"

"Yes."

"Do you have your orders for the sub skipper?" Himmler asked.

"Yes, Herr Reichsfuehrer."

"The nature of your mission when you leave here?"

"I will be flown to Kiel, where a submarine will take me to the Firth of Forth on the coast of Scotland, on the tenth. There to rendezvous with me will be an agent codenamed *Denise*. She will drive me to Dunhampton, where Hess was supposed to fly to. But I shall be the new Hess. A British welcoming committee will take me to Dungavel Castle, home to the Duke of Hamilton, where I will present the peace terms. Then I will be returned to Dunhampton to meet up with *Denise*, and she will return me to the sub."

"And what if you are asked why you did not fly as first agreed upon?"

"There was an intelligence leak and the mission had to be changed."

"Good. You've studied the Scottish countryside map?"

"Yes, Herr Reichsfuehrer."

"Perfect. Any questions? Anything you do not understand?"

"Nothing," Schubert said.

"Excellent. It's time to depart. Good luck."

"Heil Hitler!"

The three of them saluted each other, then the Gestapo leader called Geis outside the cellar.

"Is your bomb team ready at Augsburg?"

"Yes they are, Herr Reichsfuehrer. We are waiting on your orders."

"What do you think, Geis? Can Schubert pull this off?"

"He'll do it, Herr Reichsfuehrer," Geis said confidently. "He needs the money we promised him."

Himmler rubbed his chin. "Too bad he'll never see his reward. You see, Colonel Geis, when Schubert returns to Kiel, I want you there to greet him. Find out everything the British said to him. I want their reaction to the peace plan. Then do away with him as you please. And don't leave a trace. Understood?"

Geis didn't appear surprised at the explicit order. "Consider it done, Herr Reichsfuehrer."

Sixteen

London, England

"Colonel, sir, there's a call for you."

Lampert pressed the intercom to thank his secretary and picked up the receiver. He glanced at Hollinger standing in the centre of the room, twirling his fedora in his hand. "Excuse me a moment, Mr. Hollinger."

"Sure."

"Lampert here," he said into the receiver.

"Raymond. It's Charles."

"Yes, Charles." Lampert didn't expect to hear from his friend, the Director of MI-5 Twenty Committee so soon. They had spoken only yesterday.

"I have something you may be interested in. We've picked up a radio signal from Hamburg. You said to give you a ring if we catch any peculiar enemy activity on or near the tenth."

"That's right. Let's have it."

"There's going to be a sub drop off the Firth of Forth on the tenth. One of these human cargos. In daylight, of all things. Somewhere between 2000 and 2100 hours. The destination will be Dunhampton."

"Dunhampton! Yes, I certainly am interested, old top. A drop, you say."

"That's right."

"Who's it for?"

"*Denise*. There's more to it. I'll send the message up to you. If there's any change, I'll ring you."

"Yes, thank you, Charles. Keep in touch. I'll give you another number where you can reach me. I'll be in Scotland for a few days. Dunhampton, actually." Lampert read the telephone number to his friend, then hung up.

"What is it, colonel?" Hollinger asked.

"It seems we might have a last minute visitor. A sub drop. His destination is also Dunhampton."

"That's weird."

"Yes, Hollinger. Weird. I had better call Winnie."

Lampert rolled down the window of the MI-6 staff car. "There he is, Hollinger. Right on time for his morning run, as always."

From their parked position by the curb, Lampert and Hollinger watched Simon Brenwood leaving his Rolls Royce and making his way through the crowd in the light rain to the Post Office. Behind the wheel, Hollinger tugged at the brim of his fedora. He was not that impressed with the first glimpse of the rich steel man known to the Secret Service by the *Enigma II* codename of *Lion*. "Well, well, a Rolls Royce. Just a fat little runt, isn't he?"

"Hollinger, that fat little runt is the key to the appeaser lobby group and the best connection we have to Rudolf Hess. He has blood brothers in the army, navy, air force, the House of Commons, Churchill's cabinet, not to mention business ties around the world."

Brenwood's high and mighty background didn't mean a whole lot to Hollinger. "No big deal. He's going down for the count."

"Right you are, Hollinger. Do the honours."

"I thought you'd never ask, sir," Hollinger replied, grinning, tapping the holstered pistol strapped to his chest. The American left his driver's seat, flipped the collar up on his coat, and walked over to the Rolls Royce. He tapped twice, until the white-haired chauffeur rolled the window down.

"Beat it, bub," Hollinger said, standing in the rain.

"I beg your pardon."

"You heard me." Hollinger showed the man his MI-6 identification. "Move on. Shove off. Adios. In other words, get the hell out of here. We have business with your boss. We'll escort him home. And one other thing, you never saw me. Got it?"

"I understand." The man drove off.

Three minutes later, Brenwood appeared at the door, a wad of envelopes in his hand.

"Let's go, Hollinger."

Hollinger and Lampert made their move. They left the staff car, cut through the crowd and blocked Brenwood's path to the curb before he could see that his Rolls Royce was gone. Lampert stuck out his ID and in an easy, controlled voice said, "Mr. Brenwood?"

"Yes."

"Secret Service. Come with us, please. Out of the rain. Don't make a scene."

Brenwood turned pale. "What do you want with me?"

They snatched the letters and led him to the back seat of the staff car. Hollinger got in behind the wheel, while Lampert slid in the back with Brenwood. No one in the crowd noticed a thing. All at once, another car with Secret Service men pulled in behind them.

"What is this? What do you want with me?"

"Nervy little bugger, ain't yuh?" Hollinger helped himself to the letters. "Why so nervous?"

"Who are you? You're an American!"

"Good for you. Ten points to the snappy dresser in the blue suit. Nice tie, too. Too yellow, though." Hollinger pushed a Stockholm-postmarked envelope into Brenwood's face. "Now, I wonder how many points I get if I can guess what's in the letter?"

"Does the name *Lion* mean anything to you?" Lampert asked, calmly. "Cat got your tongue? How about *Deputy* or the new name, *Falcon*?" he continued. "Or *Operation Night Eagle*?"

Brenwood winced when Hollinger tore the letter open with his manicured hands. "I know it's in code," Hollinger said, "but I do happen to know it states here that Rudolf Hess—*Falcon*—will rendezvous with *Lion*—that's you, Brenwood—at Dunhampton, tomorrow evening, May the tenth. What about it, Brenwood?"

Brenwood swallowed the bile in his throat. "I don't know what you're talking about? I'm . . . I'm just a messenger. I only deliver the letters."

"Addressed to you? I'm afraid we can't believe that one."

Lampert waved to the two men in the other car. They came up and stood a short distance away on the sidewalk. The colonel turned towards Brenwood and in a slow, deliberate voice, free of emotion, said, "Simon Brenwood, you are under arrest for treason. Collaborating with the enemy in war time." He leaned his head to the open window. "Take him away, gentlemen."

"Yes, sir," one of them said.

Hollinger and Lampert watched until Brenwood was driven off. Hollinger was proud of the fact—and he showed it—that his involvement with *Enigma II* had led to Brenwood's arrest.

Lampert bent forward from the back seat and uttered, "Mr. Hollinger, this is far from over. But before you make your way to Scotland, kindly get yourself a haircut. It is not suitable for a Secret Service operative. You look like . . . like a musician."

Hollinger looked hurt. "But I just got a haircut last week."

"Well, then . . . get them to take some more off."

"Yes, sir."

Munich, Germany—May 9

Forster, the Augsburg communications man, looked flustered as he made his way into Hess's library and faced his superior.

"What's the matter, Forster?"

"I'm sorry to disturb your lunch, Herr Reichsfuehrer. It's this message I received only minutes ago on the *Enigma II* wire from Berlin. I thought it best that I run it over." He removed several sheets of paper from his shirt pocket inside his coat.

Hess took the deciphered dispatches from Forster. They were from his good friend Bremmel, one of the Board of Directors of I.S. Filberg, the powerful German business conglomerate that Hess knew had helped fund and was still funding Hitler's Nazi movement through organized international channels. Hess skimmed through the material in seconds. All the sensitive loans, including the American ones, were laid out in detail. A smile appeared on Hess's lips as he folded the sheets in half. It was exactly the information he wanted. He would take it with him to Scotland. The British would find out who their friends really were.

"Forster," Hess said, narrowing his eyes at his loyal employee, "You never saw this."

"You're right, Herr Reichsfuehrer. I didn't."

RAF Dunhampton, Scotland

Jack Croucher and Ted Jones were already in the briefing room at Dunhampton when Group Captain Walker from RAF Intelligence arrived. This was their first look at Walker, who they had only spoken to by phone before. He was a thin man of average height with a thick, sandy-red moustache. The two airmen saluted the group captain, then sat down. This was the day Jones and Croucher were waiting for. Perhaps this briefing would explain some or all of the secrecy behind the aerodrome and the two weeks of testing the "bamboo bomber", as they were calling it.

Walker brought a cloth-covered easel in with him, which he placed in front of the officers. "Good afternoon, gentlemen. So we finally meet." He threw back the cover to show a map of the east coast of Scotland, the North Sea and Denmark. The airmen moved forward. "Your two weeks of intense training has been for a special reason," Walker said. "You are now well acquainted with the Mosquito and her sophisticated airborne radar. Tomorrow you will fly towards Denmark, taking one turning point over the North Sea. Right about here." His finger pointed to a map spot as Jones wrote the location on a note pad. "From there you will circle this area to the east. A German Messerschmitt BF-110 with fuselage markings NJ-C11 will be leaving a base near Aalborg, Denmark between the hours of 1900 and 2100. Given information on German navigation, the fighter is certain to ride a radio beam along its way. Its destination will be this aerodrome. Don't ask why. It's none of your concern. We want this aircraft and it's your job to escort it in. Complete radio silence is vital within enemy coast range."

Jones and Croucher glanced at each other.

"And another thing," Walker continued, his eyes on the men. "In the next few days some, shall we say, strange newspaper headlines may be released about this particular ME-110 and its occupant. Don't tell anyone you saw it. Don't ask questions. Don't assume anything. Don't even talk about it among yourselves. That's a direct order from someone a hell of a lot higher than me."

How high up? Croucher wanted to say.

Seventeen

The North Sea—May 10

Felix Schubert had passed his first test as soon as he was taken aboard the submarine at the port of Kiel. The submariners thought he was Hess.

A day later, in the privacy of his bunk, Schubert pondered Himmler's peace terms for the umpteenth time. The trip was far from being the highlight of Schubert's sudden intelligence career. The smell of oil, machinery, cigarette smoke, and dirty, unwashed bodies lingered in the air. Living accommodations were cramped. Every available space was taken by food, equipment, and torpedoes. The constantly humming diesel engines had raised the temperature to over one hundred degrees. Fresh water was scarce, and the food tasted of diesel oil.

Schubert pursed his lips. The shock of Himmler's papers had worn off by now. The Gestapo leader was offering the British appeasers one billion pounds from a Swiss bank account to be used for influencing more Englishmen to the peace cause. The conditions were that Winston Churchill would have to be removed from office. Himmler would be the new ruler of Germany with a grand new title of Fuehrermaster and Adolf Hitler would be arrested for crimes against the state. England and Germany would cease fighting. England would remain a sea power, and not be invaded, as long as Germany was given a free hand in Europe.

Politics meant little to Schubert. It didn't matter to him who would be in power once it was all over. He only wanted to perform the mission to the best of his ability and be rewarded once he returned.

It still bothered Schubert that Hess let him go after the 1932 elections without even a word of thanks. Himmler would treat him with the proper respect due him. Himmler would look after him. He had promised.

Munich, Germany

From the window of his second-story room, Deputy Fuehrer Rudolf Hess looked over the garden he was so proud of. May had greened the lawn. It was peaceful and serene this Saturday afternoon shortly after two o'clock in southern Germany, the tenth day of the month of May. The sunshine glittered off the clear blue water of the swimming pool. He slid the window up and leaned on the ledge. The flowerbeds were full of bright colours, and the fragrance of the spring blossoms swept over him. The birch trees were nearly in full leaf and the rich-green grass had been freshly cut that morning after a solid rain two days before. Fifteen years ago, he would only have dreamed of owning such grand property.

Outfitted in his blue-grey slacks, tall airman's boots, light-blue shirt and dark-blue tie, he climbed the stairs two at a time to his secretary's office, where he scribbled a note to his wife, who was sleeping off the effects of a severe cold.

> I firmly believe that the flight I am about to make will be crowned with success.
> Should I not return, however, the goal I set for myself was worth the supreme effort. I am sure you all know me: you know I could not have acted any other way.

Hess sealed the note in an envelope and wrote on the outside, *to be opened on Sunday, my darling*. He walked to a small room that Ilse often used to read and write letters and slipped the envelope neatly inside the drawer, knowing she would look there in the next few days.

Next, he looked in on his son. Hess wondered if Ilse had found it a little unusual that for the past few weeks he had been spending more time with their four-year-old, Wolf-Rudiger, than he used to. The morning hand-in-hand strolls along the Isar River, which backed onto their garden, were more frequent and longer, and so were the trips to the nearby Hellabrun Zoo. Only yesterday, Hess and the boy had spent the afternoon with model trains and tanks. Today, Wolf was playing with some army toys. Hess kissed his son and left. Hess was still the same loving husband and father. He didn't want anything to appear out of place. Outside of this special closeness to his son, Hess was the same man he had always been.

At the front window, Hess waited, facing the high bushes and the road. He imagined he was on his way to Dunhampton . . . he could feel the cockpit deck rumbling beneath his boots . . . he could smell the pungent aroma of fuel and oil . . . he could see the props turning thousands of revolutions per minute. Then he recalled his first solo flight over twenty years earlier and how nervous he was. Today, he was anxious. He had the dream again last night. The long hall filled with Scottish and English country scenes had been more vivid this time. It only seemed right that he should have had it the night before his international peace mission, and it gave him the courage to believe he would be successful.

The wait was short. Pintsch and the chauffeur pulled up in Hess's Mercedes, a black super-charged five-and-a-half litre SSK model. The Deputy Fuehrer grabbed his blue Luftwaffe flight jacket, and his briefcase containing Bremmel's dispatches and Hitler's peace initiatives. He went upstairs to find his wife still sleeping. Disappointed he couldn't say goodbye, he closed her door quietly so he wouldn't disturb her. Then he left through the front entrance of the house.

Pintsch stood outside ready to greet his master. "Good afternoon, Herr Reichsfuehrer," he said, opening the front passenger door.

Hess took one last long look at his country home and wondered if he'd see it again. Then he recalled the dream. Of course, he'd come back. "Good afternoon, Pintsch."

Pintsch closed the door and got in on his own side.

As the chauffeur drove through the iron gates, Hess wondered how much Pintsch really knew, if anything. Hess remembered Pintsch bending over the ME-110 cockpit. Hess was angry at the time, but changed his attitude soon after. If Pintsch was spying for Goering, Himmler, or Hitler, he had to have been forced in some way against his will. Pintsch was basically a good man, dependable and hard-working. He would be forgiven.

Pintsch handed his superior the latest weather forecast for three locations represented by letters which stood for Augsburg, Aalborg, and Glasgow. Hess realized from experience that the report was only a guide. Although he had made a habit of obtaining accurate weather forecasts every day for three months, he knew the conditions could change on short notice, especially over Scotland and the unpredictable North Sea. But so far, so good, according to the new weather report. There was no stopping him now. Saturday, May 10, 1941, Hess decided, would be written in the history books as the day of the Anglo-German peace mission that had saved the world and returned to him the respect he deserved.

The chauffeur drove the car through Munich, past the Saturday afternoon shoppers, and out onto the autobahn. After fifteen minutes, Hess suddenly asked the driver to pull over to the side of the road.

"Let's take a walk and get some fresh air, Pintsch," Hess announced, startling his adjutant. "We have the time. We're running a few minutes early."

"As you wish, Herr Reichsfuehrer."

They strolled slowly through the grass.

Hess stopped inside a clump of tall pine trees about one hundred feet off the road. "Is something wrong, Pintsch? You don't look yourself."

"I'm concerned about you, Herr Reichsfuehrer. This is a very significant day, for some reason. I can feel it."

Hess agreed with pleasant eyes. His adjutant looked as if he meant his concern. "It is a special day." He held out an envelope for Pintsch. "See that you take this to the Fuehrer if I do not return from my flight after four hours. And remember to call the Air Ministry in Berlin the instant the four hours is up and ask for a radio beam to be sent from Aalborg in the direction of Glasgow, Scotland. I am conducting an experimental flight over the North Sea in close proximity to the enemy coast. And you're one of the few who knows that."

Pintsch took the envelope placed in his hand. "Yes, Herr Reichsfuehrer."

"Did you bring your camera?"

"Yes, Herr Reichsfuehrer. I have it in my bag."

They walked for another half-mile. Hess wanted to savour the moment of his beloved Bavaria, the smell of her trees and crocuses, her crisp, blue skies, and her white-capped mountains over the line of trees.

The silence between the two men lengthened. Hess was calm. He bent down and pulled up some grass by the roots. Bavarian grass. He rubbed the blades in his palms as Pintsch watched. Then their eyes met. That look relayed it all. Hess was now aware beyond any doubt that Pintsch could never have been collaborating against him.

"That's it, Pintsch." Hess threw the grass down. His mind was elsewhere, hundreds of miles away. Denmark. The North Sea. Scotland. "Let's go."

For the remainder of the forty-mile trip to Augsburg, Hess studied a file stamped REICH TOP SECRET. In it was the Fliegerkarte, an up-to-date flight map of the forbidden zones in Germany and Denmark, where every square kilometre of air space was monitored. The times and altitudes of the "safe" areas were plainly marked out for the month of May, keeping in mind the time of day. Without the map, one wrong move could lead to his being shot down by his own anti-aircraft gunners. Hess could see that in order to exit Germany he—while passing through the Hamburg and Kiel zones—was compelled to fly at three different altitudes.

Augsburg, Germany

The chauffeur braked the Mercedes and brought it to a stop on the concrete near the hangars. At his locker, Hess went about the routine he had planned. He changed into his blue Luftwaffe jacket, then searched for his leather flying suit. But it was nowhere to be found. So he took another suit nearby, which he knew belonged to the assistant airfield manager.

Pintsch watched his master's every move. He reminded himself that Hess was above suspicion. He had to be. No papers were found inside his flying suit. Pintsch had stolen the suit the day before and had cut into the lining. Unless he was carrying other papers on his person or inside his briefcase. Turning his concentration elsewhere, Pintsch went about his orders. With his camera, he snapped pictures of Hess outside conferring with the airfield staff on the tarmac and being helped into his parachute.

As Hess waited on the tarmac, the engines were fired up, giving off a brief belching spurt of white smoke. Only one engine ran at first, and the mechanics had to be called over. Once the troubled engine caught, Hess turned to Pintsch and yelled in his ear over the engine thunder, "Watch your back, Karlheinz." He offered his hand and they shook, a gesture that Hess had never before made to his adjutant.

It was also the first time he had called Pintsch by his given name.

Pintsch felt honoured. Nevertheless, Hess was warning him. Of whom? "I will always be your servant, Herr Reichsfuehrer. No matter what happens," he replied in Hess's ear. Hess smiled. They finally understood each other.

Pintsch took several more shots of the aircraft as Hess climbed into it. The Deputy Fuehrer waved and closed the canopy. Minutes later the mighty Messerschmitt gathered speed as it raced down the concrete. Pintsch held the camera by his side and watched the fighter as it accelerated with its near-full load of gasoline. It covered the length of the concrete and climbed into the sky. He saw the wheels suck into the belly. Then he returned his eye to the viewfinder as Hess flew the machine over the base, waggling his wings. It was the last picture that Pintsch snapped on that memorable day that would be locked in his memory.

The airfield manager, a stocky man with powerful hands, stood beside Pintsch and watched the fading outline of the silver-grey fighter with markings NJ-C11 head north. "I must say, Herr Captain, I can think of better things to do on a Saturday. How long do you think he'll be?"

"I have no idea," Pintsch replied truthfully. So many of his other flights had been cancelled. Maybe this one would be too.

Pintsch grew impatient as he walked around the base. One hour went by. He stopped in at the cafeteria for some dinner. Two hours went by ... then three. Where was Hess? Was he finally on his way this time?

After nearly four hours had elapsed, the manager and Pintsch returned to the dispersal site. A dense mist had covered the field. The manager appeared nervous. "I do not like this mist. I should telephone Professor Messerschmitt and tell him the Deputy Fuehrer has not returned."

"There's no need to torment yourself," Pintsch assured him. "He probably set down at another base. The Reichsfuehrer is an excellent pilot. Do you not have faith in his abilities?"

"Oh, I do. I do, Herr Captain. It's just that something beyond his control could have gone wrong. A bad engine, a broken aileron. Perhaps ..." Distressed, the manager ran out of specifics. "I don't like it."

"Do you think I do? I'll look after it. All responsibility lies with me."

The manager backed off. "Of course, Herr Captain."

Pintsch waited ten more minutes. Time was up. It was exactly four hours. He made his way to a small office at the administration building and closed the door behind him. He pulled down the shades, turned on the light, then asked the telephone operator for the Air Ministry in Berlin. Once the connection was made, he said into the desk receiver, "This is Captain Pintsch speaking from Augsburg."

"Yes, Herr Captain," a man's voice answered.

"The Deputy Fuehrer has asked me to make a special request. He wants a radio directional beam sent from Aalborg, Denmark to Glasgow, Scotland."

"That might be difficult tonight. Most of the available beams are directed towards London. A heavy raid is expected."

"How heavy?" Pintsch asked, unaware of any raid.

"Five hundred aircraft."

Had Hess known this? Pintsch wondered. "You have to give him a beam. It's vital," Pintsch pleaded. "I can't reach him."

There was a long pause, mixed with background voices. "Well, I might be able to help you with a beam, but it will only be good until 2300 hours. That's all I can do."

"Thank you. Goodbye."

Pintsch hung the receiver in place and mumbled to himself as if in prayer, "Good luck, Herr Reichsfuehrer. You will need it."

Eighteen

*A*LBORG, *D*ENMARK

Hess made an easterly approach to the German fighter base for a reason. Over the North Sea, forty kilometres offshore, he banked his Messerschmitt to check his radio-beam equipment and found it worked perfectly. Pintsch had ordered the beam as directed. He had done well.

At ten kilometres out, Hess radioed the tower for landing instructions. He landed, taxied, and followed a truck to the tarmac, where the aircraft would remain until refuelled.

Behind some trees on the road leading into the ME-110 Luftwaffe base, Colonel Wolfgang Geis saw the fighter through his binoculars. He nodded to the Gestapo agent nearby.

"There she is, NJ-CII. On time."

The first part of the two-stage flight had been completed without incident. Hess had carefully obeyed the air-zone instructions as laid out in the *Fliegerkarte*. He shut the ME-110 engines down, and saw to it that the ignition switches were off, along with the electrical services, master switch, fuel cocks, and that the radiator shutters were closed. The fuel truck appeared and an organized crew started the work of pumping high-octane fuel into the wings of the Messerschmitt. Hess filed a fake flight plan at the tower, then watched the crew go about their duties. When they were finished, Hess leaped aboard, eager to be on his way.

But, once again, the starboard engine wouldn't start.

Hess cursed his luck. No tinkering by the mechanics helped. Hess remained in the cockpit. Half an hour passed. Still nothing. He knew he couldn't cross the North Sea on one engine because the burden on the fighter would be too great. The range would be affected and the manoeuvrability would be restricted. The other concern was the letter to Hitler, although Hess knew it would take Pintsch several hours to deliver it to Hitler's mountain resort. He could call Pintsch to cancel the trip. No . . . he couldn't. He had to go . . . now . . . today. The nosey Gestapo were already asking Albrecht Haushofer questions. If NJ-C11 couldn't do it, then he'd have to take a substitute, one that didn't have the stronger radio and the added auxiliary tanks in the fuselage. His old reliable aircraft wasn't so reliable when he needed it most.

Hess took the screwdriver from inside his flight suit and with his right hand reached over to remove the plate to the right of his cockpit seat. As he did that, his left hand went to the bottom edge of the dash to steady himself. He felt something odd. He stopped for a moment and ran his hand along a metal box, the size of his fist. He bent down as far as he could, despite the tightness of the area, until he caught sight of the bottom edge of the object. It was a clock stuck to the metal with putty. What would a clock be doing under the dash? Unless . . . He yanked the device out to look at it more closely. It was attached to a series of wires running from the clock to two small sets of explosives. And the clock was set to go off in another ninety minutes, when he was due to be over the North Sea, out of visual range of Denmark, away from any land mass and any prying eyes. Who was behind this? Surely not Pintsch. Goering? Hess wouldn't put it past the fat man. Hitler? Himmler? Bormann? They were all suspects. It didn't matter who it was, because Hess would now implement Plan B. Angry, he disconnected the wires and threw the bomb under the seat. He had to go now.

Thinking clearly and rationally, Hess continued in his work without getting out of the cockpit. In great haste, he managed to undo the screws and slide out the leather folder of papers and photographs. He shoved it into his briefcase, then screwed the plate back in place.

Suddenly, the crew chief appeared on the wing. "Herr Reichsfuehrer, I've checked the electrical system completely."

"Well?"

"It could be the wiring or a dead magneto."

"Never mind. Get me another Messerschmitt ready. Immediately."

"Yes, Herr Reichsfuehrer. Come with me, please."

Hess climbed down from his fighter as a scurry of activity erupted around him. He grabbed his briefcase and made his way to the refuelling truck. With the crew chief, they drove about two hundred yards to a row of four parked ME-110's. The nearest one was new, not a mark on it, and had the fuselage letters NJ-OQ.

"What about this one," Hess said, jumping to the ground and sprinting up the wing. He looked into the cockpit and saw it had the type of radio-beam equipment he had used before.

The crew chief was right behind. "But this is a brand new one that arrived only today from the factory. It hasn't been properly air-tested."

"It was flown here from Augsburg, was it not?"

"Yes, it was."

"Is it fuelled?"

"Right up."

"Is it armed?"

"No."

"I'll use this one. Hurry! Let's move it!"

"Yes, Herr Reichsfuehrer."

The rest of the crew drove up in their own truck and made some quick electrical checks on the engines and bolted the engine covers in place. Hess watched them leap to the ground and pull the scaffolding away. He let out an audible sigh when he received the all-clear sign. He pressed the starboard engine start button. The engine cranked, smoked, and caught fire and was soon roaring on its own. Then Hess started the port engine. Another crank. Another blast of smoke. Another roar. Both engines were soon running, all twenty-four cylinders, a combined rating of 2,700 horsepower. Hess waved at the ground crew and let go of the brakes.

Half a mile away, Geis saw that Hess had switched aircraft. "Get the rifle with the scope!" he yelled to the agent.

Hess had the port window open to bring down the cockpit heat. He pushed the throttles forward. He was moving. Suddenly, his starboard window shattered before his eyes, spraying Plexiglas into the air. What was it? A gunshot? If so, someone obviously didn't want him to leave

Germany. That was plain enough. First the bomb and now a bullet. Although a thrill of fear ran cold in his heart, Hess didn't think of the impending danger because that same fear was his tonic. He grabbed the control column with his right hand, gluing his eyes to the runway. His left hand went for the throttle levers. It seemed so natural to him, like walking or driving a car. The fighter began to veer left. Hess adjusted, gradually pressing down on the right rudder pedal with his boot.

The end of the concrete was fast approaching.

Calmly, Hess eased the stick forward to get the tail off the ground. Now on the main wheels only, the fighter started to swing to starboard. Hess gave more throttle to the port engine. He was dead centre on the runway, the engines screaming in his ears. He was drifting again to starboard. More power to the port engine and he was back on course. Dead centre once again. The aircraft seemed to have control problems and it didn't have the power that his own aircraft did. He slid the port window closed and locked it.

The black edge of the runway was seconds away. But for some strange reason the lift wasn't there for a proper takeoff. He needed the right combination of speed and lift. He nudged off the throttles a touch. No sense wearing the engines down. If he didn't get off soon, he'd smash into the trees on the other side of the field. He had to wait another split second or two. The lift seemed there now. The end of the runway loomed ahead ... the grass. He heaved back on the stick ... and the fighter responded.

The runway and grass dropped away as the fighter clawed her way towards the sky, barely clearing the high trees.

BERLIN, GERMANY

Himmler took the phone call from Geis in his office.

"Yes, Geis?"

"He got away, Herr Reichsfuehrer. The Deputy Fuehrer got away!"

"What are you so excited about? He's on his way to Scotland, is he not?"

"Yes and no. He's flying to Scotland, Herr Reichsfuehrer, but he switched aircraft. He took another Messerschmitt because his own wouldn't start."

"Why didn't you stop him?"

"I tried. I sent my man over the fence. He took a side shot as Hess was moving down the runway. He got his side window. Whether he got Hess, we don't know. He took two more shots after that. They both missed. Then Hess took off."

"Geis, how could you! Where are you calling from?"

"The Aalborg Gestapo."

"Did the people on the base see you?"

"No. We were well hidden and we made a hasty retreat. It would be difficult to tell where the shots came from with the engine noise."

Himmler put his mind into high gear. They had missed killing Hess twice. They would have to get him the third time. Hess must not reach the appeasers. Hess must not return either. He'd get Hitler to use decrees to hunt down the culprits who tried to kill him. Himmler knew he had to cover the matter up quickly. "Listen to me closely, Geis," Himmler said.

"Yes, Herr Reichsfuehrer."

"Go back. I don't care how you do it, but get that bomb, and get rid of it!"

"Yes, Herr Reichsfuehrer. I will do that."

"Get our man in Hamburg to send *Denise* a message. Can you do that, Geis?"

"Yes, of course, Herr Reichsfuehrer."

"Do you have a pen?"

"Yes, I do, Herr Reichsfuehrer."

"Good. Take this down."

Nineteen

Firth of Forth, Scotland

A slim, attractive woman with dark, curly hair slipped through the broken window of the deserted two-story house on the cliff at the edge of the water. The fierce winds and salty moisture had peeled the paint in most parts to bare wood. The house had been in ruins for years.

The woman took the creaky stairs to the top floor, as she had done every day for the last week. Through the cracked window she pondered the waters. It was not the best day for a sub drop-off. The wind was picking up. However, the waves were higher during the last drop two months ago. It still wasn't impossible, except for the fact that this one would be during the day. The area was an unpopulated coastline, but still...

She turned around and searched for the loose planks in one corner of what was once the master bedroom, and found her paper pad, codebook and British-made Mark II Suitcase Transceiver. She positioned the radio on an old dusty worktable that she had dragged up from the basement the first time she had transmitted in January. She lined the frequency crystals to one side, and switched the power on. As the set warmed, she loosened the top two buttons on her coat and glanced at the window to check the aerial's position on the indoor windowsill. Then she waited.

Ten minutes to go.

At the top of the hour she placed the earphones on her head. Inside of twenty seconds she received her call sign broadcasted from Hamburg, nearly five hundred miles to the southeast. The airwaves were quiet at this hour later in the day. No distractions or jamming. The signal was clear. She removed her gloves and with small, gentle fingers adjusted her dial, thus allowing the signal on 7587 kilocycles to come in more clearly. She opened her set and began the transmitting by tapping her three-lettered call sign six times.

DLM... DLM... DLM... DLM... DLM... DLM...

Then she relaxed and waited for a reply. The receiving station answered with their call sign and followed with a coded, "WE READ YOU LOUD AND CLEAR."

The woman let out a deep, assuring sigh, reached for her paper pad, and jotted down the dots and dashes that crackled over her phones. The message was average size. There was a lengthy pause after what seemed like the message's climax. Then Hamburg's call sign was repeated, signalling the end of the transmission. The woman followed up with her own call sign. Then, as if by magic, the line went dead. Just in time. Her back was killing her from leaning over the radio.

She sat and leaned against a dusty wall and with the codebook and pad in her lap, she began to decode the garbled block of words.

RAF Dunhampton, Scotland

Jack Croucher and Ted Jones entered the operations room, each loaded down with their Mae West life-jacket, flight suit, boots, parachute and helmet.

Jones dropped his canvas bag containing his log, pencils, maps, flashlight, and compass by his feet and sat down with Croucher to go over the flight plan. Jones removed his maps and spread them out on the plotting table. Next, he drew a heavy pencil line from his aerodrome at Dunhampton to the first turning point, then along to Aalborg, Denmark. He measured the last leg at 130 miles, exactly 96 degrees. He figured that if Croucher cruised at 240 miles per hour, which was four miles a minute, they'd arrive at the turning point in just over thirty minutes. On a separate sheet of paper, he jotted down the course, the distance, and the time. From there he was to follow a straight line towards Aalborg. Ninety-eight degrees.

Croucher stood and sauntered over to the large map of Britain and Northern Europe on the wall. He saw the pinpoint marking for Aalborg. He ran his finger to the right of the turning point.

"Somewhere in here, Ted, is where we make our interception."

* * * *

Forty-five minutes later, on the sun-baked tarmac, Croucher began his methodical outside check on the Mosquito starting with the starboard side first. He made his way to the tail wheel and fin, then worked up the port side to the bomb bay. Turning to the back section, he and Jones stopped to perform their customary good-luck leak on the tail wheel.

Croucher looked up to the aircraft's belly, threw his dinghy and parachute through the hatch, and ascended the ladder. He sat in the navigator's seat first in order to position his chute behind the control stick, then he swung over to the pilot's seat once he had placed his dinghy on it. Jones followed up the ladder and squeezed through the hatch. He set his dinghy on his seat and sat down. He dropped his parachute pack on the floor. This is where it would stay until he had to use it, which he hoped he never would. He helped Croucher into his straps, then did his own. He checked to see the needed maps were in their proper order inside the metal box at his right knee. With a jar, the ground crew pulled the ladder away from the fighter.

"OK," Croucher called out. Below, the sergeant slammed the hatch door from the outside.

Croucher plugged in his intercom and adjusted his helmet. From there, he went over the internal cockpit checks with Jones's help. Lastly, he ran through his own checklist-confirm procedure that he knew by heart.

Main fuel cocks . . . on outer tanks.
Throttles . . . one-half-inch open.
RPM control levers . . . maximum.
Superchargers . . . low gear.
Radiator shutters . . . closed.
Pressure venting cock . . . on.
Fuel transfer cock . . . off.
Immersed fuel pump switch . . . off.
Bomb doors . . . shut, selector to neutral.

A yellow flare soared overhead from the direction of the tower, the prompt to start their engines.

"Tally-ho," Croucher said. He pointed to the number one engine. "Contact port."

The ground crew had the external power source in place and worked the priming pump until the fuel reached the priming nozzles. Croucher switched the ignition to on and pressed the starter and booster-coil buttons. The engine whined, growled, and kicked into perpetual power. As the oil pressure rose, he opened the throttles slowly to 1200 RPM. He pointed to the number two engine. The same whine, growl, and kick followed. Once both engines were running smoothly, Croucher made further checks of the oil and coolant temperatures and the magneto charge. He opened the throttles fully, dropped them back to minimum idle, then opened them up again to 1200 RPM. "Radio check," he said to Jones in the seat beside him.

Jones pressed the mike for his pilot who was busy eyeing the gauges. "SUNDOWN, THIS IS WILLOW TWO-THREE. DO YOU READ?"

"WE READ YOU, WILLOW TWO-THREE."

"WILLOW TWO-THREE OUT."

"Clear the chocks!"

Jones relayed a thumbs-up to the ground crew to slide the wheel obstructions away.

"SUNDOWN, THIS IS WILLOW TWO-THREE. ARE WE OK TO TAXI?"

"OK TO TAXI, WILLOW TWO-THREE."

As soon as Croucher pulled out, he tested the brakes twice for maximum pressure. They held. Ahead was nearly a mile of runway, banked on both sides by red lights. He turned onto the concrete, then rolled to a stop. He set the course on the compass ring to oh-nine-six degrees. "How's the hatches and your harness, there Ted?" Croucher yelled.

"Locked and tight."

Croucher studied the gauges again. "Ready for take-off?"

"You bet."

Croucher pressed the radio button. "WILLOW TWO-THREE TO SUNDOWN. WE ARE READY FOR TAKEOFF?"

"YOU MAY PROCEED, WILLOW TWO-THREE. GOOD LUCK."

With one forward shove of his hand, Croucher roared the throttles to maximum, and watched the revolutions rise. Then he released the brakes. They were off. Partway down the runway, he glanced over at Jones pressed to his seat. They were both thinking the same thing. What power!

When they took to the air, Jones flipped open his log and recorded: airborne 1931 hours.

* * * *

Lampert watched through Group Captain Walker's office window as the Mosquito climbed into the sky. The phone rang.

"It's for you, Colonel," Walker said. "London."

"Thank you." Lampert took the receiver. "Lampert."

"There you are, Raymond. Charles here."

"Yes, Charles."

"*Denise* picked up another Hamburg message. There's more to that sub drop. Listen to this."

Twenty

Firth of Forth, Scotland

As Felix Schubert stood inside the control room with the young sailors, his eyes examined the dizzying array of dials, valves, handles, and knobs that controlled the movement of the sub. Then he noticed Steider entering the cabin.

The boat's commander, Kurt Steider, was a whiskered lieutenant in his late twenties, a hero in the Fatherland for sinking the first British ship of the war in September of 1939, off Scapa Flow. "Down scope," he called out, motioning to a sweaty subordinate. The long, tedious trip had originated twenty-four hours earlier at the port of Kiel and they were now 350 yards off the Scottish coastline, inside the Firth of Forth. Waiting for the periscope to drop, Steider reversed the peak of his officers' cap, extracted the handles, and bent down to the foam-rubber eyepiece. He used his left hand to guide the instrument, while his right hand focused the eyepiece. Pivoting back and forth, he eyed the lonely Scottish shoreline through the sea mist and the long shadows.

"Do you see the signal, commander?" Schubert asked, his voice cracking unexpectedly. He looked down at the briefcase by his shoes.

"Nothing yet, Herr Reichsfuehrer. We're still early," the lieutenant replied, then resumed panning the rocky enemy shoreline. There was no doubt they were at the right location—the jagged point that poked into the firth. Although most of the sailors were thrilled that Hess was aboard, Steider was not, and for several reasons. The Deputy Fuehrer was his responsibility and he out-ranked everybody aboard. Letting Hess off here in daylight was too risky. And what bothered Steider the most was that Hess did not seem to recognize him. They had once conversed for several minutes at the chancellery in Berlin in 1939, at a celebration for the lieutenant's sinking of the British ship. Perhaps there had been too many people that day. Steider thought that Hess now looked different. He was older and greyer and his voice was deeper than he remembered. He had changed physically in such a short time. Was this the result of High Command pressures? If so, Steider didn't want any part of high-level politics.

Ten minutes went by before Steider saw something through the instrument.

"There we are." The relieved lieutenant saw a figure on the distant shoreline through the eyepiece. He saw the weak flashlight blinks in Morse code, despite the sunshine. Dash-dot-dot, long dash, dash-dash. "DLM. There it is again. Bring her up!"

The lieutenant gave the order to expel the water in the ballast tanks. He was only too anxious to rid himself of Hess. Going aground was another possible danger with low tide approaching. At least the Deputy Fuehrer would return in darkness. That was one consolation. "Up scope."

"Aye, aye, commander."

Schubert braced himself on an overhead bar. The pressure jerked the sub upwards, creaking and hissing until it bobbed on the surface of the North Sea.

"Open the hatch and make ready the dinghy. On the double!"

"Aye, aye, sir!"

Steider turned to Schubert. "Good luck, Herr Reichsfuehrer."

"Heil Hitler."

The sub commander flashed a stiff Nazi salute. "Heil Hitler."

Schubert clutched his briefcase, buttoned up his dark-grey trench coat, and climbed the ladder. He could feel the difference passing from the stale air below to the fresh, damp spray above. One rung to go, he looked straight up and saw the deep-blue sky overhead. He held his fedora to his head and pulled his body through the hole. On the surface he saw foaming water surrounded by walls of rocks on two sides. To his surprise, they were inside a cove, and it had to be at least thirty degrees cooler on the surface than it was inside the sub. He dug for his glasses and put them on as a flock of gulls screeched overhead. He performed a balancing act across the slippery deck, blinking in the sunshine, as two sailors held onto a rubber dinghy and waited for Schubert to reach the water's edge. Schubert boarded by lowering between them. He then glanced over his shoulder and proceeded to paddle in the direction of the blinking light, his back to the beach.

"Give them one for us, Herr Reichsfuehrer," one of the sailors said.

Schubert waved solemnly.

The sailors disappeared below deck and closed the hatch with a thud. The sub wasted no time submerging. It was not until Schubert caught his last sight of the conning tower and periscope vanishing beneath the cold, black waters that the enormous reality of the situation seized him. He would now play the part of Rudolf Hess on enemy soil. He had fooled the sailors, but could he fool the British? He was very aware that his assignment could be extremely dangerous if it did not go as planned. Himmler and his country were depending on him and his mission, however bizarre it seemed. Perhaps the outcome of the war hinged on how he handled himself.

Paddling with firm, even strokes, Schubert steered the lifeboat for the steady flashing signal. The mist cleared, and a human form appeared on the beach. Rowing closer to the figure, he felt his arms began to weaken. He should have kept in better shape. As he neared the beach, the figure—a woman with dark, curly hair—came out to greet him. Together, they dragged the raft up to dry land.

"The light of the morning," Schubert said in German to open the conversation, gasping to catch his breath.

He waited for the answer in code, his hand close to the Luger strapped inside his coat.

"Comes early in the east," the woman replied in German-accented English to the man in sunglasses. "*Falcon?*"

He too switched to English. "So you are *Denise?*"

"Yes. Heil Hitler."

"Heil Hitler," Schubert responded. He towered over the woman who was dressed in dark slacks and a plaid coat and stood only a couple inches above five feet in height. He studied her face and decided she looked close enough to Himmler's picture of her.

"We must hurry. I have my car just up the road."

"How far is it to Dunhampton?"

"Less than an hour if I take some back roads I know." Her manner was feminine, thorough and professional. "But first we have to deflate the raft and take it with us."

"Certainly."

That done, and now inside the vehicle, Schubert finally removed his hat and sunglasses, and looked over at the agent behind the wheel.

The woman froze in shock. "Rudolf Hess? Is it really you?"

"Yes, it is. You may call me by my rank of Reichsfuehrer."

"I don't know what to say, Herr Reichsfuehrer. It's an honour."

Schubert smiled. He had passed another test. "There is no need to say anything. Go."

Denise threw the car into gear as she handed Schubert a note in German—her most recent deciphered message from Hamburg—without saying a word. Schubert snatched the sheet. It was Himmler's headquarters via Hamburg. Schubert now had fresh orders that had to be carried out promptly. He had to kill the pilot of the ME-110 that was due to arrive at the base at approximately the same time as he and *Denise* were scheduled to. What pilot? What ME-110? Then he was to return by Steider's sub with the pilot's briefcase. How was he supposed to do that? And why his briefcase? Nothing made sense. Something must have gone wrong.

"Is anything the matter, Herr Reichsfuehrer?"

Schubert managed to recover. "Just drive, please. I have to think."

Twenty-one

RAF D**UNHAMPTON, S****COTLAND**
Hollinger rushed to the aerodrome with the convertible top down, his recently cut hair blowing in the wind.

Along the way this sunny afternoon, he chuckled at how his clandestine career had developed. In only a few short years he had helped break the Japanese *Enigma*, had leap-frogged across a good portion of the United States and Great Britain, and had met, drank and conversed with Winston Churchill. He had also discovered startling British Secret Service files on leading German and British figures, had been exposed to the British appeaser group, and was now about to face the Deputy Fuehrer of Nazi Germany, Rudolf Hess. Not bad for a kid from New York State who had lucked his way into the U.S. Navy Intelligence. Hollinger was having more fun than he could ever have believed possible. He wouldn't have missed all this for anything. Then he thought of Langford. She was some dame! But did the two of them stand a chance with the predicament she was in, pregnant and dumped by her navy man? He actually felt sorry for her.

Cleared through the gate checkpoint, he flew down the road to the administration building, spinning to a halt on the gravel. He undid his brown trench coat and breezed past the adjutant inside to a large office. A Royal Air Force officer looked up from behind his polished desk.

"Good evening, Mr. Hollinger. I'm Group Captain Walker."

Hollinger recognized the voice from RAF Intelligence attached to *Enigma*. "Pleased to meet you."

"You're late. We were expecting you forty minutes ago."

Hollinger smirked. "I got lost along the way."

Walker reached for a pack of cigarettes. "Care for one?"

"No thanks. Don't smoke."

"Oh, yes. So I've heard. Sit down, Mr. Hollinger. There's trouble."

"What kind of trouble?"

Walker took his time explaining the latest intercepted radio message from Hamburg. "At first," he finally said, "we thought that Hess had cancelled his flight and was going to be dropped off by sub instead, because the destination of Dunhampton is the same. Now the last message really threw us. Kill the pilot and return by sub must mean that the mission has gone awry."

"Do you think the Germans are on to us and are pulling out?"

"It's possible. Or someone or some people from Germany are out to get Hess. Nevertheless, our traps are set for both Germans, whether Hess is one of them or not. We're not sure of anything. Both Germans have the same code name. *Falcon*. Whoever these two are, they will both be caught before one can kill the other."

Hollinger looked through the wide window behind Walker's desk. The entire aerodrome spanned before them. "So how are we all set to nab Hess, I mean the pilot, or whoever he is?"

Walker handed Hollinger a flare gun. "For our benefit, let's say it's Hess, shall we?"

"Fine."

"Jones and Croucher are under strict radio silence. We can only go by Hess's radar contact off the coast. Lampert is ready outside Dungavel Castle with his men." The officer stood and pointed to one of the hangars through the window. "Those men in coveralls out there are all Secret Service men who will wait for your signal. Hess will land his fighter on the longest of two runways, runway two-six, and wait for you near the ground-crew shack over there by the dispersal site."

"Got yuh." Hollinger stood and picked out the men.

"When Hess cuts the engines, you approach the aircraft. Hess will come out and state his codename of *Falcon*. Give him the *Operation Night Eagle* codename as *Lion's* representative—remember *Lion* couldn't make it—and he hands you the proposals. One shot from your Very pistol—a green flare—to the Secret Service men will bring them over. And we have him and his peace terms. What do you think Mr. Hollinger?"

Hollinger's background in intelligence operations had taught him one thing above all others, and that was to expect the unexpected. "I hope it will be that simple," he replied, brushing his hand through his hair, glancing down at the pistol strapped to his chest holster.

Near RAF Dunhampton, Scotland

"This is as far as we dare drive, Herr Reichsfuehrer," *Denise* informed Schubert, as she braked the auto along a dirt road. She wondered what she was to do now. Where were the Secret Service men?

"The rest will have to be on foot, I take it?" he asked.

She got out first, still in awe of the passenger. "We must move fast. Patrols, you know," she said, as Schubert got out with her.

Schubert remembered what Himmler had told him. No one except the British group were to see the papers. He removed Himmler's proposals from the briefcase and stuffed them beneath his shirt, then threw the briefcase in the back seat of the car.

They began to jog up a low hill. *Denise* looked back. The peat-covered earth of the moors was soft and damp, leaving tracks.

Over the North Sea

"Oxygen on. We're climbing."

Pilot Officer Jones flipped his rubber mask over his face. He twisted his body to his left, stuck his face into the tube behind Croucher's seat and played with the knobs on the Gee box. He watched the green blips, which represented signals picked up from two Gee stations in Scotland, then took a position reading off the point where the two lines crossed. The signals were fading quickly and would soon be jammed by German controllers. As soon as he thought of that, the screen turned to fuzz. He shut the box off and stared out at the small, round alto-cumulus clouds moving slowly east. On the second leg of the interception now, they were closing in on the enemy's patrol range.

"Turn starboard four degrees for correction," Jones told Croucher. "We're off course."

Croucher eased the stick to the right and watched his compass heading. "Steady at zero-niner-eight." He pointed his gloved hand at the radar scope, and Jones flicked on the button. "I'm going to turn her around."

Croucher banked wide through the puffy clouds, the two officers stuck to their seats by the centrifugal force. They could see glimpses of the surface of the North Sea below them. Croucher brought the fighter out of the turn and straightened it, throttling back to just above a stall. Back in cloud, they were now on a westerly course, relying on instruments only.

Jones caught a mark on his radar. "Looks like a target of some sort."

He studied his two circular displays. One showed height and range, the other direction and range. The outgoing pulse fanned out horizontally on the left display until it came in contact with a downward notch on the centre baseline—the target. To the far right was the ground return. The right display, a vertical view in similar fashion, had the notch to the right of the centre line.

"We got one, Jack."

Jones calculated the distances between the outgoing pulse and target. "Target to starboard, six degrees. Range five thousand yards, five below."

Croucher dropped the nose a touch to allow the target to move above and in front of him. "Can't see a thing through this cloud. It thickened up all of a sudden." He edged the stick to the right. The radar target bulged and fluctuated on the scope, then settled down. Croucher didn't want to nose down too severely and dive after him. Building up speed and zooming in on the target could result in flying right past and not getting a good look. In this cloud, he might not even make a proper visual, let alone bear down on him with the cannon.

"Back off."

"Right." Croucher throttled back.

They were still in heavy cloud.

"That's it. Turn port three degrees. We're riding the beam."

"Turning port three degrees," Croucher acknowledged.

"Five above. Range two thousand."

Visibility was down to one hundred feet. The radar scope was approaching the minimum range.

"Fifteen hundred . . . twelve hundred . . ."

Suddenly, the target slid off the baseline and disappeared into the outgoing pulse. "We're off, Jack. Keep a sharp lookout."

"OK."

"Slow down," Jones warned.

Croucher backed off on the throttles as he strained for sight of the target. The cloud grew thicker. Then it happened. There it was. Directly in front of them. The rear view of an ME-110.

"Look out!" Jones screamed, closing his eyes. "We're going to collide!"

Croucher yanked the stick towards him.

At that precise moment, Rudolf Hess happened to glance through the Plexiglas above and to his shock saw a twin-engine plane directly above him, its whirling propellers a stone's throw away. Then it banked away right, disappearing into the cloud. Hess alertly pressed the stick forward, sending the fighter into a dive.

They came out of the turn and levelled off.

"That was close."

Croucher agreed. "Too ruddy close."

"That was an ME-110, wasn't it?"

"Yeah, I think it was."

"Whatever it is, it's back on scope. Ease up," Jones said, his eyes stuck to the display. "We have to find out if he's the one."

Croucher pulled the throttles towards him. "Give me a bearing."

"Ten below. To port. Range fifteen hundred. Throttle back."

The transmitter light flicked on, then went off. Once more the target was disappearing into the baseline of the radar scope. Croucher gave the target some distance before he dropped the nose.

"Good. That's good. That's it. Level out," Jones said, guiding his pilot. "Eight below to starboard. Great." A minute later. "Six below. Range nineteen hundred. The bugger's trying to get away. Pour it on. Let's see what we got."

"I see him!" Croucher shouted, pointing. Through the dispersing cloud, they spotted a camouflaged ME-110 below. "She's a Hun, all right. ME-110."

Hess glanced over his shoulder at the twin-engine fighter with the airborne radar following him. She was fast. Real fast, as evidenced by how quickly she was closing the gap, despite Hess giving full-throttle to his own machine. Hess was fighting for each breath, his World War I lung injury pestering him. To his surprise, the Messerschmitt 110 was not the fastest twin-engine in Europe as he had been led to believe. He felt so alone at this moment, and so cold from the onrushing air in the cockpit through the shattered window.

He wondered what an RAF fighter with an airborne radar crew was doing this far out over the North Sea in daylight hours. It was too far for a patrol. Hess didn't stand much of a chance in an unarmed fighter, and he had nowhere to bail out. He wouldn't survive twenty minutes in the North Sea.

Hess watched through his shattered window as the strange fighter blasted by and banked to port. He caught a good look at the RAF roundel on the fuselage. What speed! There was no time for evasive action, not the way that thing could fly.

"He didn't shoot," Croucher said.

"And the markings were NJ-OQ. She's not the one. Must be a stray. What do we do now?"

Croucher knew what to do. "Shoot her down. That's what. She's still a Jerry." He put the Mosquito into a stiff bank to port, his vision going grey from the pressure.

Hess realized there was still sufficient fuel for an alternative, such as neutral Sweden. Or he could head back to Denmark? But what hope did he have there? Whoever was out to get him would finish him off.

Then he had an idea.

"What's he doing?" Croucher gasped. "He's heading for the deck."

"He won't get away."

Croucher set the gun master switch to fire. The twenty-millimetre cannon was ready to do its work. He sent the Mosquito into a dive, hot on the tail of the German, applying more power to the Merlin engines, until he was two hundred yards behind his prey, whose pilot was now jinking his aircraft to stay out of harm's way.

Croucher nudged the stick left and right to line the ME-110 in the centre of the gun sight.

"He's a tricky one, Jack."

It was now a game of cat-and-mouse. Pilot against pilot. Machine against machine. The ME-110 dove, twisting and turning, and Croucher dove after him. At five thousand feet, the German suddenly climbed to starboard, then dove again. Croucher lined the German up in the gun sight, then lost him in a violent banking turn.

They were 150 yards apart, with Croucher closing fast.

"Slow down or we'll overshoot."

Croucher knew his navigator was right. At one hundred yards, the German was centred in the Mosquito's gun sight. Then he wiggled away. This Jerry was bloody good. Croucher hit the firing button, attempting a deflection shot with his armour-piercing and incendiary cannon. The fighter shuddered from the noise, and the speed dropped off dramatically, as the cockpit quickly filled with the smell of burned cordite. But he missed. Then, in a stroke of luck, the German's tail crossed Croucher gun sight. He fired again and missed again. Croucher hung on and lined up another shot, this one between the wings.

He fired. They saw smoke.

"You got him, Jack!"

Hess acted instinctively. He closed the throttle to the starboard engine and feathered the prop. The RAF fighter roared over and climbed. Hess turned off the fuel cock, switched off the ignition, and closed the shutter. The starboard prop was spinning slowly. Behind the engine belched a trail of black smoke. He could still make it to Scotland on one engine, if he had to.

But the British fighter probably had other plans because it turned and came around at him.

Hess tried to anticipate the strange fighter's next move. He chopped the throttle until the enemy machine came within seventy-five yards. Then he crossed directly in front of the plane, pushed on the power, and climbed as the enemy almost banged into him.

Croucher's reflexes weren't quick enough to avoid the German's prop wash. The engines sputtered and the wing rocked. Then the experimental Mosquito fighter turned on its side and began to spiral.

"We're going down! Do something damn it!" Jones yelled, the world spinning around in tight circles.

"I'm trying! I'm trying!"

"Try harder!"

But Croucher was powerless to gain control. He waggled the stick.

Jones banged on the glass. The ocean raced towards them. This was not good. This was not good!

Twenty-two

Over the North Sea

Eighty-five miles off the east coast of Great Britain, Hess fiddled with his beam recording apparatus, positioning himself onto the invisible radio beacon that Pintsch had arranged to be sent out from Aalborg.

Hess aimed for the wide-arcing beam by performing the required right-angle procedure. As he drew near to the tunnel of the beam, his *X-gerat*—the beam recorder—started to pick up a pattern. He heard a fast-paced DIT-DIT-DIT-DIT in his headphones. The closer he came to the tunnel, the steadier the tone became until it merged into a continuous hum. Then he heard a slower DIT. . . DIT. . . DIT. . . Now he had gone too far to the right. He nudged the stick to the left ever so carefully. The hum gradually returned. He was now on track. The line would take him right to Dunhampton. One of the gauges told him his port engine was beginning to overheat from the strain, but it should make it. His face was numb from the cold rush of air through the window. He was going in with a damaged aircraft—one howling engine—but he was going in.

The sun was casting its last few minutes of golden rays over the Scottish coastline, dead ahead. The air was calm, the sky unbelievably clear. A pale mist rested upon the water. He had been promised excellent flying conditions and he got them. He suddenly believed that the mist had appeared just for his sake. God was on his side. The side of peace and decency in a crazy world. That's if there was a God, a higher authority. Someone or something had to be higher than Adolf Hitler. Hess glanced at the altimeter—eight thousand feet—and threw the aircraft into a nose-down attitude.

Stanmore, England

The British called it RDF—Radio Direction Finding—the detection system that had saved the country during the Battle of Britain by identifying German aircraft the second they were in the air over France, well before they even hit the far side of the Channel. Twenty-four hours a day, RDF generated pulses of energy in short radio waves on high frequencies of more than one thousand megahertz. These same waves were concentrated into narrow beams, searching the far reaches of England and Scotland.

At that moment, Hess's range, course, and speed were being monitored by RAF Fighter Command Headquarters, north of London, in a room smelling of electronic machinery. One attentive woman plotter stood over the table and guided a lone black enemy aircraft marker—tagged Raid 42—into position over the giant grid-map of Britain's eastern approaches. Within minutes, Chain Home Stations sent additional reports to Stanmore of a low-flying aircraft heading west at more than three hundred miles per hour. At first, those at Stanmore took the flight to be a diversion to draw attention to a raid at another part of the island. To be certain one way or the other, a call went out to 13 Fighter Group Headquarters.

Edinburgh, Scotland

At 2200 hours, Wing Commander the Duke of Hamilton was on evening duty in the 13 Fighter Group Operations Room at RAF Turnhouse near Edinburgh when the data came through on Raid 42. For the last four nights, the duke and a handful of his officers had been on steady call due to a series of small German raids on parts of Scotland. Earlier that day, Hamilton, behind the controls of his Hurricane fighter, engaged his second in command in a fierce mock dog fight over the Firth of Forth.

Now, Raid 42 appeared on the filter board in front of him. One word from Hamilton would alert every fighter base for a hundred miles. He had to make a move because an enemy fighter was on the loose in his airspace. The two-month-old "Instruction 17" stated that on full-moon nights under good visibility, enemy attacks on nearby Glasgow and Newcastle were to be met by a sufficient fighter force.

A telephone rang.

A dark-haired airman in glasses close to the filter board caught Hamilton's attention. "Excuse me, Wing Commander, the Observer Corps at Chatton says the aircraft is an ME-110 and it's flying at *fifty feet!*"

Hamilton laughed out loud, the others in the room quickly joining in. The RAF never did take the civilian Observer Corps too seriously. "It has to be a Dornier. A 110 doesn't have the range," Hamilton informed the men. "Our observer boys did it again. They couldn't identify an ME-110 if their lives depended on it."

RAF Dunhampton, Scotland

Group Captain Walker answered his ringing telephone, while Wesley Hollinger looked on anxiously in front of the wide window.

"Thank you," the RAF officer said, hanging up. Easing out of his chair, he turned to the American. "Radar picked up a swift-moving aircraft off the Scottish coast just a few minutes ago, and several Observer Corps people have identified an ME-110 flying west at zero altitude, heading this way. It gave no IFF signal."

"Sounds like our boy."

"Indeed."

Denise and Schubert struggled through the trees, and got on their stomachs as they neared a long, thick roll of barbed wire that circled the aerodrome. They could see the runways and the dispersal ahead. To the left stood the hangars, the tower, and the administration office.

"How am I supposed to get through this?" Schubert asked, pointing at the wire.

Denise smiled. "This way."

They crawled back into the trees and ran a few hundred yards towards the buildings.

As they neared their destination, they heard noises and voices. Then a car or truck door slammed.

"Get down!" *Denise* whispered.

"What now?" Schubert whispered back. He was lying on his stomach, the woman only a few feet away.

"There's a hole in the barbed wire farther down there, fifty feet or so. You won't see it unless you're right on it. I'm friendly with an NCO on the base. Most of the men know about the opening and use it because it's closer to the pub up the road. They're too lazy to go to the gate on the far side of the aerodrome, I suppose."

Schubert didn't care. "Yes, I suppose."

"This is where I depart. Heil Hitler, Herr Reichsfuehrer," she said, then left in a hurry through the thicket.

It was up to Schubert now. He saw a line of refuelling trucks on the other side of the barbed wire. All he needed was one. Then he had to reach the aircraft, providing the pilot had made it. It would be dark soon. Schubert waited nervously, laid out on his stomach for what seemed like at least half an hour. When he finally checked his watch, he saw that only seven minutes had elapsed.

Where are they? Denise thought, scrambling back to the woods. She squatted and looked around. A tug on her arm made her jump. A stocky, six-foot man in a long, open coat stood over her.

Denise bounced to her feet. It was Snowden. "Where the hell were you?"

"I was going to ask you the same question," Snowden said.

"I took the south road—"

"I told you not to take the south road. There was a change of plans, remember. It's too winding and we couldn't see you coming."

Denise felt her sweaty forehead. "Oh, yes, I do remember. Sorry, I'm not a professional like the rest of you. I'm a throw-in, as you may recall. I'm bloody terrified as it is. Do you know who I had in my auto?"

"Who?"

"Rudolf Hess, that's who. Rudolf bloody Hess. I'm still shaking like a leaf."

"Hess? Are you certain?"

"Yes. No mistake."

"Where is he now?"

"I led him through the barbed wire."

"You did what!" Snowden exploded. "You mean he's on the base?"

"That's right."

"How could you?"

"How could I not? What else was I supposed to do? Kill him? Me? With what, my pencil? And if I could have stalled him, he would've known something was up and he would've killed me."

"Is he armed?"

"A Luger, for sure. I saw it. And he removed some papers from a briefcase and stashed them inside his coat."

"All right," Snowden grunted. "I'll let those on the inside know."

Schubert heard a sound through the trees. Thinking it was a single-engine fighter, he was surprised to see an ME-110 flying on one engine, turning to his right. There were only a few minutes left until darkness.

He found the barbed wire opening and carefully squeezed through it, mindful of the fact that he could easily get tangled in the sharp points. Free of the wire, he half-crawled, half-ran to the first of the smaller hangars, which shielded him as he scrambled to one of the trucks opposite the hangar tarmac. Once he got to the truck, he peeked over the door. Through the open window, he saw the Messerschmitt fighter touch down with a screech of tires. His heart thumped like a drum all the way up to his throat. Then to his left three men came out of nowhere and began to slowly work their way in his direction. Schubert ran behind the hangar and flew around the other side. Ahead, all he saw was a black, four-door sedan. He ran to it, opened the passenger door, and jumped in. He was about to slide over to the driver's side and start it up, when he heard footsteps. He threw himself down to the passenger side floorboards, withdrew his Luger and waited...

The steps came closer. Then the door opened. Schubert looked up and pointed the gun at the startled young man who stood gawking at him.

"Don't make a sound." Schubert warned him.

"Who the *hell* are you?"

"Never mind that. Get in and shut up!"

Twenty-three

*RAF D*UNHAMPTON, S*COTLAND*

"Now what do you want me to do?" Hollinger slammed the sedan door, eyeing the sweaty individual in the shadows, crouching down, his hat pulled down over his forehead and his collar flipped up.

"Look straight down the asphalt and drive me out to the fighter," Schubert demanded in accented English. "Keep both hands on the steering wheel."

As calmly as he could, Hollinger released the brake and put the sedan in gear. As he drove slowly past the Secret Service men, one of the men nodded. Hollinger didn't dare nod back, not with a gun barrel poking his ribs. Ahead, near the mechanics' shack, the Messerschmitt had already come to a full stop at the edge of the mile-long runway. A low-to-the-ground mist had appeared.

By the time Hollinger had braked at the runway's end, the aircraft had spun around 180 degrees to face the hangars and the base. With the sun now below the horizon, the twin-engine fighter was a profile of shapes superimposed against the orange sky. It struck Hollinger as odd to see that only one engine was running and that the right-side Plexiglas was shattered. And it had different fuselage letters than the NJ-C11 he had been expecting. These were NJ-OQ.

"What do I do now?" Hollinger asked.

"Put your head down on the steering wheel," Schubert answered.

When Hollinger leaned forward, Schubert got up and clubbed him in the back of the head twice with the Luger. With the driver out, Schubert had to act fast and with precision. The pilot was coming down the wing, holding his briefcase. Schubert recalled his orders. Kill the pilot. Take the papers. Return by sub. He slid out of the sedan to meet the pilot who by this time had come around the starboard side of the fighter.

At ten feet apart, Rudolf Hess and Felix Schubert saw each other.

"Hess," Schubert uttered, mouth open.

"Schubert!" Hess was stunned, but quickly found his tongue. "What are you doing here?"

Schubert held out his left hand, his right clinging to the Luger that was pointed at Hess. "I came for the papers. Give them to me."

"Who got you out of jail this time?"

"I want the papers."

"Who was it?" Hess persisted. "Hitler, the Austrian vagrant who never worked a day in his life? Or was it that fat cow, Goering?"

"Shut up, Hess."

"Or was it Himmler? That's who it was, wasn't it? I can read your face. Do you know he used to be a chicken farmer? Our illustrious Gestapo leader used to be a chicken farmer. What about you Schubert? Back to drinking? Still wallowing with the mud-sucking pigs?"

"The briefcase, Herr Reichsfuehrer."

Hess threw the briefcase at the imposter's boots. "What are your orders, Schubert? Take the papers? Act on my behalf? The British would spot you as a phony in a minute. Himmler is an idiot to send you. You don't stand a chance. You may be able to imitate me at a podium, but you are no negotiator."

"I'll do fine. At least my superiors will reward me."

"Reward you?" Hess laughed. "Himmler doesn't reward people. He does away with them once he uses them up. That will be your reward. I see what happened now. The Gestapo tried to get rid of me by planting a bomb in my airplane, set to go off over the North Sea. But I switched planes. While this was going on, Himmler sent you over to represent me as the Deputy Fuehrer during peace negotiations. Trouble was, I got away."

"I'm supposed to kill you."

"I thought so. But what then? They—Himmler and the Gestapo—won't let you live long. You're a dead man, Schubert. You go back, you're a dead man."

Schubert began to think twice about his mission. "How do you know that?"

"Because I know Himmler. I know his motives. I know his new plans for the Third Reich. Now if *I* was the Fuehrer, things would be different. I was the one who shared Hitler's cell for a year after the Munich uprising. Did Himmler or Goering help the Fuehrer write *Mein Kampf* like I did? No! Did they help me create and organize the Nazi Party?" Hess pounded his chest with his fist. "I'm the leader of the Nazi Party. I've been Hitler's adviser for twenty years. How dare he make Goering number two in the regime. My Deputy Fuehrer title is only a name. Goering! That fat buffoon. That idiot! He never did anything right in his life. He botched the Battle of Britain. His Luftwaffe was supposed to knock off the Royal Air Force in a few weeks. Bah! Mark my words, Goering will botch *Barbarossa*, too."

"*Barbarossa*? What is that?"

"You don't know, do you? The attack on Russia, of course."

Schubert was spellbound. "Hitler is going to attack Russia?"

"Yes. Have you ever heard of anything so insane? Another two-front war! Unless I do something to prevent it. What do you hope to accomplish by killing me, Schubert? What? You'd be playing right into Himmler's hands. He'll eventually try to get rid of you too. That's if you return safely to Germany. Do you think he'll let you play me again? Are you going to take over my identity?"

Schubert hadn't thought about it before. What would happen if he was to kill Hess and return to Germany? "Yes, I would," he said, half-heartedly.

"You fool. You won't get away with it. Another thing, how do you propose to leave here? The Brits will track you down. The same Brits who are scheduled to meet me here. They are waiting for me. They must be late." Hess then took two steps closer to his impostor.

"Stand back," Schubert ordered, the Luger pointed at Hess's chest.

"Well?"

Schubert could see that maybe Hess was making sense. "I . . . I don't believe you, Hess."

"I think you do." Hess's arms spread wide. "Go ahead and shoot me. Where will it get you? You've no place to go."

Hollinger came to on the other side of the ME-110. He looked over at the aircraft, where two men stood on the far side of the nose. He felt his aching head. He couldn't have been out longer than a few minutes, he determined, because it was nearly dark now. Did the passenger knock him unconscious? He must have. Still groggy, Hollinger slipped out of the car without making a sound and fished for the flashlight under the seat. Grabbing it with one hand, he reached for his gun with the other, and began to quietly approach the two men. Ducking under the wing and out the other side, he flicked the light on and shone it at the two men, who were only four feet apart.

"Not so fast, you two. You there, let go of the gun!" Hollinger shouted in English. When the man dropped the pistol, Hollinger's already unsteady knees almost buckled on him. Was he seeing things? Both men looked the same. Both looked like Rudolf Hess. The one on the left wore a flight suit. He had to be the pilot. The other one was taller, in a trench coat. Was he the one hiding in the car? Was he the real Hess or was the pilot? There was one way to find out.

"Give me the codename for the mission?" Hollinger said, eyeing both faces.

"*Operation Night Eagle*," Schubert snapped ahead of Hess. "I'm Rudolf Hess. I'm *Falcon*."

"No he's not," Hess exclaimed. "I'm the one. And you must be a representative for *Lion*. You are not *Lion*, I know that much. Where is he?"

Now Hollinger was thoroughly confused. Both knew the proper codenames for the operation.

"Shoot this impostor before he escapes," Hess continued. "I can prove who the real Deputy Fuehrer is?"

"How?" Hollinger asked.

"I have top secret papers and photographs that will make you hair stand on end, material that only a person of my stature would have possession of."

Schubert had to do something. He withdrew his stiletto and lunged at Hess. But the Deputy Fuehrer anticipated the move and caught Schubert's arm. They wrestled to the concrete and turned over and over, locked together.

"OK, you two, stop it!" Hollinger yelled.

They ignored Hollinger. He knew he couldn't shoot. He didn't know who was who. Then the one in the trench coat knifed the pilot and slowly crawled to his feet.

"Now, we can finally get down to business," Schubert said, brushing himself off and calmly walking over to the Luger lying on the concrete. His neck was gashed and sweat poured off his face. He held the gun loosely, barrel down. "Rudolf Hess at your service. The other was sent to foil this peace negotiation."

Hollinger didn't know what to think. The man who had been in his car was Hess? "I need more proof," Hollinger said.

"Put the gun away, please." Schubert waited for Hollinger to relax, then he flipped the gun up and fired twice before Hollinger could react. The American fell backwards to the ground. Schubert looked at the aircraft, then at Hess, then across the field. A truck with its headlights on had moved out from the hangars a mile away and was heading in his direction. Schubert turned to Hess and stripped him of all his flight gear, throwing it over his own body, and throwing the trench coat and hat loosely on Hess. Then he picked up Hess's briefcase and shoved Himmler's proposals inside. He took a step towards the fighter, then realized that he couldn't leave Hess there, yet he couldn't drag him aboard either. There could only be one Hess now. He—Felix Schubert—had to be the Hitler's Deputy Fuehrer. With no remorse, he stood over the body and fired the Luger in rapid succession into Hess's face until the chamber emptied. He glanced down at the blood on his boots, dazed for a moment. If Hess's body was going to stay behind, then no one would recognize it.

Schubert climbed onto the wing of the fighter. Stumbling to the cockpit seat, he hit the button for the port engine. The engine wound and caught. He looked out the broken Plexiglas at the truck racing to the end of the runway. Schubert hadn't flown in years, not since he had been washed out of the Luftwaffe. Would he remember how to get this thing off the ground? Worse, this would be a one-engine takeoff.

Hess was right. Schubert couldn't go back to Germany. He would fly his way to neutral Ireland. He was a Luftwaffe pilot now. If he had any trouble, he'd be Captain Alfred Horn, as the letter on his person stated. He spun the ME-110 around and faced the truck coming straight for him.

Group Captain Walker was watching through his binoculars as best he could, despite the setting sun and oncoming darkness. At the distance of a mile, he couldn't distinguish the figures at all. When he saw the flash of gunfire, he was forced to move, fearing the worst. He jogged down the hall and flew out of the door to one of the refuelling trucks, motioning for two of the Secret Service men to follow him. "Come on, let's go!" he screamed at the driver, as the other two men jumped in the truck.

As the driver raced down the runway, the occupants were shocked to see the German fighter racing head-on at them, its red wing lights blinking. The driver had no choice but to swerve onto the grass as the aircraft roared past. Walker flung open the passenger door and hung out the side and watched the ME-110 climb into the night in one of the sloppiest take-offs he had seen in a long while. The driver then drove the rest of the way to the end of the runway, where the truck's headlights revealed two bodies lying on the concrete. The four men ran out. The nearest was Wesley Hollinger lying face up. Walker bent down and checked the American's pulse. Then he saw blood stains on his shoulder and chest.

"Bloody hell, no!" Walker exclaimed. "Get him to the hospital. He's still alive."

"Yes, sir," the driver said.

Walker trotted over to the second body, this one lying on its side, dressed in an open grey trench coat, beneath it a blue jacket, blue-grey slacks, a blue shirt and blue tie. All Luftwaffe colours. A huge puddle of crimson red blood and pieces of brain covered the concrete. Walker turned the body on its back and was sick to his stomach at the ghastly sight. The face was a horrible conglomeration of blood, bones, and raw flesh.

Walker dropped to his knees. "Good God, what would make somebody do such a thing?"

Twenty-four

Firth of Forth, Scotland

She stood on the rocks and watched the surf picking up in intensity. With the countrywide blackout enforced, she couldn't see a light anywhere.

"We're coming up to low tide," Snowden said to her. A stiff wind at their backs, he studied the water with binoculars for any sign of a conning-tower showing above the water. "It'll be further out now, what with the low tide. Let it go."

Denise dug for the flashlight inside her coat. Using Morse code, she flashed her call sign several times, followed by the letters A-B-O-R-T another six times, then signed off. She turned to Snowden. "Do you think they got the message?"

"Whether they did or not, I'll radio the navy."

"And what about Hamburg?"

"Send them your last communiqué. After that, *Denise* is officially retired. We can't take any more chances. This one was horrendous enough. Despite the rendezvous foul-up, you performed quite well. Good job."

Denise smiled. "Thanks. But I'm glad it's over."

Lieutenant Steider read the Morse blinks clearly through the periscope more than six hundred yards offshore. It was an abort. Hess was on his own.

"Up scope," he ordered, pulling away from the periscope eyepiece. "And take her out to sea!"

"Aye, aye, sir."

Near Eaglesham, Scotland

A tight procession of six black sedans, headlights blacked out, chugged slowly along the tarred road. A quarter mile distant, Dungavel Castle marked the foggy landscape. Overhead, the stars were out in full force.

"Keep your eyes on the road, young man, and push on," Colonel Lampert said to the driver across from him in the front seat of the lead vehicle.

"I'm trying to, sir. But I can't see a thing."

"Hold up here," Lampert said, once the driver came alongside the castle gates.

Lampert got out and waited for the occupants from the five other cars. When they assembled for last-minute instructions, he asked them to check their pistols. He then sent two of the cars ahead with orders to surround the house in case anyone tried to escape.

"I'll knock," he said to those men remaining. "As soon as I say Secret Service, we rush inside and cart them off. Tally ho."

The estate had several cars tucked inside the gates. No sounds could he heard, even as they reached the oak front doors. Lampert knocked, waited, and knocked again. He caught the faint sound of footsteps on the other side.

The door opened, and a tall butler in his sixties appeared. "Yes."

Lampert showed his pocket identification with a flick of the wrist. "Secret Service." Then he pushed ahead, followed by the other agents. Lampert stopped and glanced down a long hall of oil paintings. At the very end was an open door with a brightly-lit room beyond, from where he heard laughter and the clinking of glasses.

"What's the meaning of this?" the butler asked, his voice shaky.

"Never you mind. That way," Lampert said, pointing to the room. "Two of you stay here at the entrance."

Eight Secret Service men rushed down the length of the hall, pistols drawn. They made way for Lampert to enter the room first. The meeting was not what Lampert had imagined. He had pictured a great party for Hess and the peace-pact signing, not nine well-dressed men, five of them seated around a long, polished table, and the other four standing and looking on. All had drinks in their hands. What was this, a Sunday afternoon bridge club? Lampert recognized two of them from news photos as prominent politicians. One other was a high-ranking officer in the army. The sight of each one—powerful as they were in their own right—drove home the fact to Lampert that these men and others had been conspiring to overthrow someone much more powerful and smarter than they were—Winston Churchill. It was up to Lampert to show that they were taking on the wrong man and the wrong team.

"Who the bloody hell are you!" the army man shouted. "I demand an explanation! How dare you march in—"

"Shut up!" Lampert held out his hand and showed his ID. He glared at the faces slowly, as the MI-6 men spread out, guns pointed. "Secret Service. You are all under arrest."

"On what grounds?"

"Treason," Lampert replied. "Collaborating with the enemy, namely Rudolf Hess. You will be held at MI-6 Headquarters until Churchill himself decides what to do with the lot of you. And by the way, your friend, Brenwood, couldn't make it. He's . . . tied up."

Lampert walked up to the table, poured himself an inch of red wine into a crystal glass, and downed it. "Not bad. Must have been a good year." He thumped the glass to the table. "Get these traitors out of here."

Edinburgh, Scotland

Wing Commander the Duke of Hamilton was flabbergasted when two different observer posts miles apart phoned RAF Turnhouse with the same information—an ME-110 was racing low over the Scottish countryside on a course southwest of Glasgow. Now Hess was in the air, again. So soon. He was supposed to land at Dunhampton, then be escorted to Dungavel. What was he doing? Did something go wrong? Whatever had transpired, Hamilton had to act to shift any suspicion away from him.

"Alert 141 Squadron at Ary to send up a Defiant and pursue the intruder," he barked at his controller, knowing that he had ordered that particular base on stand-down for the evening.

Over Southern Scotland

At six thousand feet, Schubert sighed at the sight of the glittering Firth of Clyde only a kilometre or two over his port wing. According to the crumpled map in his left hand, he was 160 kilometres from

British-controlled Northern Ireland and over three hundred kilometres from neutral Ireland. The latter seemed the only alternative.

He thought ahead to the landing, while he struggled to keep the fighter steady in the frigid, breezy cockpit. He gave left rudder to line up on his anticipated course. He felt for the parachute under the seat. If worse came to worse, he could ditch the fighter in the water and parachute in. Then... his cockpit Plexiglas crashed to his lap! Now both side windows had been blown out. What happened? A glance down at the gauges told him that the RPM and engine pressures were rapidly falling. An aircraft flew past and banked. Damn! He was under attack!

Schubert banked hard to port and dove at the same time. He didn't have a hope of making Ireland, not with a dying engine that was vibrating the entire aircraft. And a water landing was impossible at night. His only way out now was back to the mainland. He reached down and struggled with the parachute. Think. Think. Then it came to him... Dungavel Castle. The British collaborators could get him out of this.

Hold on. Find Dungavel Castle in a blackout? Fat chance of that.

Edinburgh, Scotland

At 2305 hours, another telephone call broke the silence at RAF Turnhouse.

"Wing Commander?" said the controller, receiver in hand, to Hamilton who had just entered the combat room.

"Yes, what is it?"

"The observer post at Eaglesham Moor reports the ME-110 flying an erratic course as if the pilot is looking for something."

"Is the Defiant still in pursuit?" Hamilton asked another airman.

"Not anymore, sir. He lost the intruder, but the pilot claimed some hits."

Near Eaglesham, Scotland

Schubert took the damaged fighter up to 6,500 feet, and it strained to get there. The machine was now hanging on by a thread and a vapour, the fuel tanks reading empty. He threw the gun and the stiletto out the port opening, then reached overhead and slid back the cabin roof, his right hand on the briefcase. Bailing out of an aircraft would be a first for him. To start what he thought would be a simple procedure, he made the mistake of sticking his head too far into the open, turbulent slipstream. He was thrown back. He tried again. The slipstream pushed him back yet again. Now he was terrified he'd never get out.

One more time!

He pushed, he shoved, he swore under his breath, but he still couldn't get out. Landing in the cockpit seat, he decided that the conventional method of evacuating an aircraft was not going to work. So, he heaved back on the stick to send the nose up. The fighter climbed until it stood on its tail . . . and stalled. It took perfect coordination to complete the next step. As the ME-110 hung motionless for a brief, split-second, Schubert jumped into the night.

The slipstream tore the briefcase from his grasp. But at least he was free. Tumbling at first, he managed to control his descent by spreading his body out.

Then he counted to ten . . . a bit too fast . . . and pulled the cord.

Twenty-five

Berlin, Germany

Heinrich Himmler lifted his office telephone receiver and held it to his ear.

"Herr Reichsfuehrer. This is Geis."

"Yes, Geis. What is it?"

"Hamburg has just received a message from *Denise*. Schubert did not return to her. That is all she reported."

"Any word on the submarine and Lieutenant Steider?"

"Nothing, Herr Reichsfuehrer. No one has been able to reach them."

"Return to Berlin, directly," Himmler said, then hung up. The news was not good. Where was Hess? Where was Schubert? Had they crossed paths?

Munich, Germany

Karlheinz Pintsch stalled at his home to give Hess time to return. But it was no use. Time had run out. The Reichsfuehrer was long overdue and he would not come back. He was on his way to Britain or . . . Pintsch didn't want to think about the negative possibilities. Instead, he ordered Hess's chauffeur to drive him to the train station, where Pintsch issued another order, to hook up Hess's private coach to the train leaving for Berchtesgaden.

While the work was being done, Pintsch walked the crowded platform, sprinkled with soldiers, airmen, military policemen, and their wives and girlfriends. Suddenly, Pintsch had a premonition that he would never see his superior again. And because of that it would only be fitting that he should carry out the Deputy Fuehrer's last request and take the letter to Hitler.

But what kind of mood would he be in?

Near Eaglesham, Scotland

Schubert came down hard in a field of short, grazing grass. He tried to stand, but found it too difficult. He had sprained his ankle when he hit the ground. Not only that, his back hurt from scraping the rudder on bailing out. To make matters worse, the wind was billowing his parachute and dragging him on his knees across the damp field.

"Who are you?" a voice broke the night air. The only other sound was the dying ME-110 engine overhead.

Schubert ignored the voice for the moment, concentrating more on trying to rise to his feet. He finally broke free of the chute and let it drift away. The man had a pitchfork with him and came within arm's reach. "Help me, please. I am hurt," Schubert said. He got up on one leg and placed his hands on the man's shoulders for support. It eased the agony. Schubert stood at least a foot taller than the man he took to be a middle-aged farmer.

The farmer stepped back. "Are you a German?"

"Yes," Schubert replied with his German accent. "I am a German. I want to go to Dungavel Castle. I must see the Duke of Hamilton."

"What do you want with that silly bugger?"

"I have an important message for him."

"That figures. He always did love you Nazis."

Then a loud crunch caught their attention. The Messerschmitt had crashed in the distance, lighting up the sky with a fiery flash.

"Is that a German plane?" the farmer asked.

"Yes," Schubert winced, attempting to stay standing on his own. "It's a Messerschmitt 110."

"Were there any more in the plane?"

"No. I flew alone."

"Are you armed?"

"I have no weapons. I have come in peace."

"Yeah, I bet you have."

An elderly man approached them, stopped a good twenty feet back, and said, "What's happened? Who's out there?"

"There's a German flier here," the farmer answered his neighbour. "Get some soldiers." He turned to Schubert. "Come, lean on my shoulder. My house is over the rise."

Helped away by the farmer, Schubert turned back to the parachute lying limp in the field. "I can't leave that. I owe my life to it."

"I'll get it for you as long as you promise me you won't move."

"I promise."

Schubert watched the farmer fighting with the large sheet of parachute silk, until he was finally able to roll it up and tuck it under his arm. "Thank you," Schubert said, as the farmer returned.

Each step over the rise was sheer torture for Schubert. Inside the house, an elderly woman in a patched grey nightgown held the door open. She was old and tiny and wore her white hair flipped back in a bun. Although she kept her distance, she seemed curious at the sight of this hobbling stranger in her place.

"My God, you are a German!" she exclaimed.

Schubert bowed to her. "Yes, madam. I am indeed a German."

"We'd better go in there," the farmer said.

The living room was lit by a single bulb hanging from a plaster ceiling. The farmer motioned Schubert towards a large leather armchair with wide cushions. The old woman followed the two men in. To Schubert, it was plain that the chair was the finest piece of furniture in the room, and one meant for a prominent visitor or head of the house.

"You may sit there." The farmer pointed. "Welcome to my house. I am David McLean. This is my mother."

Schubert dropped his sore and tired body into the chair. "I am very pleased to meet the both of you. My name is Captain Alfred Horn."

Mrs. McLean smiled. "Why don't I get us all a cup of hot tea?"

"Yes, do that, mother."

Schubert turned to his captor, and winced. "I have an urgent message for the Duke of Hamilton. Please take me to him at once."

"The soldiers will be here. They will deal with all that."

"How far away is Dungavel Castle?" Schubert wanted to know.

"Twelve miles, as the crow flies."

"Would you be so kind as to drive me there?"

McLean shook his head. "I'm only a civilian, although I fought in the last war. I was in the Highlanders at Arras."

Schubert recalled some of Hess's World War I background that had been fed to him at Gestapo Headquarters in Berlin. "I too was in the Battle of Arras."

"Yeah," McLean grunted. "But on the other side."

A hush fell over the room. Schubert looked away, trying to think of what to say next. So far, he was certain that the farmer had not recognized him as Hess. The woman entered with the tea.

Just then someone pounded at the door. "Open up, David," a voice yelled. "We've come for the Kraut."

McLean left his seat and opened the door. Brandishing an outdated World War I pistol, the leader, a frumpy man in civilian clothing, burst into the living room, surrounded by other men, and glared at the German in the flight suit. Schubert set his tea down and smiled at them.

"What are you doing here?" the leader asked, pointing the gun at Schubert's head.

Schubert could tell the man was nervous. "Well, I didn't come a thousand miles just for a cup of tea."

The man's eyes narrowed. "Who else is with you?"

"No one. And will you please put that gun down. Your hand is shaking severely. I flew alone, from Germany. My name is Captain Alfred Horn. Please, you must take me to Dungavel Castle. I must see Wing Commander the Duke of Hamilton before it's too late. Do you know him? I have an extremely important message for him."

The man looked at McLean then back to Schubert, his gun hand shaking all the more. "Get your bloody hands up, you Kraut bastard!"

Twenty-six

LONDON, ENGLAND—MAY 11

Roberta Langford left the train station after midnight and strained her eyes for the sight of a taxi. Cars were actually moving out there. The transformation from the bright lights inside the restaurant to the inky London streets caught her off guard at first until her eyes grew accustomed to the change. After a few seconds, she began to distinguish the outline of a taxi coming towards her. Like a few million others in the city, she had to live with the blackout. In her trips to the big city, however, she had never really gotten used to it.

She was back in London, the city of smelly exhausts and smoke odours and sand-bagged buildings. Parts of the city had been razed by German bombers, but life still carried on with a stiff upper lip. London was surviving and evolving at the same time. Langford knew of London girls who, when going out for the evening, always took their nightgowns or pyjamas with them, just in case their return route was bombed in the night and they couldn't make it back. Despite the wartime inconveniences, London was still home to the redhead cryptographer from Bletchley.

Langford hailed the taxi with a shout and a wave. With her one suitcase, she got in the back seat. The driver, a stubby old man, jammed the column into gear. She gave the address of her parents' home in the west end, then leaned back into the soft padding of the seat. She was drained. As she dozed in and out of sleep, she thought of Arthur, the man she once loved, or maybe even still loved. That was the ironic thing about the situation. She still loved him now, more than ever, knowing that she probably couldn't have him. Maybe she could get him back if he knew she was pregnant. She thought of her parents. What would she say to them? *Well, mother, father, I went and got myself a wee bit pregnant, you see. So sorry. I hope you're not disappointed with me...*

The taxi continued on its way until... long, bright, blue-white searchlights suddenly flicked on and probed the sky like tentacles. The old man ground the taxi to a screeching halt and gawked through the windshield. Sirens wailed. Cars stopped. Pedestrians ran across the street. Langford rolled down her window. Anti-aircraft fire opened up and exploded into the star-filled sky. A woman shrieked. Then another. Langford looked around in horror. They were caught in the middle of a bombing raid! The driver quickly pulled the taxi over to the curb. She had never been in the midst of a bombing raid before. And she was never so scared in her life.

"Come on, missy. We can't stay here," the driver said in a composed voice. This was obviously not the first time for him. "We've got to get ourselves to the tube."

Langford knew he meant the underground railway. Everyone in London called it the tube. But she was not familiar with the side streets the driver had been taking.

"How far is it?" she asked

"A few streets down and around to the right, missy. Follow the crowd."

"A few streets!"

He turned over his shoulder to see her reach for her suitcase. "Never you mind that. Leave it!"

Langford ignored him and grabbed it anyway. On foot, she melted into a sea of dark figures flowing in the same direction in an orderly manner. Overhead, she picked out the outlines of the enemy planes in their ragged V-formations at the end of the pencil-shaped searchlights. The shells burst in white puffs. It was like flock shooting for the ground gunners—hit or miss. But they were badly outnumbered. There had to be hundreds of planes. Engines throbbing in unison, the invaders flowed over the great capital city. More and more bombers appeared. From what she could tell, the Luftwaffe were concentrating on the east side. Then the bombs began to explode closer. The closer they came, the quicker the pace of the crowd picked up. Langford ran with it. Before long her legs were sore and she was coughing. She stopped by the edge of a brick building and reached for a handkerchief to pat her perspiring face. The tube had to be close now because the crowd was very thick.

Then she took a breath and turned the corner, only to fall. In the darkness, two people stumbled over her and she was stepped on several times. Aching, she picked herself up. The crowd was squashing her. Then the tube entrance came into view. At last. She saw explosions in the distance, hurtling flames into the sky, in stark contrast to the blackout. Two airplanes, both on fire, headed to earth as if they were falling stars. Were they friend or foe? Everything was happening all at once: the red, white, and blue colours of flames and searchlights, the stars overhead, the unique hum of German engines, the crackling of anti-aircraft, the white puffs in the sky.

In the time it took her to run from the taxi to the tube, the German Luftwaffe had rained terror and destruction onto the city. She had been raised in a proper English home, where coarse language was not tolerated. But she wasn't at home now. She looked up at the sounds of war, shook her fist, and uttered words she thought she'd never say in her life.

"You sons of bitches!" she whispered, her teeth clenched. She said it to the Luftwaffe bombers . . . to the RAF who let them through . . . to Hitler and his henchmen who started this war . . . and to the anti-aircraft batteries who weren't knocking the planes down. "You damn sons of bitches!"

"Here they come!" a young woman shouted, then disappeared with her male companion, a Royal Navy officer in dress blues, down the steps. Langford wondered if the woman had her pyjamas with her.

The crowd slowly pushed its way down the concrete steps like a huge ocean wave. Outside, the whistle of bombs sliced the air, followed by detonating bursts. More women screamed. Langford felt dizzy as she took to the steps slowly, edging her body along the wall. Down they all went into the belly of London until the bottom of the entrance opened into two long platforms to either side of a tunnel of underground rails.

Langford had to stop and stare. It was like another world. Under the curved walls, human beings covered the platforms, and with them were their belongings—cots, mattresses, bed sheets, tables and chairs, and food. Most were homeless, bombed out of existence months ago. The sour smell of cigarette smoke, dirty bodies, and urine laced the air. The place was a breeding ground for a typhus outbreak. For the many nights since the Blitz began nearly a year before, men, women, and children had to vacate their homes in the evening and dart for the underground tube stations. At the beginning, the packed-in-like-cattle London crowds were jovial and often sang and danced to pass the night. But as the months wore on they sat silently with blank faces as the steady pounding continued overhead.

With emotion that she hadn't felt before, Langford looked across the many faces in the vast throng of people. This was war—civilian style. The ugly side of war. It was war so distant from her and her work at Bletchley. Until now. She was full of admiration for how Londoners had carried on. She looked one way down the ramp, then the other. Her dizziness seemed to be getting worse. She held her stomach. Something was wrong. Everything began to flow in circles around her.

Then she dropped her suitcase and fainted.

Edinburgh, Scotland

The Duke left his office at RAF Turnhouse and headed for the ops room where he heard the news that London was facing a heavy bombing raid. Hamilton knew the Germans would leave his sector alone now because they hardly ever conducted two raids at once.

As he left and climbed into bed in his quarters nearby, the duke wondered what happened to the Messerschmitt. Was it Hess? If so, where was he now? His eyes were just starting to close when his bedside phone rang.

"Hello."

"Sir, will you please come to the ops room at once?" The night-shift controller asked.

"Why? What's wrong? Is there an attack?"

"No, sir."

"Is there another enemy sighting?"

"No, sir."

"I'm in bed. What's so damn important? Can't you take care of it yourself?"

"Well, sir, it's about the ME-110."

"I'll be right there." Hamilton dressed and walked the hall to the ops room where he saw the controller in person. "What is it?"

"Sir, the ME-110 pilot bailed out."

"He did?" The duke felt a lump in his throat.

"He's in custody at Maryhill Barracks in Glasgow. He gave his name as Captain Alfred Horn and he wants to speak to you personally."

Why me? thought Hamilton.

RAF Dunhampton, Scotland

"Is he going to make it?" Lampert asked Group Captain Walker in the hall outside Hollinger's hospital room.

"The doctor doesn't know. He took bullets to the chest and lung, not to mention a frightful lump to the back of his head. He's unconscious now, but his breathing and vital signs seem regular."

"Who shot him?"

"One of the Germans. Hess or the other one."

"None of this would have happened if we had caught Hess when *Denise* made contact with him. What did you see?"

"It was getting dark, so it was hard to tell. The ME-110 landed and waited at the end of the runway. Hollinger drove out. Hess was with him, I gather, hiding inside. The next thing I knew there was a flash of gunfire. We drove out but were too late. As near as I figure it, sir, Hess had arrived by sub the same time the pilot did. One shot the other, someone shot Hollinger, then one of them tried to fly out of Britain. Very strange."

"So, we don't know who's in the ME-110?"

"Maybe we will, soon. We just got news the aircraft crash-landed near Eaglesham. The pilot is under guard outside Glasgow."

"No positive identification?"

"Not yet. He claims to be Captain Alfred Horn and he's demanding to see Wing Commander the Duke of Hamilton."

"Hamilton? That's odd."

"Yes, it is."

"Where is this Horn now?"

"Maryhill Barracks. That's not all. There's the dead body. He was sliced through the heart and shot in the back of the head and face several times from different angles. A little bit of an overkill, wouldn't you say, sir?"

"Yes." Lampert frowned. "A little. I wonder why? Anyway, we've got to keep Hollinger alive. He's our answer to this. I know a specialist in

London who's done work for our department. I'll call him. Do you have a scrambler in your office?"

"Yes, I do. Be my guest."

Lampert knew he had better call Winnie, too.

Berchtesgaden, Germany

Upon arrival at Hitler's Bavarian hideaway later that Sunday morning, Karlheinz Pintsch saw Albert Speer, Hitler's architect, sitting in the anteroom.

"Excuse me, Herr Speer," he said. "Would you permit me to see the Fuehrer first? I have an important personal message from the Deputy Fuehrer."

"Of course. I can wait."

Pintsch bowed. "Thank you."

Just then, Hitler, in grey jacket and black trousers, slowly descended the stairs off to the side. The bright lights caught his Iron Cross for an instant. He looked tired and disturbed, another sleepless night for him. He had finished an interview minutes before with Dr. Fritz Todt, the Minister of Armaments, and he was in the midst of preparing a reception for Admiral Jean Darlan of Vichy France that would take place after lunch.

Pintsch displayed the Nazi salute. "Heil Hitler. The Reichsfuehrer asked me to deliver this letter to you in person."

"Come with me," Hitler demanded, leading the way into the nearby salon. Inside, door closed, they both sat in padded chairs.

Hitler grabbed the envelope from Pintsch's hands, placed his glasses over his eyes and read the hand-written message.

> My Fuehrer, when you read this letter I shall be meeting with my British friends. You can imagine the decision to take this step was not easy for me, since a man of forty has other ties with life than one of twenty.
> Mein Fuehrer, I will convince them and explain later. Trust me. It has been done for the betterment of mankind.

Hitler began to burn red with rage. "He's going to tell the British about *Operation Barbarossa*. I know it. I can feel it in my bones. I can always feel such things. Hess, you fool. I told you not to go." Hitler collapsed in his chair and slapped his forehead once . . . twice. "This is awful. Awful! Bormann! Where is Bormann?" Hitler shouted at the top of his lungs, rising and waving his arms.

Martin Bormann rushed in from another room. "Yes, mein Fuehrer?"

Hitler's eyes bore down on Pintsch, then returned to Bormann. "Get me Goering, Ribbentrop, Himmler and Goebbels by the fastest means possible. And confine all the guests to the upper floor!"

"Yes, mein Fuehrer."

"Quickly! Go!"

Then Hitler stomped over towards the frightened Pintsch, only inches away. But he was so mad he couldn't speak. With an abrupt swing of his arm, he left the room, slamming the door behind him.

Alone in the salon, except for an SS guard, Pintsch rubbed his trembling hands together. What was to happen now? His thoughts were answered when Bormann entered the room minutes later. Hess had reminded Pintsch more than once that Bormann was not to be trusted. *Be careful with him. Watch your back, Pintsch.*

Bormann cleared his throat, a nasty smile appearing on his lips. "Captain Karlheinz Pintsch, you are under arrest. You will be taken to Obersalzberg until a court of inquiry can be arranged to probe your part in the events of today. Heil Hitler!"

Two tall SS guards stepped forward and stood beside Pintsch. He followed them down the winding marble staircase to the main floor. Led into the back of a Mercedes, with the guards to either side of him, Pintsch gave the two men, both of whom he knew, a tormented look.

"What's this all about?" one of them asked, politely. "There must be a mistake."

"This is no mistake."

"What did you do?"

Pintsch watched the mountains through the windshield as the chauffeur drove the Mercedes through the front gate. "I don't really know."

Inside the compound, nothing that the inner circle did to pacify Hitler worked. The Fuehrer fumed relentlessly, pacing his study, Hess's message in his hand. Bormann and the others could only look on, helplessly.

Hitler didn't know what to make of Hess. At one time he had been considered a loyal and trusted subordinate. Now Hitler was feeling more sorry for the German people. What would he tell them? His eyes rested on the last sentence of Hess's message.

> And if, my Fuehrer, this project—which I admit has very little chance of success—ends in a failure, if fate decides against me, there will be no harmful consequences for you or Germany; you can always deny all responsibility—simply say that I am insane.

Hitler slapped his forehead. What a catastrophe. "Hess must have had a mental derangement. What lunacy on his part! Why did I agree to this?" Hitler turned to the men. "Where is Goering and Himmler? Why haven't they called?"

Twenty-seven

Outside Glasgow, Scotland

Maryhill Barracks was an old army training centre surrounded by barbed wire. In it, Felix Schubert was confined to a six-by-ten-foot rundown room containing a cot. He was in great distress throughout the night and was unable to fall into a proper sleep. At three-thirty in the morning he complained to a doctor about several ailments: a broken ankle, a stomach ache, and pains in his upper lumbar and back. Schubert asked for a sedative and received one. In minutes, he was fast asleep with his flight suit and boots still on, his parachute wrapped and by his side. Seven hours later he was wakened by an orderly and told to expect the Duke of Hamilton to arrive shortly.

The duke appeared at Maryhill with his intelligence officer, Flight Lieutenant Benson, and was pointed to a room where they examined the German's possessions. He had a map of Scotland, photographs of Hess and his son, and Hitler and Hess together, an assortment of vitamins and drugs, two visiting cards from Karl Haushofer and his son, and a postmarked envelope that read *Captain Alfred Horn, Munched 9*. The map of Scotland caught Benson by surprise because someone had ink-marked the approximate location of Dungavel Castle by name. Hamilton made an attempt to look astonished.

A guard duty officer appeared while Hamilton was fingering the vitamin capsules. "Strange combination of pieces, is it not, sir?"

Hamilton agreed, nodding.

He put a set of pills down on the table, recalling that Albrecht

Haushofer had said that Hess was one of those health nuts. "Take me to your German prisoner."

"Yes, sir."

The duke managed a dry smile when he finally saw the prisoner in a room down the hall. Was this Hess? He appeared to be the Deputy Fuehrer from news photos he had seen of Hitler's right-hand man. The duke was confident that Benson did not recognize the German. He would soon, once the news broke. Assuming it *was* Hess. How could this be kept silent? Albrecht had also said that Hess and the duke should meet one day because they had a lot in common.

But like this? Here?

They found the prisoner sitting on the edge of the bed, his flight suit stripped to his waist, his arms out, his hair a tangled, sweaty clump. He had casual clothing underneath and looked to be in some distress. He stood to face his visitors.

"I am Wing Commander the Duke of Hamilton. This is my Intelligence Officer, Flight Lieutenant Benson. You were asking for me?"

"I should like to speak to you alone," Schubert answered the duke in English.

Hamilton turned to Benson and the guard duty officer. "Leave me with him until I call for you."

"Yes, sir," they replied separately.

Schubert waited patiently for the men to withdraw, then said, "I saw you at the Olympic Games in Berlin. Don't you remember? You lunched with us. I don't know if you recognize me—but I am Rudolf Hess."

"Where is your proof of identity?" the duke asked, remembering the games but not the lunch. He would have known if he had lunch with someone as prominent as Rudolf Hess.

Schubert rummaged beneath his pillow for a picture of Hess and his son. "Here. This should prove it."

"I can see it's a snapshot of you," Hamilton observed. "But that doesn't mean it's a snapshot of Hess. What is the codename of your mission?"

"*Operation Night Eagle.*"

The duke was convinced now, handing the photograph back. "What do you want with me?"

"Please, with your influence, you must arrange for me to leave your country. I was trying to fly to Ireland, but I didn't make it. I was shot down."

"Ireland? Well, why did you seek *me* out? And why did you leave Dunhampton. You were supposed to be driven to my castle."

Schubert needed a good story. And he had one that he had taken most of the evening to conjure up. It would have to save his own skin and include Himmler's motives, should the papers be found. "There is a power struggle within the Nazi government. A German agent working for Adolf Hitler discovered my true plans. He flew into Scotland in my place, and I came by submarine. At the same exact time, we surprised each other at Dunhampton. I shot him, but not before he shot one of your men. I had to escape by aircraft and find you, and to give me time to sort through this. I feared for my life. I couldn't stay at Dunhampton. But I couldn't find your castle in the night. Albrecht once said you could be trusted. Please, you must get me out of your country before anyone finds out, so I can fulfil my destiny in the new regime."

"What new regime?"

"I need safe passage to Ireland where I will make contact with my own collaborators in Germany through the embassy. Then I must return and make the moves before Hitler ruins our country. It's up to me. We can live in peaceful harmony again, Germany and Great Britain, but only if Hitler's shadow is erased forever and Churchill steps down. Until that happens I want England's assurance of a temporary truce."

"Who in the German High Command knows you are here?"

"Adolf Hitler and Heinrich Himmler. I come in the name of Himmler, who hopes to be our new Fuehrer. We both wish an agreeable end to hostilities. I have planned the trip with Hitler for months. Only he believes I'm here acting on his behalf to sell his own peace plan to you and call a truce so that he can attack the Soviet Union, although I was not supposed to reveal the attack. Please you must let me go before anyone knows I'm here."

"Do you have any paperwork with you?"

"The briefcase carrying the proposals flew from my hand when I aborted the aircraft."

"You mean the briefcase is out on the moors somewhere?"

"Yes."

Hamilton did not like that. "I'll need a photograph. Anything."

Schubert returned the photo of Hess and his son. "Take this or anything else I brought with me. There is something else I must tell you. There is one billion pounds sterling waiting for your peace group in a Swiss bank to use as you wish to influence others to your peace cause."

Dumbfounded at the figure, the duke left the cell with the photograph stuffed inside his jacket. He sought the officer in charge of the sickbay. "You might have a very important prisoner here." He looked to the direction of the hall, then to the officer. "I think it would be wise to move him out of Maryhill, and keep him somewhere in secret with a double guard."

"Yes, sir. If you insist."

"I do." Hamilton then spoke to his intelligence officer in the adjacent room. "Benson. I want you to get every available man to help you."

"Help me with what?"

"To find something."

"Find what?"

"I will tell you outside."

Edinburgh, Scotland

Hamilton and Benson made their return journey to RAF Turnhouse an hour later, where Hamilton dropped the photograph into his briefcase. Next, he telephoned 10 Downing Street, clearing his name through three people until a voice came over the line introducing himself as Churchill's personal secretary.

"What do you have for us?"

"I can't say over the phone," Hamilton answered. "I'll be at Northolt in an hour and a half. Kindly have a car there."

"As you wish. I'll make the arrangements."

"Thank you."

The duke rushed to his Hurricane fighter and flew it down to Northolt, arriving there in late afternoon. When he checked in at the watch-hut, he was handed a sealed envelope. He opened it to find he had been ordered to fly to Kidlington.

RAF Kidlington, England

After nightfall, an enormous black car met the duke at the tarmac.

"The Duke of Hamilton?" The chauffeur saluted.

"Yes."

The chauffeur held the door open, and the duke slid in, holding his briefcase. He removed his leather flying jacket. "Where are you taking me?"

"To Ditchley Park, sir. To see the Prime Minister."

Covering over four thousand acres, Ditchley Park was owned by Mr. and Mrs. Ronald Tree, old friends and parliamentary supporters of Winston Churchill. The eighteenth-century Georgian mansion north of Oxford contained seven reception rooms, twenty-four bedrooms, and ten bathrooms. This was Churchill's secret weekend getaway during the war. The duke arrived to see Churchill's entourage at the end of a meal, and in good spirits. Brandy and cigars had been passed around. With Churchill were some members of his staff, including Professor Lindemann, his scientific adviser; Sir Archibald Sinclair, the Air Minister; and his Military Secretary, General Ismay. The group had just received the reports on the London raid. They were saddened to hear that the House of Commons absorbed a direct hit and was partly destroyed, and this only four days after Churchill's stirring speech that spared the coalition government defeat. But they were delighted that thirty-three enemy bombers had been shot down.

Churchill, in dinner jacket, stood and greeted the wing commander. "I'll be with you in a moment, Douglo," he said.

The other guests finished their meals and retired elsewhere, leaving Hamilton, Churchill, and Sinclair. Churchill nodded at Hamilton.

The duke sat at the table and began. "I have just come from Maryhill Barracks in Glasgow. A German officer named Captain Alfred Horn had parachuted down in Scotland last night. He now claims to be Rudolf Hess."

"Hess? Are you sure it's him?"

"Yes, Mr. Prime Minister. I'm sure of it. He asked for me personally. I saw him in his cell and spoke with him. He said he has come to Britain with offers of peace." Hamilton then showed the two men the photograph of Hess and his son. "He was carrying this when he bailed out."

Sinclair studied the photo Hamilton gave him. "It looks like Hess, I suppose."

"Hess or no Hess," the Prime Minister huffed, after a short pause,

"I'm going to watch the Marx Brothers. After that, you and I, Douglo, are going to have a private little chat."

"Yes, sir."

The entire delegation of guests withdrew to another room, where a projector was ready. The evening's film was *The Marx Brothers Go West*. Given a comfortable chair, the duke was so exhausted from his activity during the day that he dropped off to sleep.

Near midnight, the room lights flicked on. Hamilton woke, startled. He had slept through the entire movie. The others had left, except for Churchill who was now clad in an elaborate dressing robe. He lit a cigar and puffed slowly. He closed the door to the room and sat across from the wing commander. Everything up to now was a put-on for Sinclair and the others. "So, what exactly does Hess want?" he barked.

"He came to inform us that he and Heinrich Himmler are seeking to overthrow Hitler, and Himmler will be the new Fuehrer."

"Himmler? Not Hess?"

"Yes. And he wants safe passage out of Scotland, so that he can return to Germany via Ireland and the German embassy there. He said there is little time left because Hitler plans to attack Russia and he must be stopped. In fact, he begged me to get him out of the country. In the meantime, he wants England and Germany to cease all operations of war so he and Himmler can make their moves. And he said that there's one billion pounds sterling waiting for the appeaser group as blood money. He also demands that you, sir, step down."

Churchill scowled. "I will not! The nerve of him. One billion pounds! Does he have any proof, any documentation of the bank account?"

"No. He does not."

"Does he have any paperwork at all?"

"None at all."

"Then it's only hearsay. We can't believe a word he says."

"He claims he lost everything when he bailed out of the aircraft. His briefcase and the papers are in the Moors somewhere."

"Find them, damn it!"

"I have Benson on it already, sir. Another thing, Hess said that Hitler knows that he—Hess—made the trip, only he is using it for the sake of his own peace plan with Himmler."

"Are you absolutely certain it was Hess?"

"He knows the codename."

"*Operation Night Eagle.*"

"Yes, sir."

"Did Brenwood at any time suspect you've been reporting to me?"

"No, I'm sure he didn't. And that was right up to the seizure of his cronies at my castle. I hope to God no one else knows we've been collaborating."

Churchill smiled through a cloud of cigar smoke. "No one. Not Lampert. Not Hollinger."

"This incident won't help my reputation when word leaks out that Hess was looking for me. There are probably rumours circulating now that I allowed the aircraft free passage in my air space. What about the press? What about my association with Albrecht Haushofer?"

"Don't worry, Douglo. From here on in you won't be heard from. Your good name will be protected. The name Haushofer doesn't mean a thing to most of those in the press and the British public. It'll stay that way. As for Hess, I'll see to it that no one in Britain who knew Hess personally will get anywhere close to him until we sort this mystery out."

Hamilton sensed there was more to it. "What mystery?"

"Lampert filled me in. I want to know why Hess—or whoever he is—shot someone a half-dozen times in the head at Dunhampton."

"He what? He told me that one of Hitler's agents was after him. The agent had flown in while Hess came by sub and they clashed. Something smells here, sir. I thought all along that we were communicating with Hess to come to Britain by air. Then he shows up by sub. So who's the pilot?"

"We don't know. And why was he shot up so many times? It's almost as if Hess doesn't want us to recognize the body. As for Hollinger, he was shot twice and is now in a coma. He's alive, but barely. He may have some answers for us. However, if Hollinger dies, then we might be forced to deal with Hess in another way. We can't keep his confinement a secret forever. Someone of consequence may have to identify him because too many people will start asking questions. I'll send someone with you to Scotland."

"Who, sir?"

Churchill brought to mind Ivone Kirkpatrick, the present controller of European Services at the BBC, and the former First Secretary of the British Embassy in Berlin from 1933 to 1938. He was a good man. A Churchill man. "What about Ivone Kirkpatrick?"

Hamilton shrugged. "He'll do."

"You two have to stall Hess as long as you can. He's lying about something."

"Or everything." Hamilton looked down. "Dear God. Russia. Another two-front for Germany. That's what did them in the last time. You'd think they would have learned their lesson. They would be crazy to attempt it again. If that happens, though, it will take the strain off us. We'd almost invite it right now."

"We would, Douglo."

"If you had to, would you make a public announcement about Hess, Mr. Prime Minister?"

Churchill brooded over that. He could say that the Nazi empire was in disarray. Here was Germany's deputy minister fleeing his own country. Could they say Hess was a loony? "Right now, I'll stay silent on the issue. There's another factor here. The Germans. We still haven't heard from them. We'll have to just sit on our rumps before we officially state anything. Any peace talk news may only harm our war effort."

"I suppose it would, yes."

Churchill nodded, chomping on his cigar. Disdain marked his face. "Yes. One way or the other, whether Himmler or Hess is in charge or not, it's still the same disease. Britain is going to fight Germany tooth and nail, whether it's now or later. There will be no peace until we rid the world of Nazism."

"That seems rather straightforward," the duke said.

Churchill stretched. He looked weary. "It's late. You'd better head on to London and pick up Kirkpatrick. Have him call me if he wants any verification."

"Yes, sir."

Twenty-eight

BERCHTESGADEN, GERMANY—MAY 12

Adolf Hitler locked his hands behind his back and paced back and forth in the sitting room, considering his unfortunate dilemma. He feared the worst. It was approximately thirty-six hours since Hess had left. He was not returning. If no announcement or word from Britain had come by now, then assuming Hess had reached them, the English group was not ready to talk peace. Maybe he didn't make it. Even if he did, Hitler decided, and informed the group of *Operation Barbarossa*, the British would probably not feed the information to the Russians. There was no love lost between the two countries. And if they did, Stalin wouldn't believe them anyway.

Hitler reached into his coat pocket to discover he had run out of chocolates. Someone knocked at the door. "Yes! Come in!"

"Mein Fuehrer," Martin Bormann said, appearing. "Doctor Dietrich is here."

"Send him in."

Hitler's press adviser, Dr. Otto Dietrich, had been briefed on Hess's mission over the telephone. He was an astute man who was aware of complications that might arise from Hess's flight if it was not handled properly. "Heil Hitler," Dietrich said, entering the room, executing a Nazi salute.

Hitler extended his arm lazily, then dropped it. "Dietrich, we have to react now. We haven't heard from the English. Before Britain exploits this, you must prepare a radio communiqué that will discredit Hess and his one-man mission. I know that won't be easy because Germany loves their deputy minister. Our allies in Italy and Japan must see that we are not scheming behind their backs to sign a peace on our own."

Hitler picked up his pacing again. He stopped at the window and turned square to Dietrich. "I want to see your first draft in half an hour. That is all. Go."

"Yes, mein Fuehrer." Dietrich saluted and took his leave.

Hitler sighed. Hess had been his friend and confidant for twenty years. What would the German people think? They weren't fools. Hitler knew they would wonder why Hess had to suddenly take off in a plane and land on enemy soil. Many would be curious if he left with the Fuehrer's blessing. Hitler nodded to himself. Hess had the right idea in his parting letter, reiterating what he had said weeks ago. Hess must be declared insane. But how would the German people respond? If the Deputy Fuehrer was insane, then why was he still in office? What would that say for the other leaders?

Hitler slammed his hand down on the desktop. His people would swallow it because he was their Fuehrer and he knew what was best for his people.

Buchanan Castle, Scotland

Ivone Kirkpatrick's trip to Scotland to observe and interview the German pilot who called himself Captain Alfred Horn was a comedy of errors. Accompanied by the Duke of Hamilton, the former British Embassy official had left London by aircraft that evening. Strong winds forced them to land unannounced and refuel at Catterick, an airfield that had been heavily bombed during the weekend. The RAF authorities were in no hurry to send Kirkpatrick and Hamilton on their way until they were positively identified through London. That took more than an hour.

At twenty minutes to ten, the two had landed at Hamilton's headquarters in time to hear a German radio announcement on short-wave declaring that Rudolf Hess had been missing since May 10, having taken off that day from Augsburg on a flight from which he had not returned. A letter he left behind was incoherent, giving evidence of a mental derangement. All this had led Hitler's office to believe that Hess was a victim of hallucinations, and it was feared that Hess had crashed or met with an accident somewhere.

It was now imperative that Kirkpatrick make the identification as soon as possible. The duke asked his adjutant to drive them to Buchanan Castle; the prisoner had been transferred there from Maryhill Barracks. But because all the road signs had been removed the year before, the adjutant, unfamiliar with the area, lost his way. Several times he had stopped to ask for directions, but was met by blank stares from the local people who feared that they were dealing with spies on such a night.

They finally reached the castle after midnight. The commander met the duke and Kirkpatrick in the yard, then took them up a long flight of stone stairs to a tiny attic room with a slanted ceiling.

Schubert was asleep on an iron bed under a brown army blanket. He woke immediately and threw the blanket aside. He was unshaven and wore grey flannel pyjamas. He acknowledged the duke with a nod, then glared at the middle-aged gentleman with the moustache, greased-back hair and flickering eyebrows.

"Don't you recognize me, Herr Reichsfuehrer?" Kirkpatrick asked in perfect upper class German.

Schubert had never seen the man before. "Should I?" he answered in his common German dialect.

"I am Ivone Kirkpatrick. I was First Secretary at the British Embassy in Berlin for five years."

"I have met so many people during that time, diplomats from all nations," Schubert said, carefully. "But I do seem to recall your name. Why did you bring him?" he asked Hamilton, switching to English.

Hamilton didn't know what to say.

"Leave me with the duke, please?" Schubert said to Kirkpatrick.

When the BBC official withdrew, Hamilton said, "I didn't want to say too much. He's part of our group, but he doesn't know anything about your specific peace plans."

"Who else does?"

"Others who need to know. Trust me on that."

"Then I can leave?"

"Not at this time."

Schubert's eyes narrowed. "Why? You are making a terrible mistake. I cannot stay here any longer. You must give me passage out this very day."

Hamilton stood his ground. "Not so fast. How do we know that what you are telling us is true? We haven't found your proposals. How do we know if you came with anything at all? Goodbye, Herr Reichsfuehrer. We'll be in touch."

Kirkpatrick and Hamilton walked into the yard. The sky was starting to lighten to the east. Dawn was approaching. Waiting for them across the road was the duke's adjutant behind the wheel of the RAF staff car.

"That's not Hess," Kirkpatrick whispered.

Hamilton was stunned. "What are you talking about! I thought you recognized him."

"I met Hess face to face in Berlin before the war. We spoke at a Chancellery reception. Although it was only a few minutes, it was sufficient to know that the man we have in custody here is not the Deputy Fuehrer I remember. He looks to be under great stress. He is too skinny. He is too tall and too old. The Hess I knew knows how to conduct himself. He is a highly intelligent man. He speaks a distinguished German, not that gutter garbage I heard back there. I was talking with one of the guards. He said that this fellow flew all the way from southern Germany, by himself, without a single change of clothing or even a toothbrush. It simply does not make sense. Why didn't he fly to a neutral country with these so-called peace initiatives that you and Churchill told me about? Why into an enemy country, for God's sake? How did he plan to get out afterwards? Did he have an escape route? He must have known he would run out of fuel. The real Hess—at least the one I recall—is too methodical, too organized to attempt anything so foolhardy."

The duke rubbed his eyes. "We're both tired, Mr. Kirkpatrick. You haven't seen Hess in what—four or five years?"

"Six to be precise. It was 1935."

"Consider this, Mr. Kirkpatrick. A man can change in six years."

"Yes, but can he grow taller?" Kirkpatrick argued.

"He claims to be Hess. Germany says Hess is missing. The man does look like Hess. What else do you need? Your job is to identify him, and leave the rest to the interrogating authorities. I think it's Hess, at least physically. Churchill wanted a diplomatic identification of the prisoner. That's your job. You did it."

"Are you asking me to not make waves?"

"You might say that, yes."

Kirkpatrick frowned. "Why didn't Churchill insist on someone else to identify Hess? Why me? I know two London journalists who spent considerable time interviewing Hess in Germany before the war. Why not call them?"

Hamilton smiled. The last thing Churchill wanted was more people involved. Besides, newsmen were trouble. "Maybe we will. Meanwhile, let's go grab some sleep?"

Twenty-nine

Berlin, Germany

"They have found Hess."

"Who has, mein Fuehrer?"

"The British."

Himmler had mixed emotions during the telephone conversation in his study with Adolf Hitler. "What happened, mein Fuehrer?"

"They have just issued a statement on their radio. Hess aborted near Glasgow. His plane crash-landed. He broke his ankle during the fall, the silly fool, and gave his name as Horn."

"Horn?" Himmler repeated, as he felt a strange tickle at the base of his throat. Captain Alfred Horn was the name he had given to Schubert. "I wonder why he did that, mein Fuehrer?"

"I don't know. The British also said he had photographs with him to prove his identity. Do you know anything about this, Himmler?"

"Why should I, mein Fuehrer?"

"I thought the Gestapo knew everything."

"Not everything, mein Fuehrer. I knew nothing of Hess's flight."

"If you say so, Himmler. If you hear of any further developments, let me know."

"I will, mein Fuehrer."

"How are the new plans for the Jewish problem coming along?"

"On schedule. You will have your report by the end of this month, mein Fuehrer."

"I'm looking forward to reading it. Goodbye, Himmler."

Himmler hung up. What had happened? Did Schubert find Hess?

Who was claiming to be Horn, Schubert or the real Hess? Who was in the plane before it crashed? And where was the submarine? There was no word from Steider since the evening of the eleventh. Did the British find the sub and sink her? The possibilities were endless. If Schubert was in British hands—Churchill's hands—then the mission was doomed. They would know he was a pseudo-Hess after proper interrogation. British Intelligence was not composed of idiots.

Himmler had to do something.

Twenty minutes later, Wolfgang Geis answered the front door in his night robe, surprised to find Himmler waiting for him on the darkened porch in civilian clothing.

"Herr Reichsfuehrer, why are you here at this hour?"

"Let's go for a walk, colonel. We need to talk."

Geis didn't like the tone of his superior's voice.

It's late, Herr Reichsfuehrer. Can't it wait until morning? I can come to the office early."

"No, it can't wait. Now. Please."

"It's about Hess isn't it? Or is it Schubert? Or is it both?"

"We have to discuss them."

Geis had an inkling what was coming. He considered slamming the door and running for his life. He couldn't see Himmler making a house call just for a chat. "I prefer not to, Herr Reichsfuehrer," he said in the darkness.

"In that case, we'll talk right here. You bungled Geis. Gestapo colonels do not bungle."

"But, Herr Reichsfuehrer—"

Before Geis could finish, Himmler pulled out a gun from his leather coat and shot three times.

RAF Dunhampton, Scotland

Wesley Hollinger wove in and out of consciousness for nearly thirty minutes. When he finally opened his eyes he tried to focus on the white ceiling above him. He couldn't move, not with the stabbing pain in his chest and shoulder. He looked to one side and saw an intravenous machine attached to his arm. Then it dawned on him. He was in a hospital, in the land of the living. Beyond the window, it was dark. Then he remembered that for most of the time he was semi-conscious he saw the blurred outline of a woman in long hair calling his name, softly.

Gentle footsteps came towards him from across the room. He caught the whiff of lilac perfume. When the fog over his eyes gave way, he saw Roberta Langford smiling sweetly at him. Her face was bright. She wore a white blouse and matching blue suit; jacket and skirt moulded to her firm figure. Her hair was up in front, curled on the sides and down to her shoulders at the back. It was the way he remembered her best.

"Robbie?"

"Hello there, Wesley."

"What are you doing here? Where am I?" His voice was weary and gruff, his mouth as dry as sand.

"You're in the hospital."

"I know that. Which one?"

"Dunhampton."

"Oh, oh yeah. Dunhampton." He rubbed his eyes. "I need a glass of water, please."

"Hang on, I'll grab you one."

He drank from the cup she handed him. "I didn't think water could taste so good. Nice and cold, too."

Taking the cup back, Langford said, "I'm sorry, Wesley. It's all my fault."

"Sorry? For what? What's your fault?"

"I was the one who got you into this. If I hadn't let you in the MI-6 Headquarters, then you wouldn't have gotten the information that led to you being shot and brought in here."

"Hush. Don't talk like that. I did it to myself. It was my idea to search the files, as you may recall." Grimacing, he tried to pull himself up despite the dizziness in his head and the pain in his chest. "Anyway, putting all that aside, did they get him?"

Langford pressed him back down as if she was an understanding nurse.

"It's best to lay down."

"Did they get him?"

"Quiet, you. You were shot twice in the chest and you've been out for nearly two days."

"Two days!"

"Yes. Forget that for now. Colonel Lampert wants to talk to you. It's frightfully urgent, I suspect. Are you up to it?"

"I was out for two whole days?"

"Yes, you were."

Hollinger leaned his head to one side and touched the bandage wrapped around his chest. His head aching, he tried to recall the events on the tarmac. He saw two Hesses. He knew he did. Or did he? Of course he did. "Good idea, Robbie. Get me the colonel. I have to tell him something."

He waited in a comatose state until he saw Lampert standing by the bed, unlit pipe in his mouth.

"Hello there, ol' top. How are we feeling?"

"Hello yourself. I don't know about you, but I got one hell of a pain in my gut."

"We're glad you're back with us. You're going to have to take it easy for a while. But you'll be up and around soon. A bullet came very near your right lung. But the doctors pulled it out."

"Never mind me, colonel." Hollinger gasped and coughed. "Where's Hess?"

"He flew off after he shot you and the pilot. He crash-landed near Eaglesham, attempting to leave the country. We were hoping you could shed some light on the situation. Apparently, he wants to cut a deal with us."

"Where's the other guy? Is he still alive? What did he look like?"

Lampert looked puzzled. "Why would you—"

"Did he look like Hess?"

"Hess? Oh, no. You must be confused. As I told you, Hess flew off. He's in custody not far from here. As for the corpse, they just finished embalming it. It was one terrible mess. A good four or five bullets to the head. His skull and face bones were crushed to pieces."

"Of course they're crushed, damn it. That was his plan."

"Whose plan?"

Hollinger rubbed his face.

"The impostor's. Or was it Hess, and he got rid of the impostor? Oh, I don't know."

"What impostor? Wesley, you are not making sense. You're delirious. Get some sleep and we'll talk later, perhaps."

Hollinger lunged out and grabbed Lampert by the lapel of his suit. "Listen to me!" he winced. "Uh, that hurt!"

"Unhand me!"

"Listen to me, both of you." Hollinger hung on, glancing from Lampert to Langford, the pain secondary now. "There were two Hesses on the runway. Two! OK! I don't know how or why. But there were two. Got it. TWO! They were nearly identical. I must have driven one of them out to meet the ME-110 coming in. He had a gun on me and wore a hat."

Lampert tried to pull away from Hollinger's grip. "Stop it! Confound you, man!"

"They fought right in front of me! I didn't know who was who. You don't believe me, do you? You think I'm nuts." Hollinger released Lampert and fell back. Then he recalled Hess's medical reports. *The mortar wound to the chest.* He snapped his fingers. "Oh, yeah. Oh, yeah, that's right."

"Oh yeah, what?" Lampert said, brushing at his lapel.

"Hess had a mortar wound to his chest that left a scar on the front and back. It was all in the medical report. Check the body, colonel. If it has the scars, then it's him. And—"

"The buckteeth," Langford snapped, quickly realizing she had given herself away.

"So, you're the one who let him in." Lampert stared at Langford, who blushed. "You didn't tell me."

"Forget that now," Hollinger said, visibly tired and weakening by the second. He closed his eyes for a moment then opened them. "OK, look, you said he wants to cut a deal. What kind of deal?"

Lampert folded his arms. "Hess wants free passage from the British Isles with an aircraft. He promised that he and Himmler will take over the German government from Hitler, then postpone further aggressive action. He claims he has access to an anonymous and untraceable Swiss bank account worth a billion pounds sterling. The trouble is, he has no proof. We're looking for his papers near where he went down. He also claims his briefcase flew out of his hand while bailing out."

Hollinger grunted, his face twisted in shock. "One billion pounds! First, you better find out if it's Hess you're dealing with or the impostor. And the only way to do that is check the body for scars and for the buckteeth. Don't just stand there. Colonel, please check the . . . the . . . body." Then his voice trailed off and he shut his eyes.

Lampert called for a doctor, who made a quick examination by lifting back Hollinger's eyelids, then said, "He's exhausted. He'll come around again. Give him some rest."

"By all means," Lampert sighed.

He and Langford left and stood in the hall.

"I don't know what to tell Churchill. Are those medical reports on Hess the way Hollinger says they are?"

Langford nodded. "They are, sir. I saw them. I'd get a look at the body, if I were you, colonel, as crazy as it seems. Wesley was rather adamant, wasn't he?"

"That's an understatement. Well, I had better look into it. Two Hesses?"

Langford smiled. "What a war."

"Indeed."

Langford opened the door and glanced in at Hollinger sleeping.

She didn't know what to think of him. She was strangely attracted to the ruggedly handsome American whose brash ways were so different from the Englishmen she had known. She walked into the room and was struck with the impulse to hold his hand. It was as if that shaky first meeting at Bletchley when he snatched the cigarette from her mouth had never happened. She blotted it from her memory, along with his alleged statements about redheads. She squeezed his hand in hers, feeling his ring. It was a genuine diamond, all right. Yes, there was just something about him.

She blamed herself. It was her fault he was there, lying in the hospital bed. It was her fault . . . her fault.

The colonel returned to the hall in a mild daze twenty-five minutes later. In his long years in the world of Secret Service Intelligence, he had yet to encounter such a bizarre series of events.

"I called Headquarters to get the exact position of the scars," he said to Langford. "Then I went to the morgue. They were on the body, as the report had stated."

"Front and back?" she asked, lighting a cigarette.

"Yes," Lampert replied. "And that's not all. One bullet went through his mouth, but it was not enough to hide the fact he had buckteeth. Extraordinary. Hess's body in our morgue. The Deputy Fuehrer of Nazi Germany. To confirm it, I called Buchanan Castle. They performed a quick physical on the prisoner. Got him out of bed, they did. No scars. No buckteeth."

Langford exhaled a puffy, blue smoke ring. "So they are two Hesses. What do we do now?"

"What else? Call Winnie. Good grief, he won't believe it."

Thirty

BUCHANAN CASTLE, SCOTLAND—MAY 13

Schubert gawked at himself in the mirror over the sink. He hadn't shaved in days, and had been wondering for hours why the Duke of Hamilton didn't come back. Was the duke seeking a higher authority or did that person, Kirkpatrick, find a flaw during the interview? When three men in doctors' smocks entered the cell an hour later, one of them holding Schubert's flight suit, boots, and helmet, Schubert thought that the British were finally complying.

"We are ready to make a deal with you, Herr Reichsfuehrer," the spokesman for the men said, as one of them threw Schubert's flight gear inside the door.

"Where is my parachute?" Schubert demanded.

"You'll be provided with a new one."

"And the aircraft?"

The man hesitated, then replied, "A Bolton. But first, we have to give you a needle to put you out until we let you off at an RAF aerodrome."

"Why a needle?"

"Security reasons."

"Why not blindfold me?"

Schubert stood there in a long moment of silence. These men were not doctors. They were too burly. When the spokesman produced a long needle from his front pocket, Schubert kicked it from his hand. The two other men leapt towards Schubert and after a fierce struggle pinned him to the floor. They inserted the needle into Schubert's left arm and held him down until he drifted into a mindless silence.

RAF Dunhampton, Scotland

The next morning, Langford found Hollinger sitting partly up in bed and looking out the window at the morning mist rolling down the valley. He was stripped to the waist, except for the tight white bandage covering most of his powerful chest. His build reminded her of Arthur, big in the shoulders with well-developed biceps.

"Robbie, come on in," Hollinger said. He brushed his hand through his hair. He noticed she was wearing the same clothes as yesterday, and they showed signs of being slept in.

She smiled. "Now, there's an improvement, if I ever saw one."

"I'm still a little on the groggy side from the morphine. But I'm getting used to one-arm shrugs. What's up? Fill me in. Where's the colonel?"

"In London consulting with Churchill." She walked up to him, and dumped a Glasgow newspaper in his lap.

Hollinger glanced at the bold headlines:

RUDOLF HESS IN GLASGOW—OFFICIAL
NAZI LEADER FLIES TO SCOTLAND

The front page carried two pictures of the downed Messerschmitt, along with an official statement issued from 10 Downing Street and an interview with ploughman David McLean, the man who caught Hess, under the line, "I found German Lying in Field."

"Is he the real Hess?"

Langford sat in the chair beside him, and looked behind her. Then she decided to get up, close the door and return to Hollinger's bedside. "No. The impostor."

"So, he killed Hess, tried to kill me, then tried to fly out of the country. He didn't get too far and it was then he thought he could cut a deal."

"Exactly right."

"What are we going to do with him now?"

"Keep him as a prisoner of war, naturally."

"But he's an impostor. Someone will find out, eventually."

Langford shook her head and grinned. "Churchill has made it clear that anyone who knew him previously will not get within sight of him. Besides, the impostor is playing along with us."

"How?"

"I don't think he realizes that we know he's a fraud. And the clever man is faking amnesia. He claims he can't remember names and places due to the traumatic nature of the crash, and the drugging, and everything."

"You're drugging him?"

"Yes."

"Amnesia, eh? The best way out if you're an impostor."

"Exactly what the colonel said. I have some other news for you. A sub was blown out of the water in the Forth of Firth on the morning of the eleventh. It could very likely have been the impostor's drop off."

"Who sent him? Hitler? Does anybody know?"

"Heinrich Himmler."

"Damn! The Gestapo leader."

"Right you are."

"You never did tell me what you are doing up here in the first place."

"Well . . . it all started when I found out I had lost my baby."

"You what?" Hollinger sat up, slowly. "You lost your baby?"

"Yes. I called Lampert from the hospital on the morning of the eleventh to ask him for time off to recover and that's when he informed me what had happened to you. He and I drove up here together."

"You mean to tell me that you yanked yourself out of the hospital bed to come up here to see *me* in hospital?"

"Yes, I suppose I did."

"You're quite the woman." Their eyes locked. "How do you feel?"

"A little wobbly in the knees. But look at my hand. It hasn't been that steady in months."

A nice hand, too, thought Hollinger. Long, slender fingers. "Did your parents ever know?"

"No."

"Then your reputation is intact."

"Yes. What else was I to tell you? Oh, the Mosquito men never returned. No radio contact. Nothing. They just disappeared." She looked sad. "The colonel said you knew who they were."

Hollinger pictured Jones and Croucher. The poor lads probably crashed into the North Sea. "Yeah, I knew who they were."

She stood as if she was ready to go. "Another thing. According to Lampert, the Special Operations Branch of the Secret Service have been asking a lot of questions about the prisoner and they want answers. The head of the branch has been a good friend of Churchill for years, part of the inner-intelligence group before the war. But he's not been briefed about the impostor, and he won't be either. He seems to be the only roadblock for the time being. If the impostor passes the branch's scrutiny, then we're in the clear."

"For now."

"Yes."

"Then it's not over yet?"

"No, not by any means. And we still have to find the impostor's briefcase with the peace proposals before someone else does. But there's too much ground to cover."

"Like looking for a needle in a haystack."

"Now, if you'll excuse me, I'm expected back in London for a temporary assignment with the Secret Service. And you need time to get better."

Hollinger smiled. "Thanks for coming, Robbie."

"You're welcome." She strode to the door and turned, catching Hollinger looking at her. "We'll see each other soon enough. Cheerio." Then she opened the door and took to the hall, leaving Hollinger with the echo of her high-heeled footsteps.

"Adios, Robbie," Hollinger said to himself.

Thirty-one

LONDON, ENGLAND—MAY 16

Schubert couldn't understand it. One minute he was told the Brits had made the preparations for him to fly to Europe, then the next minute he was seized by three men, drugged and taken by train to the Tower of London in the middle of the night, under heavy guard.

En-route to the capital, he was shown a copy of the *London Times* depicting his flight and crash-landing in Scotland. Had the news broken the same time the British were about to make a deal to let him go? And now were they forced to keep him in custody in the Tower?

Schubert made up his mind that there was only one way out of this. He had to continue to pretend he was going crazy—without putting it on too much—to prevent the British from knowing the truth, and hope that the Germans won the war. So far, it was looking good for Hitler's forces. Britain appeared to be on its last breath. Through the train window, he saw mile upon mile of blackened frames where buildings once stood.

The Luftwaffe had done their job and then some.

Schubert stood for a man carrying a briefcase who entered the Tower of London cell and gave his name simply as Richardson. His fixed lips and dark eyes made Schubert uncomfortable, and he took an instant dislike to him.

"Sit down, Herr Hess. How is your ankle and back?" Richardson asked in fluent German.

"Better. My stomach is still bothering me, however."

"I understand you have been eating everything placed in front of you. Beef. Chicken."

Schubert sat slowly on the bunk. The springs let out a creak. "I was hungry."

"I thought you were a vegetarian. Vegetarians are usually very particular about what they eat."

"I have no choice. The British, so far, have not complied with my demands for vegetarian meals. I do not wish to starve."

"You are in no position to demand anything, Herr Reichsfuehrer. You are a prisoner of war." Richardson found the room's only chair and withdrew a thick writing pad from his briefcase. "Where and when were you born, Herr Reichsfuehrer?"

"Alexandria, Egypt in 1896. No, 1894."

"Don't you remember your own birth date?"

Schubert shrugged. "My memory has been playing tricks on me lately. It was 1894, I'm sure of it. Yes, 1894."

"Do you have any brothers or sisters?"

"Two brothers, two sisters."

"Their names, please?"

"Alfred, Gretl, Eva and . . . and . . . Hermann."

"Your mother's name?"

"Klara."

Richardson removed a sheet of paper from his breast pocket and unfolded it. "Is this yours?" he showed a hand-drawn map to Schubert.

"Yes, it is. It shows the route I took across the North Sea."

"Alleged route, you mean."

"How else did I arrive?"

"That's what I'm trying to find out. You left Augsburg, correct?"

"Yes."

"And you flew non-stop?"

Schubert tried to remember some of Himmler's background information on Hess, who, according to the Gestapo, had often used Augsburg as his base for flights. "Yes, I did fly non-stop."

"Then you reached the coast of Scotland and raced over the rooftops at more than three hundred miles per hour, according to reports from some frightened farmers."

"Yes, I did fly low-level."

"You seem quite proud of your little hedge-hopping caper."

Schubert laughed. "Yes, I am. It was quite sporting, as you Englishmen would say."

"*Sporting*? Why didn't you play it smart by landing at your destination—Dungavel Castle—without all the fanfare? Did you know that you flew right over Dungavel at one point?'

"No, I did not. I lost my way. I flew low to get my bearings."

"After all that, you lost your way!" Richardson removed a photograph from his inside breast pocket. "Who is this man, Herr Reichsfuehrer?"

"I don't know," Schubert answered, giving it back.

"You should."

"Why should I?"

"He's one of your closest friends. He was your teacher at Munich University. Don't you recognize Karl Haushofer, the Professor of Geopolitics?"

"No."

The Englishman scribbled some notes, his head down. "You must miss your sport."

"What sport is that? Flying?"

"No tennis."

Schubert stretched. He remembered that Hess enjoyed tennis. "Yes, I do miss tennis."

"According to sources you are quite good."

"Thank you."

"I am not familiar with the game. Would you mind telling me how the scoring system works?"

"I don't seem to recall very much about the past. Ever since your people started drugging me. Why am I being drugged? Why was I not freed? I came in peace. In good faith."

"I do not know the answers to those questions." Richardson stood. "Goodbye, Herr Reichsfuehrer."

In the hall, Richardson held his pen to his lips, thinking. This man Hess was very peculiar. According to the Tower of London guards, his table manners were atrocious; a big contrast to the upper-middle-class upbringing that Hess had received. He could not remember personal details about himself, or his family, or his friends. And he was much thinner than the man shown in recently published photographs.

Richardson quickly added several figures in his head, then pondered the known facts and details of the ME-110, including its range. He estimated that the alleged course the prisoner had flown came to approximately twelve hundred miles, which was far outside the range of the aircraft, even if it had drop tanks. Then there was the high-speed sprint over Scotland for an hour, which was sure to gobble the fuel at a fantastic rate.

Richardson determined that the prisoner was lying about his facts—some or all. It was impossible for him to fly from Augsburg, deep in southern Germany, climb the mountains, zigzag around the German air defences, head into the stiff Westerlies over the North Sea, then make a straight dash to Scotland without refuelling. The information would go into Richardson's evaluation report.

When his MI-6 Special Operations interrogation of the prisoner at the Tower of London was completed three days later, Richardson came to one of two possible conclusions—either this man was a lunatic or he wasn't Hess at all. However, what Richardson thought didn't matter. What his boss, Churchill's friend, thought didn't matter either. The report did not get any further than 10 Downing Street.

Prime Minister Winston Churchill saw to that.

Thirty-two

London, England—June 23
Churchill stood and flicked the cabinet radio off. The news was thunderous. Germany had attacked the Soviet Union the day before at exactly three-fifteen, and now three main army groups consisting of 140 divisions were pouring across the Russian borders on a front a thousand miles long. One Panzer division had already advanced fifty miles into Lithuania. The Luftwaffe was pounding the Russian Air Force, destroying hundreds of airplanes on the ground and disrupting Soviet communications. The mighty onslaught was not unexpected to a handful of individuals in Great Britain, three of whom had been listening to the day's BBC broadcasts in the 10 Downing Street library.

Cigar in mouth, Churchill turned to Lampert and Hollinger. "We tried to warn Stalin, but he wasn't listening. Over three million German soldiers is a lot of manpower. Our prisoner was right. Hitler was going to do it. The same mistake Napoleon made. If the Nazis don't make Moscow by winter, they're finished. They'll never survive a winter war." The Prime Minister faced Hollinger in particular. "And how are we doing young man?"

Hollinger sighed. He had arrived at Churchill's smoky residence part-way through the BBC broadcast. He had been out of hospital less than a week and was still fighting off morphine withdrawal. "My chest still hurts, but I'm happy to be out of bed, finally. And I'm glad the bandages are gone."

"You were lucky. Hess, of course, wasn't. The curse of the Doppelganger legend caught up with him."

"What legend is that?" Lampert asked, relighting his pipe.

Churchill sat down. "Wesley, you know German. What is a Doppelganger?"

"A double."

"Precisely. It's a German legend by the way. Somewhere in the world is a double of yourself." He pointed his finger at Hollinger. "There is another one of you, Wesley, somewhere, some place."

"God forbid," Lampert said, smiling.

The three laughed.

"And that goes for you too, colonel. If you can imagine that. If you and your double ever come face to face, so the story goes, one of you must die." Churchill let his visitors absorb that. "How's the prisoner doing, colonel?"

"Fine, considering he's trying awfully hard to be crazy. He's becoming a little moody and almost suicidal. But we're keeping a 24-hour watch on him."

"If he gets out of hand, drug him some more. But we still want him alive. Don't let anyone near him who hasn't been cleared through my office first. And no pictures of him. The appeaser group is cooperating fully now. We've cut a deal."

"What if he squeals?" Hollinger asked. "You know, tells somebody who he really is?"

"If he hasn't yet, then he probably won't. Himmler and his Gestapo are brutal people, Wesley. They undoubtedly intimidated him and his family. That's the way the Gestapo have always done things. As long as he keeps playing along, he's content to stay where he is, with the belief that his family will be safe."

Hollinger played with the knot in his new silk tie. "What deal did you strike with the appeasers, Mr. Prime Minister, if you don't mind me asking?"

"We've placed a one-hundred-year secrets stamp on the affair, until the year 2041. By that time, every name will be mentioned, the appeasers, Hess, the impostor, whoever he is, and us. Your name is in the file, Wesley, although you will not be listed as the Tyrant of Hut Nine."

"I should hope not," Hollinger laughed. "But why a hundred years?"

"I promised to protect the 'good' name of the appeasers, along with their generations to come. In a hundred years no one will care that they were traitors to their country. I gave the appeasers an ultimatum. Help me fight Hitler or be exposed to the public and tried for treason. And that includes Brenwood. We also threw the homosexual ring at them for good measure. With their messenger boy in our hands, who they take to be Hess, they had no choice but to agree to our demands."

Hollinger thought back to his discovery in April of the proposed flight. It had been two months of shock after shock. "What about the duke?"

"Ah, yes, the Duke of Hamilton has been working undercover for me for nearly a year."

"He has?" Hollinger and Lampert said, almost together.

Churchill nodded with a sly grin. "He was the intermediary. One of my agents of ungentlemanly warfare since the beginning of the war. As soon as Hitler attacked Poland, he changed his allegiance and secretly joined us. A little persuasion helped. We used the file on him. The same one you found, Wesley. However, as far as I know he did not recognize the prisoner as the impostor. Hess and the duke had never met before. The duke is one less person to tell the truth to."

"What about this money the colonel told me about?" Hollinger asked the Prime Minister.

"There's a problem." Churchill twirled the smoking cigar in his fat fingers. "One billion pounds in a Swiss bank is a lot of money."

"We made a breakthrough, sir," Lampert cut in, crossing his legs. "Just this morning, an agent at our embassy in Zurich cabled me. He is concocting a plan to forge Himmler's signature and gain access to the account. Since we know the number now and that it's in Himmler's name, we are trying to transfer it to a bank draft in pound sterling, where it can be turned over to an English bank."

"Excellent. Now, if we could just find some way of pulling the Americans into this war, then we may stand a chance." Churchill stared at Hollinger through a swell of blue cigar smoke.

"You've been doing pretty good on your own so far, sir."

Churchill shrugged away the compliment. "At least Stalin is in it. If we lose the war, the Council of Peace plan of Hitler's might come about sooner than we think."

"What Council of Peace are you referring to?" Hollinger asked.

Churchill peered over his glasses at Lampert. "Colonel?"

"We have the peace proposals in our hands; three separate ones, by the way. It took over a month, but a combined RAF intelligence and MI-6 group found them spread over a wide area, in some trees, bushes, and open fields not far from where the ME-110 went down. We never did find the briefcase, but everything probably blew out anyway. This is what we arrived at. Hess—the real Hess, we presume—had Hitler's blessing to fly to Scotland to meet the Brenwood appeaser group with peace terms from Hitler. I couldn't see even the appeasers agreeing to them."

"What were they?"

Lampert removed a small pad of paper from his suit jacket and read from it. "Hitler would be the figurehead of what he called the Council of Peace, a coalition board of European countries. There would be a common currency for all of Europe, including England. Based in Berlin, naturally. Our British parliamentary system and the pound sterling would be abolished, and all our financial interests would be monitored or controlled outright by the German business monopoly of I.S. Filberg. And last but not least, Hitler promised he would never go to war with Britain again."

"Hell of a lot of good his promises are," Hollinger said. "Try the Munich Agreement."

"The next set. I'll skip Hess for the moment and go straightaway to Himmler."

"Himmler? So the impostor was telling the truth?"

"Yes, Wesley. The impostor was in cahoots with the Gestapo chief, who was using the peace negotiations for his own advantage. The funny part of it is that anybody who knows anything about the German High Command also knows that Hess and Himmler have been mortal enemies for years. Hess never would have worked for Himmler behind Hitler's back. For himself, yes. And that's what Himmler's proposals are, a stab in the back. A Hess impostor was found and convinced to represent the German side during peace negotiations with the appeasers, providing that Himmler was the new Fuehrer with an impressive new title—Fuehrermaster. The rest of the points, the money, and so forth, were quoted verbatim. Now to Hess. He was seeking asylum."

"Really?"

"It's true. He wanted us to snatch his wife and son out of Germany, and he was going to hand us all the information and secrets that he could on the Nazi regime. To begin with, he had already obtained documents of atomic secrets complete with formulas. He had information and blueprints of new twin-engine jet-powered Messerschmitt fighters capable of speeds in excess of 550 miles per hour, and some blueprints of what he called Vengeance weapons. One of these is a small, unmanned jet machine and the other is an intercontinental rocket that will hit the ground at three times the speed of sound. He also had a detailed military report of the attack of Russia. Then there is something much more evil than anything else we can comprehend. Himmler, with Hitler's written permission, is already forming plans to systematically exterminate the Jews and other undesirables. Hess had photographs of these new death camps, most of them in Germany and Poland. Hess had had enough. We know that his power was slipping recently, anyway. Last year, Hitler appointed Hermann Goering second in command. It must have been a terrible blow to Hess."

Hollinger swallowed. "So, Hess was going to spill the beans on the operation? Geez, a Nazi with a conscience. What do you know?"

"Our agents in Europe will have to confirm these death camps and this new jet and atomic technology. I'm sure our American friends in Washington will want a full-scale report."

"They will, sir," Hollinger replied with enthusiasm.

Lampert leaned forward. "Wesley, I like how you've handled yourself these last few months, although your methods were a bit out of the ordinary. The Prime Minister has talked it over with Mr. Donovan. The MI-6 could use a man like you over here. Kind of a go-between for us and Washington. It would mean an increase in pay, without the increase in danger. We don't want you shot at again. There will be some traveling involved."

Hollinger hadn't heard Lampert talk this way before. "Is that my only choice?"

"Oh . . . continue working for the MI-6 in England on loan, of course, in various duties suitable to a man of your experience. However, to keep you out of trouble, I'll give you an able-bodied assistant. The Prime Minister and I are hoping you'll accept the latter."

"With an increase in pay?" Hollinger braced for an answer.

"Yes. You don't have to decide now," Churchill explained. "Give it a few days."

"OK, I will." Hollinger sighed. "I do have two things to ask you that have been bothering me."

"And they are?"

"Why wasn't the impostor apprehended right after the sub drop?"

"Good question. I'll let you answer this one, colonel."

Lampert smiled. "Ever hear of the Twenty Committee, Wesley?"

"No, sir. I haven't."

"It's an MI-5 subcommittee, a spy interrogation organization. You see, every German agent who has landed on our soil has been captured."

Hollinger was taken aback. "Every one! You're kidding."

"Then they are given their choices. Either work for us and return bogus radio information to Hamburg as if they were on the loose, you might say, or be executed. Most of them have been quite cooperative. The Twenty Committee runs the whole thing. Each spy has a case officer who works very closely with the captured agent in sending the signals. Do you recall the phone call I received in London about the sub drop?" Hollinger nodded. "The director of the force, a friend of mine from the first war, was already putting matters in motion with *Denise*, one of Hitler's spies. She landed in Scotland at the beginning of the year and was caught within hours."

"So, she's a German agent working for us?"

"Not exactly, Wesley. We couldn't take the chance and have the real *Denise* meet the sub drop, in case she turned on us. So we ordered one of the case officers for another spy who bore a close resemblance to the real *Denise* to cut her hair and act like the real thing when the time came. She's an amateur in the field, really."

"You took a big chance."

"Yes, we did. But it worked at first. However, what didn't pan out was the rendezvous between *Denise* and two of our agents who were to seize the German before he got anywhere close to the aerodrome. The impostor's original orders were to come by sub and represent Himmler as the new Fuehrer. We in the Secret Service speculate that Himmler had tried to either seize or kill the real Hess in Germany, so that he couldn't make the flight. But he got through. That's when the orders changed. Instead of performing the orders to kill the pilot and return by sub, where we were certain to nab him, the impostor mutilated Hess, took his identity, and flew off to hopefully escape. Neutral Ireland was the likely destination. But he was shot down before he could cross the Irish Sea. Now, we have him and the papers. When the fake *Denise* gave the impostor the last radio message from Germany, she used her common sense and deliberately held back the last part of it. The impostor was supposed to snatch Hess's paperwork and destroy it and his own. He didn't and we have it."

Hollinger smirked. He made a quick evaluation of MI-6's thoroughness. They had rubbed shoulders with the MI-5. They had caught every spy. They knew in advance that Hess was coming. And Churchill had an inside man. These Limeys were far from being on their last legs.

"What was your other question, Wesley?" Lampert asked.

"The markings on Hess's airplane. It wasn't his personal one. I noticed that as soon as I drove up to it."

Lampert nodded. "I know. NJ-OQ. He switched somewhere. Mechanical failure, more than likely. Who really knows?"

"I guess that about wraps it up."

"One other thing," Lampert said. "For your information, we are trying not to let on that we know that Hess is an impostor. We'll leave it that way for the time being."

Churchill opened the library doors and waved down the hall. A manservant appeared, pushing a trolley containing a large bottle of champagne and three crystal glasses. Churchill puffed out his chest. "Let's toast to our British-American Alliance."

"Wesley," Lampert said with pride. "You don't mind my calling you Wesley?"

"Of course not."

"You would have made a good army man. I could have used you in the Great War."

It left Hollinger speechless. Lampert wasn't such a stiff after all.

Hollinger put on his fedora and sunglasses, and fortified by two tall glasses of champagne left 10 Downing Street on unsteady legs an hour later. It was a beautiful afternoon, and the bright sun suddenly made him dizzy. He walked to the end of a side street until he saw his MG sports car—top down—ahead, its rear bumper shining between two trucks. He didn't remember leaving the top down. From several feet away, he saw someone behind the wheel. As he drew closer, he caught a whiff of lilac. The person turned around. There was Langford, smoking with one hand, her other hand on the floor shifter.

"Hi there, cowboy. I told you we'd see each other again." A sliver of wind touched her hair, and the sun caught some highlights. Her expression was bright and she had a thin smile on her lips. She was wearing a tennis outfit, the same as in the picture—sweater, white shorts showing creamy, long legs and white runners.

"Robbie," he said, leaning over at her, his hands on the passenger door. They were face to face. "I find you in the strangest places lately," he said. "You come out of nowhere, like a cat."

She threw her head back and removed her sunglasses. "I was stood up on a tennis date. Hey, nice tie. Well, did you talk with him?"

"Who?"

"You know who. Winnie." She dragged on her cigarette. "Which of the two jobs are you taking?"

"How did you know about that?"

"I knew before you did. I'll be your assistant, providing you take the MI-6 position." She grinned.

"So you're the able-bodied assistant Lampert spoke of?"

"Well, wasn't that a nice compliment. But I don't wish to influence you in any way."

Hollinger held back a smile. "Come to think of it, I'm getting to like Britain more and more. I might hang around for a while and get to know the people a whole lot better."

"It's up to you," she said.

Hollinger opened the passenger door and got in. This particular redhead with the great-looking legs might place a whole new emphasis on the situation. "So much for being stuck at Bletchley, eh? We both got out."

"Yes, indeed we did, Wesley. I didn't think it was possible."

"If this was another time, I'd ask you out for a drink, but I think I had a little too much already. So, instead, how would you like it if I took you out to dinner?"

"I might be persuaded," she said, holding out her hand.

He quickly plopped the car keys in her palm and said, "Yeah, I kind of like Britain."

"Do you?" she said, firing up the convertible, checking the traffic, and moving out with a roar. Turning a corner, she sailed past the Prime Minister's row house.

"You know, Robbie," Hollinger grinned, looking over at her, "this is going to be one interesting war."

Wesley Hollinger's exploits continue in

The Filberg Consortium

Book two of 'The Falcon File' series.

Afterword

Many of the characters in this novel are fictional. They include Wesley Hollinger, Raymond Lampert, Roberta Langford, Spencer Winslow, Wolfgang Geis, Earl Walker, Jack Croucher, Ted Jones, Simon Brenwood, Snowden, and *Denise*.

World War Two in Europe
In Russia, the mighty German assault reached as far as the gates of Moscow before they were met by stiff resistance and one of the worst winters in Russian memory. For the next four years the Red Army pushed the Germans all the way back to Berlin, while the other Allied powers, joined by the Americans, drove from the west. The Hitler dream of a new world order under his control collapsed almost four years to the day after Hess's peace flight to Scotland.

The remaining German ringleaders were rounded up. At Nuremberg, Germany, November 20, 1945, the world witnessed what would be the most newsworthy trial in history. Twenty-two Nazi leaders, including Hermann Goering and the man known as Rudolf Hess, faced an international tribunal on charges of war crimes. Fourteen months later, three defendants were acquitted, seven were sentenced to life imprisonment, and the others were sentenced to death.

Adolf Hitler
Many leading German generals and industrialists questioned his leadership, and tried to assassinate him in a bomb blast in July, 1944, a month after the successful Allied D-Day landings. He survived. His revenge was brutal and swift, resulting in a purge of hundreds of officers and civilians.

Recent Russian KGB files indicate that the Fuehrer and his longtime mistress Eva Braun committed suicide in Hitler's Chancellery bunker days before the war ended, and their bodies were taken away by the Red Army.

Hermann Goering
was found guilty of war crimes in Nuremberg for his knowledge of the concentration camps and his association with the secret police. But he beat the hangman by taking poison before he was scheduled to be put to death.

Martin Bormann
Hess's Chief of Staff moved up a notch in the German High Command after Hess's strange departure. Bormann was appointed Head of the Nazi Party Chancellery. Between 1941 and 1945, he was responsible for ordering millions of "undesirables" (Jews, Russian prisoners of war, Poles, and Czechs) to their deaths.

He disappeared at the end of the war. Huge rewards were offered by post-war German governments and Jewish organizations for any information leading to his capture. The West German government officially declared him dead in 1973.

Karl Haushofer
Arrested soon after the July bomb plot on Hitler's life and imprisoned at Dachau concentration camp. He survived the war and was brought to Hess's cell in Nuremberg, where Hess did not recognize him. Depressed that his Geopolitical vision had fallen apart, among other things, he and his wife committed suicide together in March, 1946.

His son, Albrecht, who was only mentioned by name in the novel, was also interrogated after Hess's flight. Arrested by the Gestapo and flown to Berchtesgaden, he was ordered by Hitler to list his peace connections in Britain, people who had contact with Hess. At the top of the twelve-page list was Albrecht's friend, the Duke of Hamilton. Albrecht was released within days, then was later investigated for a series of alleged homosexual affairs and was arrested again as a conspirator in the Hitler bomb plot of 1944. Sent to a prison in Berlin, he was murdered by Himmler's SS on April 23, 1945. He missed the end of the war by two weeks.

Karlheinz Pintsch
Was sent to prison, then let out and banished to the Russian Front, where he was captured and suffered terrible treatment at the hands of the Russians once they discovered he had been Hess's adjutant. He was released after the war and died some years later in Munich.

Heinrich Himmler
While still maintaining his iron-fisted control over the Gestapo and the SS, he also became the Minister of the Interior in 1943, and the Minister of Home Defense in 1944. In addition, he carried out Hitler's orders to exterminate the Jews, by organizing the Final Solution death camps that will forever remain a dark stain in the annals of human history.

During the war, he sent out several peace feelers to the Americans through Switzerland. One of the plans was to kidnap Hitler and hand him to the Allies. In 1944, he had infiltrated the German conspirator movement prior to the Hitler bombing and waited to see if the group of discontented generals and industrialists were successful. When Hitler lived through the blast, Himmler moved swiftly to carry out his Fuehrer's revenge and to cover his own tracks.

Unable to kidnap Hitler and sue the Allies for peace, Himmler committed suicide when American troops captured him in May 1945.

Rudolf Hess
Whether the man who had crashed his airplane near Eaglesham, Scotland was the real Hess is debatable to this day. Rumours have persisted for years that the British had an impostor on their hands.

Claiming amnesia while in British custody, the prisoner later announced at the Nuremberg Trials that he faked the condition to fool the British. But few fell for it, especially when he couldn't recognize Karl Haushofer during a cell visit. Furthermore, the prisoner refused to see any family members. Four days before the trial was to commence, Hildegard Fath, one of Hess's secretaries prior to the flight, confronted Prisoner Number 125—the prisoner's Nuremberg designation—in an interview. The prisoner told her he had lost his memory and that he did not recall her. Fath shoved a picture of Hess's family in front of him, saying, "Here, maybe this will help you remember." The prisoner waved his hand at her and replied, "I do not want any help."

One day, an Allied officer came to the prisoner's cell to ask some questions to which the prisoner answered, "Sir, there is no such person as Hess here. But if you are looking for Convict Number 125, then I'm your man."

Prisoner Number 125 was sentenced on October 1, 1946. He was found "Not Guilty of War Crimes and Crimes against Humanity," but "Guilty of Conspiracy and Crimes against Peace." Despite constant demands for the death penalty from the Russians, the prisoner received life imprisonment. A few months later, he was led through the doors of Spandau Prison in West Berlin. He was now Prisoner Number 7. His companions in custody were Erich Raeder, Walter Funk, Baldur von Schirach, Baron Constanin von Neurath, Karl Doenitz, and Albert Speer. By 1965 all had been released, except for Prisoner Number 7.

For twenty-eight years the prisoner refused to see any family members. Then, near death while suffering from a perforated ulcer in 1969, he finally allowed wife, Ilse, and son, Wolf-Rudiger to visit him. Once he had recovered, he urged more visits. Since 1967, Wolf-Rudiger had been trying desperately to free the prisoner, believing he was his father. But he was told by British and American sources that the Russians were the ones blocking the prisoner's freedom because to them Rudolf Hess was the last surviving symbol of the dreaded *Operation Barbarossa*, Hitler's attack on Russia. Now there is reason to believe it was the British blocking the prisoner's release.

Prisoner Number 7, believed to be in his nineties, died on August 17, 1987, an apparent suicide by hanging. However, he was too old and too feeble to stand and could barely tie a piece of string or his own shoelaces. Was he murdered? Was he finally talking after forty-six years? Did he finally admit to not being the real Hess? And was he silenced for it by either British intelligence or an underground German group, remnants of either the SS or Gestapo?

The Hess flight

A remarkable thing happened following the flight. The progress of the war slowly turned in favour of the British. Talk of peace with the Germans came to an abrupt end. Suddenly, England pulled together and fell into step with Churchill.

Today, parts of a two-tone green Messerschmitt BF-110 D model are kept on display at the Imperial War Museum at Duxford, England. The

Daimler-Benz engines and the fuselage sporting the letters NJ-OQ are all that remain of the fighter aircraft that crashed mysteriously near Eaglesham, Scotland on the night of May 10, 1941.

Who really flew it and why? Where did the flight originate? Did he fly non-stop from Augsburg, Germany, as the pilot claimed? And why do we have to comply with the official One-Hundred-Year Secrets Stamp placed on the affair by the Churchill government?

Enigma

The meticulous code-breaking process kept the Allies informed of enemy concentrations during the Battle of the Atlantic; General Irwin Rommel's movements in Africa; *Operation Torch*, the invasion of North Africa; and *Operation Overload*, the invasion of Europe and what followed until Germany was defeated.

Enigma was instrumental in winning the European war. The Germans never suspected a thing.

Duke of Hamilton

Kept a low profile after the Rudolf Hess flight, pleading innocence and shying away from interviews until his death in 1972.

Ivone Kirkpatrick

Later wrote a book called *The Inner Circle* in which he gave rise to Hess's sanity after three meetings with the German in 1941, stating that the German's peace mission seemed "out of character."

Winston Churchill

Despite his strong leadership through the war, the British voted him out of office in 1945, with the idea he was great in war but would be lousy in peace time. Six years later, 1951, the voters had a change of heart by voting him back in at age 76. He was knighted in 1953. To his dying day in 1965, he always carefully avoided discussing the Rudolf Hess incident.

"I never attached any serious importance to the escapade," he once wrote.

CPSIA information can be obtained
at www.ICGtesting.com
Printed in the USA
BVHW03*1111270918
528675BV00003B/6/P